PRAISE for *I*

"R.C. Goodwi.　　　　　　　 .... leads the reader through Chicago streets and venues, begging the question all the while, What causes a good man to commit a terrible act? Psychiatrist Hal Gottlieb grabs the reins in this literary pysch thriller to prove that layers of ugly truth can be uncovered through persistence, and that life carries on so long as there is hope."

--Dennis Foley, author of *The Drunkard's Son*

Also by R. C. Goodwin: *The Stephen Hawking Death Row Fan Club*

ACCLAIM for *The Stephen Hawking Death Row Fan Club:*

"Goodwin's potent debut drama is a series of stories about the U.S. rehabilitation system and how criminal acts affect the lives of criminals and victims alike. . . a collection of prison-centric stories that astonishes with its vibrancy and strong characters."

--Kirkus Reviews

"This is storytelling at its finest and I found myself truly caring about some of these characters, even the ones who were guilty of committing heinous crimes. Goodwin gives each character and story a human element that allows the reader to slip into the story in a way that few authors can achieve. . . 'The Stephen Hawking Death Row Fan Club' is a very strong short story collection that is sure to satisfy any reader."

--examiner.com

To Thomas, Kathleen, and Erin, and the grandchildren.

MODEL CHILD

"Nothing is easier than to denounce the evildoer; nothing is more difficult than to understand him."

--Fyodor Dostoyevsky

CHAPTER I

JAMES SHANNON MADE THE SIGN OF THE CROSS as he stood outside the bedroom of his daughter, Christina. In his left hand he held a heavy brass candlestick, brought by his great-grandmother from County Kerry, and a piece of clothesline. Despite the cool of the early summer night, beads of sweat lined his forehead. His undershirt was wet around his neck and below his armpits.

He opened the unlocked door with tiny movements, as careful and deliberate as a safecracker. Moving forward in stocking feet, he made his way to the middle of the room. As he gathered in a deep silent breath, he took a moment to collect himself. He looked around the moonlit room: meticulous as always, not a piece of paper or a hairpin out of place. The room had a certain austerity about it despite its red-and-white-striped wallpaper. Its furnishings consisted of a plain walnut desk with a straight-backed wooden chair, a bookcase, a bureau, a bed, and bedside table. On the back of the door hung a full-length rectangular mirror. A smaller oval mirror sat on the bureau.

Christina was fifteen, but the room held little teenage paraphernalia. No stuffed animals, no bottles or jars of makeup, no posters of rock stars or actors. No souvenirs or knickknacks from trips or parties. Her desk lay bare except for a box of drawing pencils and her ever-present sketchpad. The surface of the bedside table was bare as well, except for an alarm clock and a box of Kleenex.

A calendar with National Park scenes and a small framed

drawing of Christina herself broke up the monotony of the empty walls. This month the calendar featured Oregon's Crater Lake, its brilliant blue water prominent even in the room's dim light. The drawing, done in pencil, was a self-portrait. Christina had always liked to paint and draw, had done so for hours at a stretch from the time she could barely hold a pencil or a brush. The framed drawing showed her head and neck turned slightly to the right. It captured an unsmiling girl of indeterminate age, who could have been eleven or seventeen, a girl who regarded the world with slightly bored indifference or possibly annoyance. Shadows bathed the right side of her face.

Shannon took a step toward his daughter's bed. He tried to find the word that captured her. *Beatific.* That was it, beatific. He drank in the details of her blonde hair splayed against the pillow like a halo, her chiseled features, her ever-so-slightly parted lips. He didn't know much about fine art, had only been to an art museum three or four times in his life, but he always thought his daughter looked like a painting of a Renaissance angel.

She stirred in her sleep. Unlike her, to stir that way. She usually slept like a log. *Please, don't let her wake up*, he prayed to no one in particular. He wasn't sure he could do it if she did.

He put the clothesline on the floor and held the candlestick with both hands, near its top. Lifting it above his head, like an ax, he saw Christina stir again. She opened first one eye, and then the other. Christina, who could sleep through a tornado or a train wreck, was awake now.

She looked up at him. "Daddy?"

He swung the candlestick down with all the strength he could muster. The base struck her left temple with a thud and a crack. Christina made a sound like a wounded animal, a kind of shrill groan, and tried clumsily to shield her face with her hands. He swung the candlestick again. This time it landed above and behind her left ear. Her second groan sounded lower and more muted, almost whispered. A rivulet of blood began to trickle from her ear. Her eyes, still open, looked towards him, glazed and unseeing. The background music of her shallow breathing was irregular and gasping now.

He dropped the candlestick and bent down to get the clothesline. Encircling her neck with it, he crossed his hands, pulling each end as hard as he could. The gasping turned into choking, and a fine white froth began to form around her mouth. Her arms and legs flailed; her torso buckled. At least the room's darkness kept him from seeing her too clearly. He had an image of her flawless face, purple and distorted now, as his hands held fast to the clothesline.

He'd lost all sense of time. He might have had the rope around her neck for five minutes or fifteen—maybe thirty, or maybe half the night. TV and movies made strangulation look much easier, or at least much faster. His hands burned from the clothesline, with a searing pain that cut across his palm like a hot poker. At the same time a duller pain, more of a deep excruciating ache, began at his wrist and rose almost to his elbow. This was the most physically grueling work he'd ever done.

When the writhing and the choking finally stopped, when her body fell back against the bed as limp as straw, he let go of the clothesline. Feeling along the side of neck for a pulse and finding none, he put his head on her chest and listened for a heartbeat. Nothing. Only then, his last reserves of strength exhausted, did he allow himself to sink to the floor. He lay there, not moving, barely breathing himself, for most of an hour.

⚜

It was close to three, according to the clock on Christina's bedside table, when he finally felt steady enough to walk again. He went downstairs, holding on to the banister like a drunk. He made directly for the kitchen phone but checked himself. *No. I can just as well call later.*

Instead, he poured himself a glass of milk and thought he'd try to eat something. Something light and unthreatening, a piece of toast, or a dish of cottage cheese, or a scoop of raspberry sherbet. He hadn't eaten dinner, not more than a few mouthfuls of leftover canned stew. Par for the course, these last several weeks. But even as his stomach growled for food, the thought of eating brought him close to retching.

He picked up the glass of milk and took it to the living room. Setting it on a coffee table, he stepped over to the CD player, his CDs stacked nearby. He regarded the CDs fondly. Mainly easy listening, vocals by Tony Bennett and Frank Sinatra, several of the Boston Pops. Shannon, fifty-five, had tastes in music more common to someone half a generation older. He never had much regard for rock and roll, even when still in his teens and twenties; the Doors and the Grateful Dead and their like had never touched him. Most jazz was too unstructured for him, with too many flights of fancy. He liked classical music in a casual way, but he often felt intimidated by it. Easy listening was just right.

The CD player afforded him more pleasure than any other possession. He'd miss it terribly when they locked him up.

He looked through his collection and took out a Sinatra, a collection of duets. Margaret's favorite. On it was a number that Sinatra did with Barbra Streisand, "I've Got a Crush on You." He and Margaret had picked it as their theme song. A line from it summed up their time together perfectly, as far as he was concerned:

> I never had the least notion
> That I could fall with such emotion.

Margaret had died eighteen months ago. They would have been married twenty years this summer.

He put the CD on, sat back in his easy chair, and drank the milk as he let his mind drift, as Sinatra and his cohorts belted out familiar standards: "Come Rain or Come Shine" . . . "They Can't Take That Away from Me" . . . "I've Got the World on a String." He noticed that their theme song failed to bring a tear to his eye the way it usually did. It struck him, almost in passing, that he had no feelings of any kind. No grief or fear, no relief or nostalgia, and no regret. The rest of his mind, as best he could tell, was in order. He could remember, he could reason, he could go logically from *A* to *B* to *C*. But it felt as though the part of his brain that housed emotions had been scooped out and filled with sawdust.

He thought about putting on another CD when the Sinatra one was over but decided against it. Instead he went upstairs, where he showered and shaved. Indifferent to his dress, he reached for the first things he found in his closet, a pair of tan slacks and a short-sleeve blue shirt.

He went downstairs again, poured himself another glass of milk, and reached for the phone. The 911 dispatcher answered before the second ring. He identified himself, gave his address, and paused, but only for a fraction of a second. "I've just killed my daughter," he reported, the last words he would say for nearly two weeks.

CHAPTER II

JUST WEST OF DOWNTOWN CHICAGO, in the shadow of the Eisenhower Expressway, almost lost amidst the sprawl of the city's largest medical complex, sits a nondescript grayish building of three stories. If it caught your eye at all, you'd notice it as different from its neighbors: recessed from the street, for the most part lacking windows, surrounded by impenetrable fencing. A forbidding place despite its small size and unassuming presence.

You might think it looked more like a correctional facility than a place of healing, and you'd be right. It's called the Greater Chicago Forensic Institute—more commonly known by its initials, GCFI. Its patients came from the jails and lock-ups of Chicago and its environs, inmates whose disordered mental states made them unfit or unsuitable for routine incarceration.

On the second floor, near the back of the building, was the office of one of the GCFI psychiatrists, Dr. Harold Gottlieb. His official title: Consultant Psychiatrist and Chief of Section. He ran the GCFI admission unit. Despite the tedious yellow-brown paint job, which Gottlieb likened to butterscotch or dog doo, depending on his mood, despite the tiny windows that let in scant light, Gottlieb had imbued his niche with a degree of warmth. Pictures of his wife, son, and daughter sat on his desk, along with two small potted plants. Some framed prints of dancers hung on the wall, from the 1996 Degas exhibit at the Art Institute. Gottlieb, a large ungraceful man of forty-eight, had always been drawn to dancers. He loved the silky fluidity of their movements, in contrast to his own, which were often jerky and awkward. He loved the way they seemed to revel in their physical being. Gottlieb himself had never felt a high degree of comfort with his body. Tipped slightly backward in his desk chair, he looked at the charts on his ample lap. Across from him sat Norma Caldwell, the social worker who served as unit administrator, and Dwight Sanderson, the first-shift charge nurse. They were the members of the GCFI staff with whom he worked most closely. It was Monday morning, and they'd convened to go over the weekend admissions.

"Just three of them," Norma opened. A short trim woman in her early forties, she beheld life with bright hazel eyes, perpetually bemused. "The first one came in Friday night, about eleven. Jerry Fouts, eighteen-year-old high school senior. White kid, drunk, sent from the lock-up in one of the Northwest suburbs. Tried to strangle himself."

"Hang himself, you mean?" asked Gottlieb.

"Not quite. See, he got hold of duct tape somehow. Wrapped it around his neck, and then he twisted himself around and around on the floor of his cell."

"Gotta give him points for creativity," grunted Dwight. "'Least it's a switch from tryin' to hang his sorry ass with his undershirt." Dwight's voice had a booming resonance, even when he tried to talk quietly, which he rarely did. A dark-skinned black man in his thirties, six two and a solid 230, his face was enlivened with a single earring and a stud through one nostril. Once in a while, he enlivened it further with a *soupçon* of dark green eye shadow.

"Well, I guess he came pretty close to succeeding," Norma went on. "That duct tape is strong stuff. He *would* have succeeded, except one of the cops needed to take a leak, and he had to walk past the kid's cell to get to the john."

Gottlieb glanced through his chart. "Okay. What's he been like since we got him?"

"Sullen," Norma answered. "A bit sheepish. Told the weekend crew he's sorry he didn't make it, but they think he's probably relieved. Thing is, Hal, his situation's not so bad. Assault second, but the guy he assaulted had been drinking too, and there's a question about who started it. He's also a first offender, and the family can afford a private attorney."

"Shee-it," scoffed Dwight, "he'll be bailed out so soon, he still gonna have those tape marks on his neck." Dwight affected a speaking style which Gottlieb characterized as "fake Ebonics." Highly articulate when he chose to be, he was also exceptionally well read, a perpetual student who availed himself of the evening courses offered by Chicago's plethora of colleges and universities. A typical example: *Selected Russian Novels in Translation, from Dostoyevsky to Solzhenitsyn*.

Norma gave a few more particulars about Jerry Fouts, and they put together a plan for his evaluation and treatment. Then she moved on to the second admission, a thirty-six-year-old Hispanic named Hector Morales.

"We got him yesterday from Cook County. They had him for a week, for cellulitis." She put on her reading glasses and scanned his transfer summary. "His whole left arm was a mess. Almost twice its normal size, with swollen lymph nodes all the way up to his axilla. Got it from a self-inflicted puncture wound with a paper clip. They think he dipped it in feces first."

Gottlieb tapped the chart distractedly. "Do we have any idea why he did it?"

Dwight shrugged. "I'm guessin' it's the usual. Wanted to break up the monotony, spend time in a hospital instead of a jail. Or else his voices told him to. Or else he's just the curious type, wanted to see what would happen. Who the fuck knows?"

Gottlieb felt acutely tired. Nothing new; it was a tiredness that waxed and waned but never left him, not fully. A tiredness that had nothing to do with lack of sleep or physical exertion, that went to the core of him. A tiredness born of years of ministering to the lost and feckless, the pointlessly bizarre, the frankly sickening. Of ministering to those who often met his efforts with indifference—more than that—who would have spit in his face in a split second if they had the chance.

He asked a few *pro forma* questions about Hector Morales without the smallest jot of interest. They hashed out another treatment plan as he sipped the remains of tepid coffee.

"I've saved the best for last," said Norma. "James Shannon. They transferred him Saturday, from the Cook County Jail."

She didn't have to give particulars. The Shannon case had been front-page news for a week, had been at the top of every local newscast. In a city where violent crime was an intrinsic part of the folklore, from Al Capone to Richard Speck to John Wayne Gacy, the case had seized the public's interest like few others. It fascinated and mystified. James Patrick Shannon, a devout Irish Catholic, a law-abiding sort who hadn't so much as gotten a speeding ticket before his arrest, had killed his daughter in her bed without a known reason or provocation. He'd made no effort to conceal his crime. To the contrary. He poured himself a glass of milk, sat down in his living room, and listened to a CD before calling the police. He confessed while his daughter's body was still warm. And then he turned mute.

Gottlieb looked up sharply. "I assume we have his records from the jail?"

Norma nodded. "They're much more complete than usual. Every time he passed gas, someone wrote it down."

"Good. I want to take my time going over them. Now tell me, did he maintain a total silence?"

She nodded. "He talked to no one. Not to his brothers or sister, or his lawyer, or even his priest. The thing is, they're supposed to be a tight-knit family. His lawyer—that's something else, his lawyer's also a close friend. They've known each other forever."

"Maybe he's catatonic," Dwight volunteered. "Or maybe he's puttin' on some kinda catatonic act."

She shook her head again. "They said he paced around the cell, sometimes for hours at a time. When he wasn't pacing, he read or wrote. He keeps a notebook or a journal or something."

Gottlieb brought his fingertips together, like the steeple of a church. "Do we know what he was reading?"

"The Bible."

"Shee-it," muttered Dwight. "Mo'-fo' cracks his kid's skull, chokes her, and then he gets hisself religion."

"Maybe he's a schizophrenic with religious delusions," said Norma. "God told him to do it and so forth."

They fell momentarily silent. Gottlieb had followed the case since the onset, had become as caught up in it as most of the population, and now he was about to meet its central figure. "So they finally sent us the infamous James Shannon. I was wondering when we'd get him."

⚜

Gottlieb knocked on the steel door to Shannon's cell before unlocking it with an oversized key. They'd put him in a camera cell, a routine precaution. His every moment, waking and sleeping, reading and writing and pacing, eating and defecating, would remain under scrutiny.

He lay on his bunk, on his back, staring at the ceiling, his arms crossed in front of his chest, as his visitor introduced himself. "Mr. Shannon, my name is Dr. Gottlieb."

Shannon turned his head and glanced at him, but otherwise he gave no acknowledgment of Gottlieb's presence. He resumed his fixed gaze at the ceiling a second later. For want of something else to do, Gottlieb scrutinized his new patient. Of course, he had seen many pictures of him on TV and in the papers, but he was still ill-prepared for the stark normality of Shannon's appearance. A man of about five ten and 160 pounds, he had dark blue eyes and thinning black hair flecked with gray. A trim mustache, neither thick nor narrow. Apart from a slightly weak chin, his features were blandly regular. He had a face, observed Gottlieb to himself, that was made to be lost in a crowd. If he'd committed a stickup instead of a murder, and ten people witnessed it, they would have described him in ten different ways. The Banality of Evil. If James Shannon had committed the crime of which he stood accused, thought Gottlieb, the notable phrase caught him perfectly.

"How are you feeling?" he began.

No answer.

"Do you know where you are?"

Shannon kept silent, so Gottlieb answered his own question. "It's a place called the Greater Chicago Forensic Institute. A kind of hospital, a psychiatric facility for people in trouble with the law. They transferred you here from jail. Do you know why you were arrested?"

Again, no answer, but he thought he caught the faintest quivering of Shannon's lower lip.

Gottlieb's eyes fell upon the cell's small table, bolted to the floor, which also served as a makeshift desk. Neatly arranged on it were a Bible, a pair of reading glasses, and a Polaroid picture propped against the wall. The picture showed a pleasant-looking woman with warm eyes and reddish-blonde hair who appeared to be forty, give or take a few years. The camera caught her smiling, but something in the set of her face suggested wariness and tension.

He picked up the photo carefully by the edges. "Attractive woman. Your wife?"

Shannon shifted on top of his bunk and turned towards him again, acknowledging the question with the briefest nod. His eyes begin to well up. He wiped them brusquely with the sleeve of his tan regulation sweatshirt.

"She passed away, I understand," he pressed on. "A year and half ago, it was? It must have been a difficult time for you."

Shannon shifted on the bunk again. This time, he turned on his side and faced the wall. Gottlieb took another step towards the desk and picked up the Bible. It was open to the book of Job. He read to himself:

"And the Lord said onto Satan, Hast thou considered my servant Job . . . A perfect and an upright man, one that feareth God, and escheweth evil?"

"I see you've been reading the book of Job," he noted casually. "I'm no expert on the Bible, but that particular book has always fascinated me. It tackles the basic question, doesn't it? Why does a benign God allow evil? I think all of us can relate to Job at one point or another in our lives." He replaced the Bible on the desk. "I'm wondering if you feel like him right now. If you feel as though you're being tested."

Still no answer, but Shannon had moved his head on the pillow, as if to cock an ear towards his visitor. Despite the silence, Gottlieb sensed that he paid close attention.

He switched to a different tack. "I'm wondering if you're afraid to talk to me. If you think it would hurt your case in court." He shifted his weight from one leg to another. "You should know this, Mr. Shannon. Psychiatric testimony can't be used against you, not unless it has been obtained with your knowledge and permission. That's not something I just made up. It's based on a Supreme Court ruling. If you don't believe me, ask your lawyer."

Gottlieb took a step towards the cell door. "I'll be back to see you tomorrow, Mr. Shannon. If you want to talk to someone before then, there are people available to you. I believe Ms. Caldwell and Mr. Sanderson have already introduced themselves to you. They're willing to do what they can for you, but you'll have to meet them halfway."

He closed the door, locked it, and walked slowly back to his office. There, he found himself thinking of Iago. In his view, one of the most intriguing villains in all of literature. Another banal man. Iago, whose motives Shakespeare had left so tantalizingly vague, whose guilt propelled him into lasting silence.

Gottlieb wondered if he'd just crossed paths with a latter-day Iago.

✥

When Gottlieb went to see him Tuesday morning, Shannon was sitting on the edge of his bed instead of lying on it. Again, he met Gottlieb's greeting with a stony silence.

His breakfast tray sat on the desk. Shannon had consumed about half a bowl of cold cereal and most of a cup of coffee, but he'd ignored everything else. Gottlieb glanced at the neglected banana, the barely touched wedge of crumb cake, the unopened carton of orange juice. "You don't have much of an appetite, I see."

No response.

"You haven't had a full meal since you came here. I went through your records from the jail. You didn't eat much there either."

He paused. "I'm wondering how long it's been going on, your loss of appetite. If it started when they arrested you, or before. A loss of appetite can mean a lot of different things. A physical problem, or depression, or an overwhelming fear. Sometimes people fear they're being poisoned. Perhaps you've had those fears yourself. If that's the case"—he walked over to the desk, ostentatiously broke off a piece of the cake and ate it— "if that's the case, I wish I could make you believe that your fears are unfounded."

Nothing.

Gottlieb spied the notebook on the desk, an ordinary grade school composition book with a black-and-white speckled cover. "Sometimes we find it easier to write things down than to say them aloud. We have thoughts and feelings we can't give voice to. You often write, you've done it since they arrested you. If you'd rather communicate to me that way, I'm willing to read whatever you've written."

For the first time, Shannon looked Gottlieb in the eyes. He

shook his head, visibly alarmed. Gottlieb raised a hand to reassure him. "I won't read what you've written without your consent. Standing offer." A partial truth: Gottlieb would certainly read it if Shannon maintained his silence. But for now, he wanted his patient to maintain a small measure of control over his circumstances.

Gottlieb moved toward the door. "I have to go now, Mr. Shannon. We're getting an emergency admission. But I'll be back tomorrow. Don't forget what I told you about your journal. I'll read it when you want me to, but not before."

Shannon looked away from him, holding on to his silence like a life buoy.

⁂

The third time Gottlieb saw him, he tried a number of ploys. He suggested that they meet with members of his family present, or his lawyer, or any combination of them. He speculated aloud about Shannon's depression or anxiety, his shock at finding himself trapped in a waking nightmare, his frustration that no one could possibly understand him. He brought up the book of Job again. Knowing Shannon's staunchly Catholic background, he suggested another visit from his parish priest. He asked the standard, predictable psychiatric questions—about his family, his upbringing, his neighborhood, his job—in as calm and unthreatening a manner as Gottlieb could muster. And he tried to keep his own frustration in check, even as it mounted by the minute. Gottlieb had considerable but not inexhaustible patience.

At times, he sensed that Shannon wished to talk to him, was on the verge of talking to him. At times, he sensed it took an act of will for him *not* to talk. Once or twice, he even thought he saw the man's lips tremble.

Gottlieb moved towards the door. Just as he prepared to leave, another stratagem occurred to him. *What the hell, I might as well give it one last shot.*

He turned around, faced his charge, speaking slowly and softly. "It doesn't matter where we are or what we've done. Most of us, almost all of us, have a need to be understood. Now this is what I'm trying to understand, Mr. Shannon. A man of fifty-five kills his only child one night while she lies in her bed. This man has never been in trouble with the law, and he has no known history of mental problems. By all accounts—and I've gone through the case record file pretty thoroughly—he's a decent man, hardworking, steady, the manager of an office supply store. He held the same job for twenty years, or was it more than that? He's religious, he goes to Mass regularly. He makes no effort to hide what he's done. To the contrary, he calls the police immediately."

Gottlieb paused. "The question is a very simple one. Why does such a man do such a thing?"

Shannon looked at him, drew in a long deep breath, and spoke in a thin reedy voice, the voice of a patient recovering from throat surgery. The voice of someone in his seventies. "To save the world from her."

CHAPTER III

"TO SAVE THE WORLD FROM HER," repeated Gottlieb. His first reaction: *He went into a psychotic depression when his wife died and somehow turned his daughter into the Antichrist. He's off his rocker. Probably thinks that his wife was the reincarnation of the Virgin Mary, and the Holy Ghost lived in his microwave.*

But Gottlieb's face betrayed none of this. Through the years, he'd learned to keep his reactions under wraps. He'd also learned to treat his first impressions with a healthy skepticism.

"I wouldn't expect you to understand," said Shannon. "No one would. No one could."

"Let me try."

His patient lapsed into another silence, but Gottlieb pressed on, gently but firmly. "What kind of danger do you think she posed to the world? How do you know she was so dangerous?" He took a step towards the desk and lay a hand on the Bible. "Were you receiving some kind of unusual messages? Did God tell you Himself?"

"God doesn't talk to me directly. I wish He did." Shannon leaned towards him. "You think I'm crazy, don't you." Not so much a question as a statement of fact.

"I don't know you well enough to have an opinion about your mental state."

"I'm not." His voice was slightly stronger now. "I don't hear voices. I don't have visions. I don't think people are out to get me, except for the ones who want to lynch me because of what I did to Christina."

"Would you like to talk in my office? It's more comfortable than here." *Maybe he'll be more forthcoming if I get him out of this dungeon.*

"All right."

Gottlieb escorted him down a long bleak corridor, past the hostile eyes of other patients, past a pair of locked doors. Shannon regarded the office with a measure of interest as he took in the bookcase, the posters, the potted plants. He studied the photos on the desk, seeming to take particular interest in Gottlieb's daughter. "Your family?"

Gottlieb nodded, waiting for further questions. None came. He signaled his patient to sit down and tried to pick up where they'd left off. "Your daughter. . . can you tell me more about her?"

He shook his head. "I suppose I will eventually, but not yet."

"Then tell me about yourself."

"Not a lot to tell. You may not believe this, but I'm the most ordinary man in the world." Long pauses broke up his sentences, as though each one required Herculean effort.

"Go on."

"Where do you want me to start?"

"Wherever you want."

He sighed. "I grew up in Chicago, the far North Side, near the Evanston line. One older brother and sister, one younger brother. My father was a firefighter. My younger brother is one too. My older brother is an optometrist. My sister's a secretary for two accountants." He sounded apologetic for having to provide such boring details.

"What were things like at home?"

"No complaints. Our parents were good people. Didn't gush all over you with their emotions. I guess not many Irish parents do. But they worked hard, they provided for us. They were there if we needed them."

"Are they living?"

He shook his head. "That's the only blessing, that they died before all this happened."

"Were they devout?"

"To the marrow of their bones. It wasn't just that they went to Mass and took the sacraments. They *believed.* I'd be surprised if they ever had the smallest doubts about the Church."

"And you?" Gottlieb asked him.

"I've had my share of doubts. Especially these last few years. But in the balance, I'm still a believer. I believe in God and the Holy Trinity . . . God as the absolute good. I also believe there's such a thing as absolute evil." His glance turned to one of Gottlieb's small windows, and he fell back into the well of his own silence.

CHAPTER IV

GOTTLIEB, DISTRACTED AND VAGUELY UNSETTLED, stirred a container of strawberry yogurt in the GCFI canteen. A dull buzz of conversation filled the room, counterpoint to the low rumble of distant traffic. He'd just concluded his fourth meeting with James Shannon.

Dwight and Norma sat across from him. "So, whatcha think, Doc?" Dwight asked between bites of a ham sandwich.

"I'm not sure. It's hard to get a handle on him."

Norma washed down a forkful of pasta salad with the last of her diet Pepsi. "Is he crazy?"

"I don't think so, initial gut reactions to the contrary. If he is, he keeps a very tight lid on it."

"Maybe he's just smart enough to hide it. Just smart enough to know what sounds real crazy to the rest of us." Dwight chomped noisily on a potato chip. "Well, how 'bout a full-blown psychotic depression?"

"Still the main contender, I suppose, but I'm not too happy with that one either. Grief is one thing. Major depression is something else. Considering what's happened and what he's facing, you could argue that he's entitled to more depression than he's showing."

"How 'bout drugs and alcohol?" the nurse asked.

"For what it's worth," replied Gottlieb, "their initial drug screen came back negative. He denies using any kind of drugs, prescription or otherwise. The cops checked his medicine cabinet, found nothing more exciting than Maalox and extra-strength Tylenol. We can't be sure about how much he drinks, but he says a six-pack lasts him a couple of months."

Dwight rolled his eyes. "And we know folks don't tell lies

'bout their drinkin'. Especially Irishmen."

"He's not the type," opined Norma.

"Meanin' what? Meanin' he's a nice whitebread homeowner instead of a brother, so he can't be no junkie or juicer?" Standard banter between Dwight and her, lacking bite.

Ignoring him, she turned to Gottlieb. "How about a physical illness? Some kind of seizure disorder, say?"

"No memory gaps, no déjà vu or jamais vu, no auras. No indication of altered consciousness. No signs of any physical ailment, but let's see what the blood work tells us. That reminds me, I want to order a neuro consult."

"Which means he's gonna get the works. EEG, CT-scan, MRI, the whole nine yards," said Dwight. "Wonder what that mo'-fo' gonna cost us before we're done with him."

"Why don't we just give him a lethal injection here and now?" Norma bristled. "We could do it today, after two o'clock meds. Think of what we'd save the state by doing *that*!"

"Well, it's a real nice thought." Dwight turned serious. "Now here's what *I'm* thinkin'. Ever since his old lady died, he's gettin' lonelier and hornier. One night he's feelin' worse than usual, he has a few more beers than usual, maybe a shot or two of hard stuff, too, and he bangs her. And lo' and behold, he finds out he likes it! Gets to be a habit. But somewhere along the line she gets sick of it, tells him she's gonna blow the whistle on him. All that good old Irish Catholic guilt catches up with him, and not only that, he's scared shitless. He's been in bad shape all along, but now the fear and guilt put him over the edge. So he kills her."

Gottlieb shrugged. "I suppose it's as credible as any other theory."

"Maybe we should ask *him* why he killed her," suggested Norma.

"I already did." They looked at him, surprised. Gottlieb usually opted for a slow, deliberate style of interviewing. He took a thorough history, did a careful mental status examination; above all else, he let relations with a patient develop gradually. Not like him, starting off with such a loaded question.

"Come on, Hal, don't be a tease. What did he say?"

"He said he wanted to save the world from her."

Dwight broke the silence that ensued. For once there was no banter, no fake Ebonics. "Worst thing is, he probably believes it. Christ, I hate this fucking job sometimes."

✦

Gottlieb left GCFI shortly after lunch and drove to the office where he conducted his private practice. He fell into his afternoon routine: opening mail, answering messages, dictating a few letters and insurance forms. Then he began to see a steady stream of patients. He finished at six thirty, and pulled into his driveway three quarters of an hour later.

Fighting a losing battle to keep his spirits up, he made his way slowly to the house. He wondered what lay in store for him. More precisely, what his son had in store for him. Peter Gottlieb had turned fifteen the previous April. Thoughts of him besieged his father throughout the day, and not uncommonly throughout the night, slipping in and out of his dreams like wraiths. Thoughts that took him back and forth in time . . .

✦

First, there was the newborn son, inconceivably beautiful with his round perfect face and his wealth of black ringlets. Gottlieb scarcely believed he could have fathered such an exquisite creature. The newborn son, the link to generations stretching forward to the end of time, the holder of infinite possibilities. And then there was the little boy with the serious bright dark eyes and the laugh that boomed like a trombone. The little boy who favored his father's company over everyone else's, even his mother's. Whose idea of a perfect afternoon was to drive around with him while they did errands, and take a walk together in a park, and end it with an ice cream cone or donut. The little boy who didn't know his father was too fat, with unruly, kinky hair—his father, still deeply self-conscious about his acne scars, and his eyes too close together, and all the rest of his aesthetic failings. The little boy who not only loved his father but accepted him unqualifiedly. Who saw him (was this possible?) as something akin to a hero. Gottlieb's wife and his mother and brothers loved him—his own father had died when he was nineteen—but not like that.

And then there was the schoolboy who invariably did well, who never needed prodding to complete his homework or turn in book reports on time. Who took a B+ as a personal affront. Not gregarious, but with a solid coterie of friends. Not athletic, but strong and healthy. Given to walking and swimming, like his father, instead of more pulsating sports. Like his father in a lot of ways: quiet; a creature of understatement; demanding of himself, intolerant of his own errors. An avid reader who vastly preferred books to television. A curious child who asked unanswerable questions. What made them so sure that George Washington never told a lie? How could they prove he didn't? Why were some people, like his best friend Cal Utley, left-handed? Do animals know they'll die someday? Why didn't Jews like them believe in Jesus like everyone else? Could they be wrong? What if he really was the son of God?

And then there was the boy of nine, blindsided when his parents split up for more than half a year. One evening he did his homework as usual, and he drank a glass of milk and ate a couple of gingersnaps, and his parents said goodnight to him, and he went to bed. Everything was fine. He woke up an hour later to the unaccustomed din of their fighting, which lasted all night long. The next night his parents told him that they wouldn't be living together for a while. How long was a while, he asked them. They didn't know. Neither one of them looked him in the eyes when they told him. That was spooky. Unprecedented. It bothered him as much as the news itself.

And then there was the boy of six months later, reunited with both parents, relieved but wary. Untrusting and shaken. They told him everything had been worked out. That made him feel better, but he had no idea what they meant. He didn't know they'd had things to work out in the first place.

Then they moved away, one thousand miles away, to Chicago. He left behind his best friend, and everyone and everything else familiar to him.

And then there was the eleven-year-old, still reeling from the near-demise and resurrection of his parents' marriage, still reeling from a move he'd had no say in, and now he had a baby sister. The apple of his parents' eye, just as he had been, the new focal point of their time and attention. Eleven years of an absolute monopoly, and now he had a baby sister. Sarah Gottlieb, a beautiful child, with her mother's fine features and fair coloring, resembling her father only in her dark eyes, soft and inquisitive. Sarah Gottlieb, an adorable usurper.

He'd tried to be the good big brother. He'd held her proudly, chucked her under the chin, enjoyed her smiles and coos. He even loved her in his fashion, even when he resented her the most forcefully, even when he wished she'd die—a thought that filled him with intolerable guilt. The truth of the matter: he didn't know how he felt about her.

And now there was the boy of fifteen, the man-child who'd grown too fast for his own or anyone else's comfort. Whose added girth was disproportionate to his added height. Increasingly unhappy, Peter had turned to food for solace. He might eat three oversized muffins at a sitting. But other times, he scarcely ate at all.

His smooth boyhood skin had given way to the acne his father knew too well. His openness had given way to little more than a sullen yes *or* no, *more commonly* yeah *or* nah. *He withdrew from the rest of the family at every opportunity, sequestering himself in his room. His room, with its slag heaps of clothing and its always-unmade bed, with its scattered books and CDs. His room, with its indescribable smell which Gottlieb could only liken to the office of a busy vet. Gottlieb saw the room as metaphor, as a mirror of his son's emotional disarray. And somewhere deep within this homely, sad, reclusive youth still lurked the beautiful child, serious but happy, still possessed of a sharp wit and a wide-reaching curiosity, still full of infinite promise. Or so believed his father. A belief which sustained him, however much he had to struggle to hold on to it. If he lost it, a large part of him would die.*

⚜

Gottlieb let himself in the front door. As he made his way across the living room, he heard a joyous high-pitched shriek.

"Hi, Daddy!" Sarah flew towards her, throwing her chubby arms around his knees. The highlight of his day, most days.

He picked her up, kissed her, and went to the kitchen. Sharon, his wife, was getting dinner ready. They greeted each other with a casual hug, which didn't interrupt her tossing of a salad.

"Where's Peter?" he asked, a few minutes later.

She pursed her lips. "In that squatter's camp of a room of his."

"Has he eaten?"

"In a manner of speaking. Tuna fish, straight from the can, and a couple of Pop Tarts."

He thought about going upstairs to Peter's room, trying to cajole him into having dinner with rest of them. Trying to break through to him, somehow. He thought about it but lacked the heart to carry out the good intention. After dinner—he'd go then. He now had to steel himself to see his son, his one-time greatest joy in life.

The three of them sat down to eat at the kitchen counter. A light summer supper of salad, jellied consommé, leftover meat loaf. Sharon rarely had the time or inclination to prepare elaborate meals. A clinical social worker with a small private practice of her own, she also worked part time for a nearby office of Catholic Family Services. The token JAP, she dubbed herself.

Gottlieb glanced across the counter at her. Dark circles lined her eyes, and her crow's-feet looked more pronounced than usual. Sharon was forty-three. She'd always had a girlish aspect to her, but the gap between her age and appearance had narrowed lately. A sun lover who'd spent hours at the beach or on the tennis court at every opportunity, she'd begun to pay the price for it. Wrinkles had begun to line her oval face; her smooth hands were roughening and showing spots.

"You look tired."

"No more than usual. I didn't get out of the office till almost three. An hour later than I planned on." She took a forkful of salad. "How was *your* day? How's life among the bottom feeders?"

His face darkened. "Damn it, Sharon, I've asked you not to call them that."

"Sorry, I forgot." She tapped her chest in mock contrition.

He reached over to Sarah's plate and helped her cut the meat loaf into manageable pieces. "As a matter of fact, my day was pretty interesting. I had another meeting with James Shannon."

Her curiosity heightened. "Tell me more."

"No dramatic revelations, no big insights. He still describes himself as the most ordinary man in the world. He is, too, in most respects. Except for the little matter of what he did."

"Is there any chance he *didn't* do it?"

"None. But *why?* Now that's the overriding question." He recounted the theories posited during lunch, paraphrased and full of circumlocutions lest Sarah become too curious.

"Maybe he has some weird kind of secret life," she offered. "Something you'd never guess from outward appearances. Like, he's a Satanic cultist, and he dispatched her as part of some ritual."

"Of course. I should have thought of that. Late at night they sneak into the back of the office supply place where he works. They lock up, perform a Black Mass amidst the reams of paper and the laptops, and drink bodily fluids and sacrifice virgins."

"What's a virgin?" Sarah asked.

"A young girl," her father answered quickly, hoping that she'd let it go. She did.

"So give me a better theory," his wife challenged him.

He and Sarah helped her clear the table, and she brought in dishes of lemon sorbet. "By the way," she said, "you got a call from that woman from Public Television. Fuller, Fullerton, I forget her name."

"Melanie Fuller."

"That was it. Anyway, she said to tell you everything's all set for Thursday."

He frowned. "I can't wait."

"Spare me the coyness, *please.*" She made a clucking sound. "Admit it, Hal, you've come to love the media attention. If they offered you your own TV show, you'd take it in a minute."

Gottlieb snorted. "You make it sound as if they're badgering me around the clock. As if *People* magazine was getting ready for a cover story on me." He'd edited a book on forensic psychiatry, written for a professional audience but noticed favorably in the popular press too. He'd also appeared as an expert witness in several high-profile criminal cases.

"I've done what," he continued, "six interviews spread out over the last two years?"

"And each time you've gotten just a wee bit itchier for the next one."

"Nonsense."

"It's interesting, Hal. You really don't believe that. Doesn't matter, it's still true. So what if it is? All of us enjoy a bit of narcissistic gratification, even you." She turned towards him. "You don't find it ever so slightly gratifying when they quote the eminent Doctor Gottlieb? When you read about yourself or see your face on TV?"

"Of course I do. So what? It doesn't mean I yearn for the public eye."

"Doesn't mean you'd shun it either."

She stopped to load the dishwasher. Sarah skipped outside to play in the backyard, so her parents had the kitchen to themselves. A silence fell over them. Not an awkward silence, but not an altogether comfortable one either. Not an angry silence, but not particularly friendly. A silence that meant a conversation had been abandoned, rather than resolved. They'd begun to have a lot of them, he noticed.

CHAPTER V

"GUY COMES HOME FROM WORK, he finds his girlfriend packin' up her suitcase. 'Whass goin' on,' he asks her. She glares at him, says, 'I'm leavin' you!' Guy's so stunned he can't hardly talk. 'But WHY? We been gettin' along so well!' 'Because,' she says, 'I just found out you're a pedophile!' He looks at her, real proud like, smiles. 'What a big word for a nine-year-old!'"

It was Dwight's offering for joke of the week, a tradition they'd maintained for more than a year. A tradition like the homemade brownies Norma brought in every month or so, or the Danish pastries Gottlieb brought, or their occasional lunchtime game of Hearts. Anything to ward off the GCFI doldrums.

Norma laughed. "Not bad," she acknowledged. "Very sick, as we've come to expect from you, but not bad."

The three of them sat in Gottlieb's office drinking coffee and eating Norma's brownies. Gottlieb hadn't come to GCFI the day before and wanted updates on his patients, his most notorious one in particular. "How's Shannon?"

"About the same as when you saw him last," Dwight answered. "Maybe a little more talkative, but still not sayin' much unless you ask a direct question."

"How does he spend his time?"

"Same as before. Sleeps a lot, paces, reads the Bible. Writes in that composition book of his. Shee-it, I'd like to know what kinda stuff he's got in there."

"We'll find out, one way or the other. But I'd rather have him give it to us voluntarily." Gottlieb knew, they all knew, that he could order a shakedown of Shannon's room at any time and examine anything they found there.

"Any new evidence of psychosis?" he went on. "Strange speech or mannerisms? Posturing?" They both shook their heads.

"He had some visitors yesterday," said Norma. "His sister and older brother. His lawyer, too, but that was later. I'd left by then."

"Did you get a chance to speak with them?"

She nodded. "We both did. I spent about an hour with them. Dwight was with me for fifteen or twenty minutes. I haven't dictated anything, but the notes are in my office. We could go over them, if you'd like."

"Okay, but first just tell me about them."

"The sister's quiet, kind of mousy. The brother's more outgoing. Looks like James, but bigger boned. Pushing sixty, I imagine. Gray hair, not much of it left in front, pot belly. They seem to be regular sorts. Unpretentious, on the somber side."

"I think they're still in shock," Dwight added. "Can't say I blame 'em. I mean, here they are, these whitebread types, none of them ever been in real bad trouble, and now they got this brother who maybe gonna find hisself on Death Row."

"Did they shed any new light on the family?"

"Not really." She took a sip of coffee. "They describe their parents just as he did. Devout, hard-working, not given to great emotional displays."

"Any history of mental illness James neglected to mention?"

"None. No hints of abuse either."

"But we saw 'em together. We might get a different story if we saw 'em separately," Dwight speculated.

She shrugged. "We might, but I doubt it."

Gottlieb leaned slightly forward. "What did they have to say about their brother?"

"Mundane details. Good baby, didn't cry much, did the normal things at the normal ages. Had his tonsils out at seven, only time they knew of when he'd been in a hospital. Got the usual playground scrapes and bruises. Nothing big, nothing broken, no head injuries."

"How about school?"

"Just what he tol' you," Dwight replied. "Always in the middle. Respectable grades, nothin' woulda got him into Harvard."

"Bedwetting? Fire setting? Cruelty to animals?" These traits made a classic triad in children who often turn out to be sociopathic adults.

Norma shook her head. "Negative on all counts. The joy of his life was a cocker spaniel named Buster."

"Any suggestions of neurosis? Separation anxiety, thumb-sucking, and the like?"

She shook her head again. "I tell you, Hal, he must have been the most boringly average kid who ever lived. Except for one thing. It sounds like religion was more important to him than it is to most children. Did I mention that he'd been an altar boy?"

"No, but I'm not surprised." Gottlieb began to tap his legs impatiently. Shannon's stark normality was starting to oppress him. "What about his adolescence?"

"No big storms. One night when he was sixteen or so, he came home after he'd been drinking. His father blew a fuse and grounded him for a month but didn't hit him. Beginning and end of his substance abuse, to their knowledge. Let's see, what else? One year he skipped school to catch the opener at Wrigley."

"He a real hellion, all right," muttered Dwight. "Just like the guys I grew up with."

"When did he start to date?"

"They weren't sure. They weren't even sure if he dated at all in high school. Girls never seemed to be important to him."

Dwight made his eyes bug out, like a caricature of an agitated black man. "Maybe they figured he was one of those *ho-mo-sex-uhls* we hear about."

Norma looked towards him. "I didn't ask them, but I don't

think so. Not their brother Jimmy, not in a million years."

"Shee-it, I wish I had a buck for every former Irish Catholic altar boy I been with."

"They didn't say this," she went on, "at least not directly, but I think they had him pegged as a lifelong bachelor. It caught them off guard when he got married. They knew he'd been seeing Margaret, but they didn't know—how did the sister put it?—they didn't know it had been that sort of thing."

How did they feel about Margaret?"

"They liked her. They thought she leaned over backwards to make their brother happy, which was their chief concern. They considered her a good wife, a good mother." Norma hesitated. "This is interesting, though. I don't think they were all that crazy about their niece. Not that they badmouthed her, but they didn't say much good about her either. When they did, it smacked of lip service. I didn't pick up on any grief about her death."

Gottlieb jerked his head up sharply. "What do you make of that?"

"I don't know yet."

"Makes you wonder 'bout the late Miss Shannon," Dwight reflected.

"There's a lot I'd like to know about the late Miss Shannon." Gottlieb tapped a pencil on the desk. "Okay. Anything else, before I see him?"

"Yeah. Nordstrom called back yesterday." Dwight checked a scrap of paper on which he'd jotted down a time and date. "Gonna meet with him a week from tomorrow, three thirty." Roger Nordstrom was the neurologist they'd called in.

"Okay. Anything else?"

Norma rose to leave. "The brother and sister are eager to meet with you, said they'd come in whenever you wanted. I think there might be stuff they want to tell just you."

He nodded. "I'll check my book and give you a time."

Gottlieb brought Shannon to his office and waved him to a chair. "I know there are many areas we haven't touched on yet," he opened. "Are there things I haven't asked you that you'd like to tell me at this point?"

Shannon took a moment to gather up his thoughts. "Only this. There has never been a child more wanted or more welcomed than Christina. I think I told you, Margaret had a hard time getting pregnant. In fact, we'd almost given up. We were just about ready to go to one of those fertility specialists. If that didn't work, we planned to adopt." He paused. "She called me at work as soon as she found she was pregnant. She called me from the doctor's office, didn't even wait till she got home."

"How did you feel when your daughter was born?"

"Very happy, but more than anything else, relieved. Like I said, there'd been some problems with the pregnancy. I was glad it was over. We both were."

"What was Christina like as a baby?"

He spoke with obvious deliberation. "She was . . . different. I haven't had much contact with too many other ones, mainly my niece and nephews, but she was different. Margaret thought so too."

"Different in what way?"

"For one thing, she didn't like to be hugged or kissed. Didn't like to be touched at all, in fact. She'd tolerate it, but you could tell she didn't like it. She'd tense up, sometimes she'd even shudder."

Gottlieb wondered, *Had she been autistic?* Unlikely: her impairment would have been more severe and obvious. A teacher or pediatrician would almost certainly have picked up on it. But she could have had autistic traits without the full-blown syndrome. He filed away the question, planning to come back to it later. "All right. In what other ways do you think she was different?"

"Well, she almost never smiled. I know how strange this must sound, but it seemed to take real effort on her part. An act of will, you might say. But sometimes she smiled in strange circumstances."

"Such as?"

He stopped to think. "Here's an instance. Christina was close to four. It was a Saturday morning, and the three of us were in the kitchen having breakfast. Margaret was bringing a cup of coffee to the table, and she dropped it. Most of it landed on her foot. The coffee was scalding hot, of course. Must have hurt her like the devil; I remember how the pain made her jump up and down. Christina smiled, and then she laughed! She laughed like it was the funniest thing she'd ever seen. She clapped her hands, and this is exactly what she said: *'Do that again, Mommy!'*"

"What happened then?"

"I'll admit, I was short with her. I said it wasn't nice to behave like that when people had been hurt. I said we should try to help them, not laugh at them. But she kept on laughing anyway. So, I took care of Margaret's foot, put first aid cream on it to keep it from blistering, and then I sent Christina to her room."

"Did she apologize for her behavior?"

Shannon's facial muscles tightened. "Christina never apologized for anything."

Gottlieb took a few seconds to regroup. "How else was she different?"

"She had no friends, ever. Not one. She had a few acquaintances, not many, but certainly no friends. And she disliked being part of any group, disliked it intensely. To be alone didn't bother her in the slightest."

"Did other children make overtures to her?"

"From time to time but not often. They seemed to shy away from her."

"Did they pick on her or tease her?"

"Not that we knew of." He folded his hands into their customary prayer-like position. "It troubled us, the lack of friends, not that it ever troubled *her*. We told her, over and over, that she was free to invite other children to the house but she never did. Every fall—her birthday was late October—we'd ask her if she wanted to have a birthday party, and she always turned us down." He paused briefly. "Once we sent her away to summer camp. We thought the contact with other children would be good for her."

"How did that go?"

"The camp was supposed to last eight weeks. They sent her home after four or so. They said she couldn't adjust, never got over being homesick. We didn't buy that at all about the homesickness. She wasn't the homesick type, Christina."

"What really happened, do you think?"

He shrugged. "I suppose I'll never know. They were always vague about the details. I'll say this, though. They must have been terribly eager to get rid of her. Sent us a refund for the whole summer, even though she'd been there for more than half the session."

Despite his curiosity about the summer camp, Gottlieb moved on to less weighty matters. How she ate (heartily), how she slept (like a log). The ages at which she crawled and walked and talked (all normal or early). He ascertained that she'd had the usual childhood illnesses but no serious ones, no injuries or operations. No speech impairment, no learning disabilities. In school she always made good grades with minimal effort, had never posed disciplinary problems. No hyperactivity, no trouble with attention or concentration. Cats made her eyes water and her nose run, but she had no other allergies. The late Christina Shannon had been a model of good health.

"How did she play?" asked Gottlieb.

"That's an interesting question. She didn't, not really. We bought her the usual, dolls and stuffed animals and so forth, but she ignored them."

"Even when she was a baby?"

He nodded. "You know those toys that hang on cribs like a mobile, made of different shapes and colors? We got her those, and she ignored them too."

"If she didn't play, and had no friends, how did she spend her time?"

"She read a lot. Learned to read early, before her fifth birthday. She was always a good reader. And she always liked to paint and draw. She liked that more than anything. She also had a great capacity for doing nothing."

"Do you mean that she was lazy?"

"Not really. She could work very hard when she wanted to."

Gottlieb prepared to end the meeting. "Anything else before I take you back?"

Shannon looked up distractedly. "You asked about how Christina was different. I told you how she was when Margaret spilled the coffee on herself. I remember another incident. She had a streak . . . like a mean streak, but something more than that. I should tell you about Joe and Moe."

"Who were they?"

"Her goldfish."

"Uh huh," Gottlieb grunted with faint interest. While increasingly curious about Christina, he had no desire to delve into the story of her goldfish. He also had to see other patients.

"This would have been when she was six or so. She had these goldfish, Joe and Moe, which she kept in a big bowl on top of her play table. One evening I came to her room to tell her dinner was ready. The goldfish were on the floor. They were thrashing around, poor creatures, obviously about to die. Christina was sitting on the floor, just watching them, totally caught up in it. I don't think she even heard me enter."

"Go on," said Gottlieb, more interested now.

"'What happened?' I asked her. She told me Joe and Moe fell out of the tank. I tried to get them back in the water as soon as I could, but one of them died anyway. Then I turned to her, 'Christina, goldfish don't fall out of tanks. Don't lie to me!' She looked at me with those big blue eyes. 'All right. I *took* them out.' 'Chrissy, you can't do that to goldfish,' I told her. 'They need water the same way you and I need air!'"

"What did she say?"

"She looked at me with that stare of hers. That stare, I can't describe it. She looked at me and said, 'I *know* that, Daddy!'"

⸙

"We'll be eating together," announced Sharon when he came home. Sarah sat at the counter, engrossed in a coloring book. "All four of us, believe it or not."

"Well, there's a welcome change."

"I made curried chicken salad. You know, Beth Kaylin's recipe, the one with crushed walnuts. We'll have that, and corn on the cob, and I picked up fresh strawberries for dessert. Three of his favorites. I thought he might like a real meal for once, on a plate, in spite of himself." She picked up tongs, extracted ears of corn from the boiling water. "Want to get him, Hal? Dinner's almost ready."

He nodded, left the kitchen and went upstairs. Standing outside his son's bedroom, he waited a moment before knocking.

"Yeah?"

"It's me, Peter. Dinner's ready."

When the door opened, Gottlieb averted his eyes from the room's interior. The foul jumble that lay within did not improve his mood or appetite. A few seconds later, his son emerged. He wore a T-shirt from the San Diego Zoo, baggy gray shorts, and well-scuffed sneakers without socks. Gottlieb discerned at least three kinds of stain on the T-shirt. What looked like catsup and iced tea in the front, sweat below the armpits. He wondered if the boy had slept in it.

"Hello, son. How was your day?"

"Okay." Peter could not have sounded more indifferent.

His father glanced again at the T-shirt, embarrassed that his son would wear such a thing. He tried to make a feeble joke of it. "You, uhm, might want to change the shirt, Peter. It looks like you're testing some new antibiotics on it."

Peter scowled, but he did go back into his bedroom. He emerged in a plain yellow jersey, almost fresh.

At the table, he tried again to engage his son. "So, what did you do with yourself today?"

"Nothing much. Took a walk this morning, then I sat on the patio reading. Then it got too hot to read outside. Spent the rest of the day in my room."

"What are you reading?"

"Magazines. A *Time* and *Harper's* that were lying around. A couple of issues of *National Geographic*."

"I'm working a short day tomorrow," his mother broke it. "Just one to four. I was planning to go the library in the morning. You're welcome to go with me if you'd like, pick up some books."

"Maybe."

"Can I go, Mommy?" asked Sarah eagerly. She couldn't read yet, but she loved the picture books.

"Sure, hon."

They fell silent as they ate. Then Gottlieb turned to his son again. "I was listening to the weather as I drove home. It's going to be over ninety. You should go to the club and take a swim."

"Maybe." Peter spoke in the same flat tone, the tone of a hanging judge.

His mother turned her eyes into slits. "It would be nice if just *once*, for old time's sake, you showed a jot of enthusiasm about *something*."

"I'll work on it."

With that, the older Gottliebs gave up the battle to engage him. They turned their attention to Sarah and each other. Sharon told him about a call she'd received from an aunt in Arizona, and he told her about the latest doings at GCFI, and Sarah asked why corn on the cob looked so different from popcorn, and was it really the same thing? Peter fell into a silent funk. He ate hungrily but without an iota of discernible enjoyment. Or, if he did enjoy it, a perverse stubbornness kept him from admitting it. *Yeah, I suppose it's good*, he might have been saying, *but so what?*

From time to time, Gottlieb stole glances at his son. He looked for fleeting evidence of contentment, for a sign that the boy saw life as more than a penance or burden. None came. Gottlieb recalled something he'd heard a speaker say, years earlier, at a seminar on adolescent psychiatry. The speaker, an eminent professor at an Ivy League medical school, had passed along this aphorism: Adolescence is an illness. Those who recover, we call adults. Those who don't, we call schizophrenics.

CHAPTER VI

GOTTLIEB AND HIS FELLOW GUESTS sat stiffly around circular table in the main studio of WKLN, Channel 33. The table held only a pitcher of water, glasses, and pencils and notepads. Behind the guests hung a photomural of the Chicago skyline at dusk, shot from Lake Michigan, the studio's sole decoration.

Trying to distract himself, to defuse the anxiety he always felt before TV appearances, Gottlieb scrutinized their moderator. Melanie Fuller, a thin woman in her mid-thirties, had short-cropped red hair, chiseled features, and a clear creamy skin. She would have been exceptionally attractive, he decided, if it weren't for her hunched-over posture and her small gray eyes, too close together.

His reveries broke off sharply as a camera approached her. All of a sudden they were on the air.

"Good evening," began Fuller, "and welcome to *Roundtable*. Our discussion tonight should be a fascinating one. It deals with a subject that has captivated us, perhaps *obsessed* is a better word, since the dawn of human consciousness." She paused for emphasis. "It is nothing less than an exploration of the phenomenon of evil. Of course, we may approach this from a number of perspectives—religious, psychological, and historical, among others. It is our good fortune, then, to have with us experts from three different fields. To my immediate right is the Reverend Burton Evers, Senior Pastor at the Grace Congregational Church here in Chicago, and a former Professor of Religion at . . . ." She quickly went through the clergyman's credentials. "In addition to his degree in divinity, Reverend Evers also has a master's degree in philosophy. His dissertation dealt with concepts of evil during the late Middle Ages." The camera panned to a round-faced man with owlish eyes behind horned-rimmed glasses and a neatly trimmed salt-and- pepper beard.

"To his right," continued Fuller, "is Professor Cassandra Wirth, an expert in modern European history, whose field of special interest is the Holocaust. She has written several books on the subject, most recently *Silent Professors: The Academic Response to Hitler's Rise to Power.* She is also a contributing editor of one of the major journals of Holocaust studies." As she went on, the camera panned to a tallish buxom woman with long blonde hair and a square face, her hands folded placidly on the table in front of her. She looked to be a few years older than their moderator.

"To her right," said Fuller, concluding her introductions, "is Dr. Harold Gottlieb, a practicing psychiatrist who serves as a consultant to the Greater Chicago Forensic Institute. In this capacity, he has often evaluated and treated those accused of heinous crimes. He has recently edited a book, *Beyond Good and Evil,* a compendium of writings on forensic psychiatry." She went on to mention his position as an assistant professor in one of the city's medical schools. The camera panned to Gottlieb, who responded with a small grim smile.

Fuller addressed her first question to the clergyman. "Reverend Evers, in your career you've taught comparative religion at several institutions. Can you tell us a bit about how religions differ in their perceptions of evil?"

Evers cleared his throat. "Well, Melanie, your question could easily be the subject of a year-long course in a seminary. The best short answer I can give you is this one: they differ profoundly. Some religions, the Eastern religions in particular, pay relatively little attention to it, or regard it as mainly the absence of good. Some have a powerful embodiment of evil, something which corresponds to Satan, and others don't. Others—these would include many of the Native American tribal religions—have a central figure who's more mischievous than evil; sometimes he's referred to as the Trickster. And some religions show discrepancies themselves in their treatment of evil. A good example would be Christianity. The four Gospels vary markedly in the extent to which they mention evil, as well as the importance they give to Satan." He illustrated his point with brief quotations.

She nodded and turned her attention to Cassandra. "Professor Wirth, your focus as a historian has been on Nazi Germany, the best known instance of the flourishing of evil in the twentieth century. Can we understand what made the Holocaust possible?"

"I think so, but only partially." She spoke in a precise, no-nonsense voice. "We can analyze important contributing factors, such as the catastrophic unexpectedness of Germany's defeat in World War I. Many Germans, possibly the majority, thought until the very end that Germany would win the war. We can analyze German rage resulting from the Treaty of Versailles, and the abysmal failure of the Weimar Republic. We can analyze Hitler's malignant charisma, his intuitive knowledge of how to bring the German people to his cause. We can talk about the roots of German anti-Semitism through the centuries."

Stopping to take a sip of water, Wirth resumed. "We can analyze these things, and more. But can we ever understand *fully* what made Nazi Germany possible? Personally, I doubt it. This is part of what makes the Third Reich such an enigma, as fascinating as it is terrible."

Fuller turned to Gottlieb. "There's an obvious parallel here to the study of a given personality. Suppose, Dr. Gottlieb, we consider a violent criminal who repeatedly commits horrific acts. To what extent can we understand him?"

"Considerably, if he allows it. That's an important point, Melanie. There are violent criminals who spend most of their lives behind bars, who tell us nothing of their actions or motives. But if they do allow us access, we can learn much about them. We can learn about childhood patterns that affect their later life, and about the interplay of familial and cultural influences. We can learn about subtle neurological impairments they often have." He touched briefly on some current research about the brain physiology of violent offenders, about their CT scans and MRIs. "Now all these factors," he concluded, "may play a role in the creation of personalities we know as evil."

Fuller turned first to Evers, then to Gottlieb. "There was a time, gentlemen, when your fields overlapped quite a bit. People attributed mental illness to demonic possession. Do we still find much of this kind of thinking?"

Evers responded first. "Perhaps not in contemporary Chicago, but we can surely find it. My colleagues who work in isolated areas, with, uhm, less sophisticated parishioners, might see it frequently. This is more Dr. Gottlieb's area than mine, but I believe we've always had a tendency to demonize what we can't understand."

The camera turned to Gottlieb, who nodded. "Let's try to put ourselves in the places of our ancestors of five hundred or a thousand years ago. They saw these strange people, these misfits, whom we now would deem mentally ill. These people were buffeted by baffling and terrifying forces, for which there was no everyday frame of reference. Our ancestors' understanding of human behavior, like their understanding of the natural world as a whole, ranged from limited to none. So they created demons to explain the inexplicable. To do so made perfect sense, from their perspective. Most likely we'd have done the same, if we'd lived then."

"The notion of creating demons to explain the inexplicable has value to a historian as well," Professor Wirth broke in. "Again, we might consider the case of Germany after World War I. Despite a strong work ethic, high productivity and great valor on the battlefield, Germany lost the war. Instead of the fruits of victory, a once-great nation faced humiliation, economic collapse, and universal suffering and deprivation. It was easy to create a demon to account for this, and Hitler did it: international Jewry. It was relatively easy for him, given the context of German anti-Semitism."

Fulton turned to Wirth again. "Does this tendency to demonize account for the other great modern Holocausts? The Turkish experience in Armenia or Cambodia of the Pol Pot era, for example?"

"Yes, it plays a role in them. The particulars vary, as do the historic animosities which underlie them, but that common thread runs through all of them. I suppose it really has to be that way. It's hard to do away with millions of people unless you believe they're demonic in some way."

The camera pulled back to capture all the panelists at once before it fell again on Fuller. She faced her right again. "Reverend Evers, let's go back to religious views of evil. The most dramatic representation of evil, of course, is Satan. Do contemporary theologians see Satan as reality or metaphor?"

He stroked his beard before answering. "You'll find no consensus on this, Melanie, but I believe that many theologians nowadays, perhaps the majority, would interpret Satan as a metaphor. As an embodiment of selfishness . . . malice . . . arrogance. Put simply, an embodiment of everything we think of as ungodly." He took a sip of water and went on. "I should add that the Bible itself is inconsistent in how it deals with Satan. In the Old Testament, for instance, Satan is a minor figure, mentioned by name on only four occasions. In what is arguably his most important appearance, in the book of Job, he's almost a *necessary* figure, whom God needs to test the faith of Job. In the New Testament, he's much more a figure in his own right."

Fuller pressed him further. "If we accept the notion of God as omnipotent, the Creator of everything, then wouldn't we have to accept Him, logically, as the Creator of Satan too?"

"There are theologians," he replied slowly, "who argue that

God was obliged to create the opportunity to do evil, or else to do good would mean little. Now, if by creating the opportunity to do evil—in effect, by giving us some choice in the matter—He created Satan, I suppose the answer would be yes. He would have had to create Satan as an agent of our freedom of choice. Again, it comes down to our notion of what Satan is. Is he a metaphor, or a discrete embodiment of evil?"

Wirth interjected: "The notion of a powerful, discrete embodiment of evil . . . of Satan, if you will . . . may be outdated or even archaic, but it's hard to give up if you've made a close study of the Holocausts." The quiet precision of her speech did not conceal an understated passion. "It's hard to give up if you've made repeated trips to Auschwitz," she concluded, "if you've walked around the gas chambers and crematoria."

Fuller broke the silence that ensued. "This question is addressed to Dr. Gottlieb, but I'd like to hear our other panelists' views as well. From medieval representations of demons to the latest Stephen King novel, the western cultures have paid great attention to the diabolical. Why does evil fascinate us so?"

"I believe there are several reasons," began Gottlieb. "We explore the nature of evil to understand our worst behavior, and our enemies' behavior. Why are they like that? Why are *we* like that? When we contemplate the evil acts of others, we wonder about our own capacity for evil. Could *we* behave that way? But part of its appeal, if that's the right word for it, may go back to our basic physiology, to something as basic as adrenaline. Evil makes us fearful, and fear can be exciting, even pleasurable, to a point. Look at the popularity of roller coasters or horror movies."

"I agree with Dr. Gottlieb," Evers added, "especially about the contemplation of our own capability for evil. Mankind has always waged a battle to keep his own worst tendencies in check. Sometimes we win this battle, although God knows we often lose it. Maybe part of how we fight this battle is to remind ourselves, over and over, about the presence of evil. That certainly could be a piece of our fascination with it."

"The battle to keep our own worst tendencies in check reminds me of a well-publicized psychology experiment of several years ago," resumed Gottlieb. "I'll try to summarize it. Students were instructed to give their subjects increasingly painful electric shocks, under the supervision of the experimenter, *and acting on his orders.* The subjects were actually accomplices, and they weren't being hurt at all, but the students didn't know that. They followed orders and continued to administer electrical shocks, even when their subjects screamed in pain."

He paused. "Now these were *ordinary college students.* It's unlikely that they were secret sadists or sociopaths. But they taught us a great deal, regrettably, about how most of us could be coerced into committing what we classify as evil acts."

"As a historian, I find such an experiment very interesting but not surprising," Wirth commented. "Most of the perpetrators of Nazi atrocities were ordinary men and women. A reasonable cross section of lower middle class German society. I don't know as much about the other recent atrocities, but I suspect the same was true of those who tortured and exterminated in Cambodia, Bosnia, and Rwanda. "

The discussion was taking a troubling turn for Reverend Evers. A wan smile flickered across his face. "But let's not hold too dim a view of humanity here. There have always been people—the majority, one dares to hope—who simply wouldn't torture or exterminate. There have always been people, ordinary decent types, who resisted evil, often at a terrible risk to themselves. There were, for instance, many German Christians who took a stand against the Nazis, sometimes at the cost of their lives."

"There were, indeed," retorted Wirth. "Just as there were church leaders, both Catholic and Protestant, who turned a blind eye toward what was happening. Some of them tacitly condoned it, and that includes some bishops and cardinals.

"I'd like to go back to Melanie's question about why we find evil so fascinating," Wirth went on. "I don't pretend to have the answer, but it occurs to me that evil almost always interests us more than good. Let's face it, serial killers captivate us more than saints. A book about Hitler will always do better than one about Mother Teresa. Look at our literary classics. I challenge you to find more compelling characters in all of Shakespeare than Richard III and Macbeth."

While the camera was still on Wirth, Fuller stole a quick glance at the studio clock. "I wish we could carry on indefinitely, but unfortunately we're running out of time. I'd like to pose one last question, a very broad one, to our panel. Do you believe there are genuinely evil people or merely sick ones? Perhaps Dr. Gottlieb could take the first stab at it."

Gottlieb took a moment to collect his thoughts. "I suppose," he said finally, "that that's the basic question, isn't it? The one that cuts to the heart of all our disciplines. My own view is this: there are people who commit terrible acts, for reasons we can't fathom, and we've grown used to thinking of them as evil. They aren't sick, at least not in the same sense as schizophrenics or those with a bipolar disorder, but they're certainly *impaired*. The English philosophers of two or three centuries ago described them as suffering from moral insanity, and that might be a useful way to think of them. The fact is, we're just beginning to study them seriously. We're about where our surgical colleagues were a century or so ago. Give us another hundred years, another two hundred, and my guess is that we'll view them as truly sick."

In fact, Gottlieb had his doubts about this. Through the years, he'd encountered a small number of violent criminals who fell into none of the standard diagnostic pigeonholes, whose actions went beyond the merely sociopathic. Shortly after he'd started to do forensic work, he evaluated a thirty-four-year-old who'd plunged a pitchfork repeatedly into his seventy-year-old father on their small family farm. The last time, he'd plunged it in so hard that it came out the old man's back. Their previous relations had seemed all right, and there had been no obvious provocation. When Gottlieb met him in his cell, the perpetrator munched on an apple as he leafed through a *Sports Illustrated* and hummed "Jingle Bells" (it had been the week before Christmas). He talked about what he'd done with a blandest indifference and not the smallest scintilla of remorse. Gottlieb had encountered inmates who'd committed worse offenses, but none with that degree of sangfroid.

"I should add," continued Gottlieb, "that many psychiatrists would vehemently disagree with me. They'd maintain the view that there's a small number of genuinely evil people, whose evil natures have nothing to do with the traditional psychiatric illness."

"As a historian," Wirth offered, "I have to side with them. I believe that many of the ranking Nazis—the lesser lights, too, some of them—were truly evil. The perfect example might be Himmler, an even better example than Hitler himself. Here was a man who, as head of the SS, conceived and organized the machinery of death that took perhaps ten million lives. But I agree with the brilliant British historian, Hugh Trevor-Roper, who wrote that Himmler was not a sadist! By all accounts he took no pleasure in the deaths he caused. Of course, he took no displeasure in them either. A profoundly stupid man, albeit with a certain flair for administration. Naïve, and callous beyond our wildest reckoning, and incapable of an original thought. Fairly ordinary, in most respects—a chicken farmer, before he joined the Party—except that he just happened to be evil."

Fuller turned to Evers. "And your view, Reverend?"

The clergyman spoke slowly. "I've bandied this question around for years. There were times when I've felt certain that evil people did exist, and other times when I've felt just as certain that they didn't. And now, at this point in my life, I don't know. I believe there are weak, misguided individuals who, under certain circumstances, commit what we know as evil acts. They're often poorly educated, but not always. Nazi Germany's Mengele and Haiti's Duvalier were doctors, and Pol Pot was a teacher. But there's a key distinction, I believe, between evil acts and those who commit them.

"When we speak of those who are evil," Evers went on, "we often mean *beyond redemption.* I believe one of religion's chief purposes is to allow us to redeem ourselves, to escape and transcend the burden of our worst and most shameful deeds. And I believe redemption is obtainable, even by those who commit them, should they be open to it."

"And on that encouraging note," said Fuller, "we have to end. Let me take this opportunity to thank our panelists for their participation in a lively, provocative discussion. I hope our viewers have enjoyed it as much as I have. Please join me next week for another edition of *Roundtable.*" The camera pulled back for one last shot, framing all four of them against the backdrop of the Chicago skyline.

⚜

Melanie thanked them again, and the three guests left the studio together. It was after seven when they emerged from the air-conditioned lobby, but the temperature still hovered in the eighties.

Gottlieb turned to them. "I wouldn't mind getting something cold to drink. Would either of you care to join me?"

"Sounds good," replied Cassandra, but the clergyman declined. He said good-bye, shook their hands, and headed towards a parking garage.

She looked down the block and pointed to a smallish building with a red-white-and-green striped awning. "That Italian restaurant might have a lounge."

"Let's see," said Gottlieb. They walked down the street in silence; the evening made it too hot for idle chatter.

The restaurant did have a lounge, cool and dark, almost empty. Subdued lighting softened the garish crimson wallpaper. They sat themselves in a booth, and the waitress took their orders: a Michelob Light for him, a white wine spritzer for her.

"So, Ms. Wirth—"

"Please call me Cassandra," she broke in.

"All right. And I prefer to go by Hal."

He patted drops of sweat on his forehead with the edge of a cocktail napkin. "So, Cassandra, how do you think it went?"

"Pretty well, I guess. I don't have much to compare it to. I do a lot of lecturing, but I don't appear on many panels."

"Same here," he said. "I thought she did a good job, though. She kept bouncing it around from one of us to another, she kept it well paced. And she didn't let anyone get too ponderous."

"She also did her homework. Not all of them do, believe me. I've been on programs where we were supposed to be discussing one of my Holocaust books, and the host didn't have a clue about it. I was once in some wretched corner of Nebraska, on a local talk show, and some breathless bimbo asked me if they allowed Jews in the SS. You'd be amazed by people's ignorance about the Holocaust." She caught his look of incredulity "Hard to believe, I know, but true."

"How did *you* become so interested in it?" he asked, after the waitress brought their drinks.

She drank a hefty swallow of the spritzer and set the glass on its coaster. "Oh, there are several reasons," she said finally, "but I really don't feel like going into them just now. To tell you the truth, Dr. Gott . . . Hal . . . I can get burned out on the Holocaust, and the nature of good and evil and the rest of it. It all gets to be so *heavy*. Why don't you tell me about yourself?"

He shrugged. "It's what she said when she introduced us. I'm an assistant professor of psychiatry, and I also have a small private practice. Most of my work is at GCFI, though. Every so often I testify in criminal cases."

Her interest picked up. "What's that like for you, the

testifying?"

"At first it made me sick. I mean literally. I'd have an upset stomach and diarrhea for a day beforehand. It's better now, at least *that* doesn't happen. But the courtroom's not my favorite place. It never will be. The whole experience is stressful as hell, and full of pitfalls. An expert witness can easily wind up sounding like an idiot. And testimony takes huge chunks of time. Not just the time in court, the preparation too. The case files can run to four hundred or five hundred pages, sometimes more."

"Why do you do it, then?"

"That's a long story," he replied, not curtly but making it clear that he didn't want to answer.

They said little as they sipped their drinks, enjoying the coolness and quiet. He caught her looking at him more intensely than he was used to being looked at. "Tell me more about yourself," she pressed him.

He took a moment to summon up a few details. "I grew up in Minneapolis, went to medical school here in Chicago. Always thought I'd become a neurologist, but kind of got sidetracked into psychiatry. When I finished my training, I practiced downstate for several years. Then we moved to the South. We came back here four or five years ago." He wondered if this sounded as dry and banal to her as it did to him, but he plugged along anyway. "I'm married. Two children, a fifteen-year-old son who makes my wife and me slightly crazy now, and a four-year-old daughter we dote on shamelessly. What else?"

"Do you look forward to going to work in the morning? Do you sleep well? Are you happy?"

He was too taken aback to evade her. "As a rule, yes . . . less so recently; and no; and it depends on when you ask me. Do you usually ask such blunt questions when you've just met people?"

"Only if I think they're worth the bother." Her voice lost its hint of truculence. "The blunt ones are the only ones I know how to ask. I've never been worth a damn at small talk, and I never liked it anyway. Cocktail parties! I'd rather have my gums scraped! Faculty parties are the worst. As soon as I got tenure, I stopped going."

He wondered if her fondness for candor worked both ways. "How about you? Tell me more about yourself."

"Here's the quick version. I'm an Illinois native, grew up in Champaign. German background, as you may have gathered. BA from the University of Chicago, PhD from Cornell. Never married, no children. I've been fascinated by history since grade school. As an undergrad, I never considered majoring in anything else, not for a moment. I care about my work, my cat, reading, writing, cycling, traveling, and that's about it. I lead a life that many others would find boring if not stultifying, but it suits me fine."

"Do you travel much?"

"Every chance I get. It's one of the academic world's few perks. The long vacations lend themselves to travel. I also lecture here and there. Ottawa, Boston, and Denver in the last six months alone."

"Why are you so obsessed with history?"

She sipped the spritzer and shrugged. "Why is anyone obsessed with anything? I guess because I think it's so important. The most important field there is, debatably."

"A rather sweeping statement!"

"So it is, but I'll stand by it. I firmly believe the old cliché that those who don't understand it are condemned to repeat it. Here's an easy example. I grew up during Vietnam. If Americans had known more about the French experience there, do you think we would have gotten so enmeshed ourselves?"

He considered. "Maybe not, but it might have happened anyway. People have an extraordinary capacity for making wrong decisions."

"Can they be taught to make the right ones?"

He took a long swallow of the Michelob. "In a way. We can help them discover why they made the wrong ones in the first place. Then, so goes the theory, they become freer, and maybe more likely to make better ones."

"That's kind of close to what I said. If you understand your personal history, maybe you're not condemned to repeat it. By the way, does it really work like that?"

"Sometimes."

"Were you ever in therapy yourself?" Her blue eyes skewered him. Again, evasion was not an option. "Yes, when I was in medical school. It's the main reason I became a psychiatrist."

"It was useful, I gather."

"More than I could tell you. I fear to think what my life would have been like without it." He finished the last of the beer. "How about you? Were you ever in therapy?"

She shook her head vigorously. "The thought of it scares me shitless. Very little frightens me, but *that* does! Suppose I will, if I absolutely have to. If my demons make my life unmanageable. But they haven't, not yet. They only make it terribly uncomfortable from time to time."

Gottlieb raised his eyebrows, saying nothing.

She finished her drink, and he signaled the waitress for a bill. "You don't fit my image of a forensic psychiatrist," she said, as they waited for her to return with it. "Not at all."

"What kind of image do you have of one?"

"A slick glib man who wears thousand-dollar suits and a top of the line Swiss watch. A Concord or a Rolex, say. Someone who'll testify to anything if he's paid enough. Someone who would have made O.J. sound like the picture of husbandly concern."

Gottlieb glanced at his blue-and-white seersucker sports coat and his five-year-old Seiko. "Yes, that's me, all right."

"How *did* you get involved in forensic work?"

"By accident. It started when I was working in the South. I

did it because no one else would. Defendants wound up in prison, sometimes on Death Row, even though they were blatantly psychotic. And then I got more and more caught up in it."

"Do you like it?"

He strummed the table with his fingertips. "I find it fascinating, more than any other part of psychiatry. Whether or not I like it is another matter."

The waitress brought their check. He looked at it, left the appropriate bills, and checked the time. "Well, I suppose I should be heading off. It's been very interesting talking with you."

She gave him a brief slight smile, her first of the evening. "Same here."

"We . . . we could do this again if you'd like." He suddenly felt tongue-tied; he hadn't been so forward with a woman in two decades.

She pulled a pen from her purse, tore off a piece of her napkin, jotted down her number, and handed it to him. "Call me, if you'd like."

"I will."

The temperature outside had fallen, and a breeze was coming off the lake. She turned to him as they prepared to part. "Why don't you sleep well?"

He didn't answer right away. Instead, he turned his gaze upward. The sky was putting on a brilliant twilight spectacle, swatches of orange and magenta against the fading blue. In the east were darker streaks of indigo.

"It's another long story," he answered finally.

CHAPTER VII

"WE'RE GRATEFUL FOR YOUR TIME," began Rita Tierney, diffident and ill at ease, as she and her brother sat in Gottlieb's office. She was gaunt, with poorly dyed reddish-blonde hair, the dark roots still apparent. Her plain black dress would have been suitable for a modest funeral. No makeup; no jewelry except for a wedding band and a small gold cross around her neck. *She hasn't expected much from life,* thought Gottlieb, *and she's had her expectations met.*

"We know how busy you are," added Timothy, her brother. "But we really wanted to have the chance to talk with you." A beefy man, he wore a white shirt open at the collar, a tan sports coat, and neatly pressed khakis. The open collar displayed a narrow strip of undershirt.

"If there's any information we can give you, if there's anything we can do to help Jimmy . . ." His voice trailed off into a whisper.

"We're hoping that you'll help us too," implored Rita. "Help us understand what happened. It's been what, close to a month now? I still can't make myself believe it. It's just a nightmare, I keep thinking. I'll wake up any minute now."

"I'll try to answer your questions the best that I can," responded Gottlieb, "but I still have more questions of my own than answers. Now I know you met last week with Ms. Caldwell and Mr. Sanderson, so forgive me if we go over some of the same ground."

"Where should we start?" asked Rita.

Gottlieb crossed his legs and folded his hands on top of his knee. "Wherever you want."

Timothy leaned towards him. "Let me start by saying this.

Of all the people I've ever known—relatives, friends, neighbors, everyone—Jimmy's the one least likely to commit a violent crime."

Rita agreed with a forceful nod. "He hated violence, always did, ever since he was a little boy. The other night I was thinking about something I hadn't thought about in years. It was when our father took all of us to see professional wrestling at the old International Amphitheater. You know, over on Forty-Second and Halsted." Gottlieb nodded. "This would have been in 1956 or '57." She turned to her brother. "Do you remember, Tim?"

"Of course I do! I used to love those wrestlers! Gorgeous George, Argentina Rocca, Killer Kowalski, and the rest of them. They put on a great show, those guys."

"So, the whole family went," continued Rita. "Now everyone knew that most of the time those wrestlers faked it. They slammed each other left and right; they'd jump up and crash down on each other's faces, but it was all like a script. No one got hurt, at least not usually. Everyone knew they were faking, but it bothered Jimmy anyway. A lot of times he'd turn away, he wouldn't look at what was going on. I think he was glad when it was over. The rest of the family wanted to go there again, but not Jimmy. He never did."

"Did you ever see him become violent with anyone, under any circumstances?" They shook their heads in unison. "How about when he drank?"

"I only saw him once when he'd been drinking. That is, when he'd had more than a beer or two." Rita recounted the story she'd told Dwight and Norma, the only such occasion that they knew about.

"He never had much taste for alcohol," Timothy elaborated. "I also think he had a fear of it. The whole family does. We're Irish, we know what it can do."

"He must have gotten angry once in a while. When he did, how did he show it?"

"Well, it didn't happen very often," Rita answered him, "but when it did he'd keep it bottled up. He'd get real quiet. Vincent, he's our other brother, was the one with a temper, but not Jimmy."

Gottlieb went quickly through their brother's formative years. There were no startling new revelations. Then he turned to James's relationship with Margaret. "I believe you told Ms. Caldwell that you were surprised when he got married."

"I can't speak for the rest of the family, but *I* was," acknowledged Timothy. "It's not that he *dis*liked women. I mean, it's not like he was, uh, queer or something." Gottlieb tried to keep from smiling as he recalled what Dwight theorized the week before. *Maybe they thought he was one of those homo-sex-uhls we hear about . . .*

"Tell me about your sister-in-law," he forged ahead.

"Margaret was a sweetheart," said Rita. "She had a sunny, even disposition, and it was just about impossible to get her riled up. I couldn't imagine her being mean to anyone. It simply wasn't in her."

"She was always there if you needed her; she always did what she could to help," her brother added. "Danny and Mary, that's my son and daughter-in-law, they had a terrible thing happen a couple of years ago. Their house burned to the ground. So there they were, this young couple with a three-year-old daughter, and they had nothing. The whole family helped them, gave them clothes and money, did whatever they could for them. Margaret was wonderful. Apart from giving them all kinds of stuff, from sheets and blankets to pots and pans, she was practically a full-time babysitter while Danny and Mary went all over Chicago trying to find a new place, and that was in addition to their regular jobs. She cooked and baked for them, did their laundry, did everything. And she never waited to be asked, she just volunteered. I remember thinking at the time, she's one of the kindest people I've ever known."

"Were they happily married?"

"Yes." Tim hesitated momentarily. "At least, I think they

were."

"You're not certain?"

"Can anyone be certain about someone else's marriage? There was this foot doctor, had an office down the hall from me. Nice enough fellow, or so we thought. A real family man. He'd talk your ear off about his wife and kids. Well, last year, he skipped town with his secretary. I heard he was in Florida—"

"They *seemed* happy," Rita broke in impatiently. "Not that they were lovey-dovey. None of us are. But they seemed comfortable together. They liked the same things. They shared the same beliefs and values. They seemed to want the same thing out of life."

"What was that, do you think?"

"To get through life honorably," replied Timothy, "with as few complications as possible. If they enjoyed themselves along the way, they'd consider that a bonus. But it wasn't their chief aim."

"How did he cope with her medical problems?"

Rita twisted the gold cross around her neck. "Better than I would have guessed. Now I wouldn't call Jimmy exactly spoiled, but he and Vincent were the younger ones, and they were used to being taken care of. But as Margaret got sicker and sicker, Jimmy did more and more. More of the cooking and housekeeping, more of everything. He never made a big deal about it. He just did it."

"How did he cope with her dying?" Gottlieb asked quietly. He still posited a lingering severe depression as the most likely cause of what had happened. A depression severe enough to turn psychotic.

"He was heartbroken," answered Timothy. "He went through the motions. He would come to family gatherings, he'd try his best to be a part of things, but he *wasn't there.*

"He did what he had to do," went on Timothy." He went to work, he cared for Christina, but all the joy, all the contentment had left his life. He didn't put it into just those words, but that was the sense you got from him."

"I don't think he ever thought of suicide," elaborated Rita, "but a couple of times he told me that he would have liked to be with her."

"We're talking about right after she died, the first nine months or so," said Timothy. "And then he seemed to get a little better."

"How could you tell?"

"By small things. He walked more briskly, his shoulders didn't slump so much. Someone would tell a joke at a family get-together, and maybe he'd laugh. Once in a great while he'd even tell one himself."

"Vincent's birthday is in March," Rita added. "This year, Tim and I made plans to take him to a Blackhawks game and out to dinner afterward. We invited Jimmy to come along. And he did, he came too. I was pleasantly surprised, I guess I really didn't think he'd do it. He wouldn't have considered it the year before."

Gottlieb sipped cold coffee from a Styrofoam cup and contemplated his next round of questions. He wanted to steer the discussion towards Christina. "I'd like to know more about his relationship with his daughter," he resumed. When he mentioned her, he noticed their expressions stiffen.

"It wasn't bad, as best we could tell," Rita answered slowly. "He did his best to be a good father."

"Not that she made it easy," bit off Timothy.

Gottlieb turned towards him. "You didn't like her?"

The optometrist picked his words carefully. "She wasn't the sort of child you could warm up to easily. It was like she had a wall around her, ten feet thick."

"I would have *liked* to like her." The tinge of distaste on Rita's face gave way to sadness. "Vincent has no children, and Tim here has two sons, so she was my only niece. I would have liked to like her, but . . ."

But what?" Gottlieb prodded.

"Like Rita said before, we're not a lovey-dovey bunch," her brother elaborated. "We may not hug and kiss a lot. We don't spend all our free time together. But we care about each other, in our fashion. We may not advertise our emotions on billboards, but we have them. But Christina! If she had them at all, she kept them locked up behind that wall of hers."

"She was the coldest person I've ever known, adult or child," his sister added. "No one else came close." Gottlieb sat back in silence, not wanting to interrupt the flow.

"I'm no expert on kids," added Timothy, "but I always had a sense that she was *different* from most of them. The things that other children care about—their friends and families, their pets, their toys and games and everything—she could take them or leave them. There was an amazing self-sufficiency about her."

"I'll never forget the way she was at Margaret's funeral," recalled Rita. "Well-behaved, like she always was, *but she never shed a tear*. Not through the wake, the funeral mass, not even the burial. Never! Some of the people thought she was in shock. Myself, I didn't believe that for a second." She paused. "God forgive me for saying so, but I didn't think her mother's death meant very much to her."

Her brother turned towards her, surprised. "You felt that way too?"

Gottlieb waited for further elaboration, but none came. "How *were* things between her mother and her?"

"Calm enough. At least, that's how it looked," Rita answered. "There was none of that mother-daughter nonsense you hear about, no yelling or hysterics. Margaret never complained about her. Of course, Margaret never complained about anything. But I'll tell you something, Doctor. She worried about her. They both did, they felt she wasn't right. They even took her to some kind of psychologist."

Gottlieb jerked his head up sharply. James Shannon hadn't

mentioned this to him before.

"You have to understand," broke in Timothy, "that's a real big step for a family like ours. We tend to keep our business to ourselves."

"How old would she have been then?"

They turned to each other, uncertain. "Eleven or twelve?" Rita answered tentatively. "It was around the time they tried to send her to that camp." Gottlieb reached for his note pad, jotted down a quick memo to himself.

Changing course, he asked more questions about the period between the death of Margaret Shannon and the present, especially the very recent past. The answers jibed with what Dwight and Norma had said to him. James Shannon showed no obvious changes in behavior, speech, or personality just prior to his daughter's murder. He gave no evidence of suffering from a physical illness. He made no allusions to major changes in the offing; he gave away no possessions; he gave no hints that others would have to take care of things. He made no threats, however veiled, to kill himself or anyone else.

"Just one final question," concluded Gottlieb. "When was the last time you saw your brother before Christina's death?"

"It was five or six weeks ago," replied Timothy. "Early June, the first real hot spell of the summer. We have an in-ground pool, and we invited Jimmy and Christina over for a swim. An ordinary day, as I recall. We swam, we talked about this and that, and I made us burgers on the grill. Jimmy had his customary beer or two, no more." He pointed to his sister. "We invited Rita and her family too, but they'd gone out of town for the day."

"What was he like? What were they like together?"

"He was quiet, the way he usually was. He didn't seem upset or worried about anything. They didn't fight, didn't seem disturbed with one another."

"And Christina?"

"Same as always. Not snotty, but just this close to it." He

held his right hand in front of him, keeping his thumb and index finger a fraction of an inch apart. "She stayed off by herself, for the most part. Impossible to tell if she enjoyed herself or not.

"Maybe I shouldn't have said that she was snotty," he backed off. "The thing is, Christina had decent manners. Polite enough, and she always said *please* and *thank you*. But—I don't know exactly how to put this—it's as if she was polite to you because she didn't care enough about you to be rude."

"The last time I saw him was a week or two before that," Rita said. "My husband was away on business. I called Jimmy and asked if they'd like to go out for a pizza or something. *He* came, but Her Nibs decided to stay home."

"How was he then?"

"Exactly the way Tim described him. You'd never have guessed that he was about to . . . you know . . . ."

Gottlieb settled back in his desk chair. "I'm sure there are questions you'd like to ask me. I'll try to answer them as best I can."

Timothy spoke first. "I only have one. Is he crazy?" He clearly feared the answer, any answer.

"We see no present evidence of that," Gottlieb answered, "but we can't rule it out completely. Psychotic thinking can be obvious, but it can also be very subtle. I should also tell you that a number of physical conditions can have a powerful impact on someone's behavior. We're looking into those possibilities too." He gave a quick summary of the work-up still in progress.

Rita chewed on her lower lip. "But if he *isn't* crazy, then *why*—?" With that, her diminished stores of self-control gave way. She began to cry, to sob, burying her face in shaking hands. Gottlieb said nothing as her brother tried to comfort her, awkwardly but kindly, taking her head against his shoulder. "Now, now, Rita, it will all turn out all right. Now, now, we have to keep the faith and trust in the Lord . . . ."

Gottlieb hearkened back to what the optometrist had said before. *We may not advertise our emotions on billboards, but we have them.*

⸸

The day after his interview with Timothy and Rita, Gottlieb talked to someone else with a keen interest in the Shannon case. Brendan O'Connell, a heavyset man with a florid complexion and a boxer's pug nose, sat still only with great effort; he clearly would have liked to pace. Even when he sat, his body crackled with near-palpable tension. He bounced his knees, tapped his fingers and twitched his toes in a nonstop flurry. O'Connell was James Shannon's lawyer.

"Jimmy isn't just my client, Doctor," he began, scrutinizing Gottlieb with brown eyes at once fierce and beseeching. "He's one of my best and oldest friends."

"How long have you known him?"

"Forty years, give or take." O'Connell rhythmically dug the heels of his perfectly shined black shoes into Gottlieb's carpet. Gottlieb had seen the same shoes advertised in *Esquire*.

"We started kindergarten together," the lawyer went on. "Played baseball together, served as altar boys together at St. Claire's. It's hard to remember when I *didn't* know him."

"And you've stayed close through the years?"

"Not as close as when we were growing up, but we've stayed in touch. We went to each other's weddings and the christenings of each other's children. When I saw him, it was usually in church. Once in a while I did some legal work for him. Nothing big. The closing on his house, wills for him and Margaret." The tempo of the tapping and twitching quickened. "I never thought I'd be defending him in a case like this one, not in a million years."

Giving up the effort to sit still, he stood up and strode towards the window. "I should tell you this right off, Dr. Gottlieb, I'm not a criminal lawyer. We're a small firm, just two partners and me. General law. Most of our criminal work involves domestic violence. Someone gets loaded and beats up his wife, or they pick him up for drunk driving. Or someone's kid gets in trouble with drugs. That's what I told Jimmy. I offered to find him the best criminal lawyer I could, but he said he wanted me. Given his predicament, I felt I couldn't turn him down."

Gottlieb raised his eyebrows. "I thought he didn't talk at all after his arrest."

"He didn't. The first two times I met with him, he wouldn't speak to me. Christ, he wouldn't even look at me! Finally, now this would have been a few days after they brought him here, we managed to have a conversation. Not an ordinary conversation; he mostly nodded yes or no. But at least he said a few words now and then."

"Did he sign a release?" Gottlieb couldn't talk about the legal issues in a case, not even to the defendant's own lawyer, without his written permission.

O'Connell nodded, reaching for the inside pocket of his suit coat. He retrieved a single sheet of paper and handed it to Gottlieb, who read it carefully. Then the lawyer turned to business. "The first thing I want to talk about is motive. He said he tried to save the world from her. Now, people give lots of reasons for what they've done, but that's a new one for me. I'm no shrink, but that sounds pretty crazy, doesn't it?"

"Yes, it does, but so far there's been no other evidence of craziness. I'm not saying it won't turn up later, but so far I haven't seen it. Neither has anyone else."

"Are you saying what he did was sane?" the lawyer shot back irately. "That a *sane* man, middle-aged, without a criminal history of any kind, would kill a sleeping child *to save the world from her*?"

"I'm saying nothing of the kind, Mr. O'Connell," he answered calmly. "I'm only going by what I've learned so far about your client. That's subject to change. You should know this, though—it's hard enough in any case to sell an insanity defense to a jury, but it's particularly hard when there's only one psychotic act. If there's only one thread of psychotic thinking."

"It might be easier in this case than usual," O'Connell said. "I admit, I'm working on a hunch here, but I think a jury might *want* to find him crazy. They could understand it more easily than they could if he were sane. People have been known to lose their minds, and when they do, they've been known to do some awful things."

"And sometimes they do awful things when there's not the smallest hint of insanity."

O'Connell chewed on a knuckle. "If the jury thinks he's sane, he's a dead man."

The lawyer returned to his chair and sat down. The tapping and twitching was much less now, little more than an occasional jerk. "I'm also considering a defense based on diminished capacity."

"Well, you might have a better chance with that one," agreed Gottlieb. He'd often seen attorneys use this stratagem. Diminished capacity meant different things in different jurisdictions, but the gist of it was this: a defendant's mental state at the time of an offense had been significantly compromised. The standard of proof was less rigid than it was for the insanity defense. A lawyer could sell it more easily to the jury.

They fell into a momentary silence. Gottlieb compared him to other attorneys he'd worked with. Not as shrewd as most of them, not as polished. Certainly not as experienced in criminal law, as O'Connell himself was first to admit. On the other hand, he brought a special commitment to his client, born of years of friendship. A commitment bordering on fervor. He'd spare no effort on behalf of James Shannon, he'd try anything.

Gottlieb felt a passing wave of sympathy for Brendan O'Connell. He wondered what it must be like for him, defending a lifelong friend, in a capital case—the DA's office had made it clear they'd seek the death penalty. So here he was, a man who lacked expertise in criminal law, who now found himself enmeshed in a capital case, with overwhelming evidence against his client. And his client had made a full confession in the first place.

CHAPTER VIII

CASSANDRA WAS ALREADY WAITING at the table when Gottlieb rushed into the restaurant, frazzled and apologetic. They'd arranged to meet for lunch, at a Japanese place equidistant from GCFI and her office at the university. He'd arrived ten minutes late.

"I'm sorry. Terrible morning . . ."

She waved off the apology. "Relax, Hal. To tell you the truth, I enjoyed a few quiet minutes. First time I've had them all day."

They presented a study in contrasts. She looked cool and crisp in a mint-green cotton dress. He wore a rumpled tan jacket, a loosened red-and-blue-striped tie and a white shirt that needed to be tucked in here and there. She regarded him with slight amusement, not unkindly. "I must say, you do look somewhat *thrown together.*"

"Thanks, you look nice too." He started to sit down but checked himself. "I think I'll straighten up a bit. If the waiter comes around while I'm gone, would you please order an iced tea for me?"

She nodded, and he headed for the men's room. Once there, he washed his hands and face, loosened his belt and tucked in his shirt, retied his tie and straightened it. Finally, he took out a small pocket comb and tried to do something with his curly, unruly hair.

A mirror over the sink allowed him to take in the results. He made the usual survey of his aesthetic failings. A face too long, a nose too prominent, a coarse complexion. Eyes too close together. Still, his appearance pained him less than it used to. He was one of those men who looked better at forty-eight than twenty-eight. Sharon told him that he'd grown into his face. More important, he'd grown to accept his appearance, to a point. *I can fret all I want, but I'll look the way I look.* Gottlieb did not believe in banging one's head against a wall.

He turned to the table just as the waiter brought them two iced teas. "I gather it's been hectic," she said when he sat down.

"It's always pretty hectic at GCFI. Today was just a bit worse than usual."

"What exactly do you do there?"

He sipped the iced tea. "We evaluate and treat mentally ill inmates from the correctional facilities in the area. Anyone they can't handle, for whatever reason, is likely to wind up with us. We also get inmates who don't look like they're competent to stand trial."

"What determines competence?"

"Three things, essentially." Gottlieb grew more relaxed as he fell into a familiar teaching role. "A defendant has to know the charges that he's facing. And he has to have a basic knowledge of the legal system. What's the judge's job, who's for him, who's against him, things like that. Finally, he has to be able to work with an attorney to defend himself in court. In other words, he has to be psychologically as well as physically present in the courtroom. If he's not, the law says he can't receive fair treatment there."

She stirred her iced tea with the straw. "Do you think people get fair treatment there anyway?"

"Not always, but more often than not."

"All right, let's say someone's incompetent. What happens then?"

He pushed his chair back slightly and crossed his legs. "He receives treatment until he's competent. Then we send him back to court."

"And what if the treatment doesn't work, if he can't be restored to competence?"

"There are several possibilities. He might be sent to a state hospital for long-term treatment. He might even be sent to a nursing home. That is, if he isn't dangerous, and if his care is likely to be custodial. Or his lawyer may waive competence and proceed directly to an insanity defense. Or—if the charges are minor, as is often the case—they may simply be dropped. Judges have tremendous discretion. One judge might find someone competent, but not another one." He paused. "I don't mean to bore you with all these details."

Cassandra shook her head. "It isn't boring. If it were, I'd tell you." She took a swallow of iced tea. "What's your typical patient like?"

"Impossible to generalize. He might be eighteen. First arrest, let's say. He's facing a long bid, he's terrified and sees no way out. So he tries to hang himself. He might be forty-five, a chronic schizophrenic who obeyed his voices telling him to kill someone. He might be an old man arrested for breach of peace, with a brain turned to slush by fifty years of booze, a man who thinks Eisenhower's still in the White House."

They broke off while the waiter took their order, sushi and sashimi deluxe for two. "Do you work them up for undiagnosed physical illness?" She resumed, "neurological problem, hyperactive thyroid and so forth?"

He raised his eyebrows. "We order whatever studies we feel appropriate. We call in consultants. Do you come from a medical background?"

She nodded. "My father's a doctor, my brother too. My grandfather taught medicine in Berlin before the war. His name was Friedrich Wirth. There's a story about him that's part of the family folklore."

"I'd love to hear it," Gottlieb said. Cassandra smiled.

"Okay, so one day his boss, the head of the department, told him, 'Friedrich, from now on we must greet our patients with *Heil Hitler!*' This would have been in 1934 or '35. 'That's no way to address a sick man,' my grandfather said. 'I shall take a vacation.' And he did, he took the family to the US and never came back."

"Hmm," muttered Gottlieb, impressed. "It must have been hard for him to uproot himself like that."

She shrugged. "I suppose. We never talked about it. We never talked about much of anything too serious. He was content to be a doting grandfather, to bounce me on his knee and read to me. Mind you, that was fine with me. I was only ten when he died. I wish he'd lived longer."

"You were very fond of him."

"Yes, but it was more than that. I would have liked to talk to him about . . . oh, about all kinds of things."

"Such as?"

"Such as details of family life, what all of them were really like, the kinds of things you can only get from an oral record. Such as, his impressions of life in Germany between the wars, especially before Hitler's rise to power." She hesitated for a moment. "My father says he carried a lot of guilt because he left."

"Why?"

"Well, bear in mind that this comes to me secondhand, but my grandfather felt people like them were precisely the ones who should have stayed. Educated Christians, upper middle class. He felt they should have stayed and tried to fight against what was happening."

"As a historian, do you think it would have made a difference?"

"If more of the intelligentsia had stayed and fought?" She mulled it over. "I don't know, but I doubt it. As far as I'm concerned, the central truth about the Holocaust, and the hardest truth, is this: *The German people made it possible.*"

Gottlieb broke the silence that ensued. "So, is that how your passion for history started?"

"You could say it had a bearing."

They fell silent again, as the waiter laid a tray of sushi and sashimi before them. Bright red bubbles of the salmon roe, *kura*; the chartreuse cucumber rolls, *kappamaki*; fat pink strips of tuna, and the rest of it. Apart from the taste of sushi, Gottlieb loved its appearance and presentation.

When talk resumed, she sought to bring the focus back to him. "Why don't you sleep well?"

"Racing thoughts. My head hits the pillow, and it's as if I just threw down a couple of espressos. Doesn't matter how tired I am, how long the day has been."

She placed a piece of pickled ginger on a piece of mackerel and deftly lifted it to her mouth with chopsticks. "What do you think about?"

"Anything. A book I'm reading, a movie I've just seen. It's all grist for the mill. My son—first and foremost, him. Whether he'll survive his adolescence, and whether the rest of us will. My patients. After all these years, I still obsess about them after hours. My wife, our marriage. Where we've been, where we're going."

"How long have you been married?"

"Almost nineteen years. I'd just finished my residency."

"First marriage?"

He nodded. "First and only one for both of us."

She pushed her chair away from the table and folded her hands in front of her. A tacit invitation to talk at length. A familiar gesture to him, one he'd often used himself. "How has it been for you?"

He brought a piece of calamari to his mouth and chewed it thoughtfully. "Interesting. At times a great comfort, at times excruciating. In the balance, there's been more good than bad to it."

Gottlieb felt acutely vulnerable, and on the verge of becoming twisted in his words. It seemed urgent that he turn the conversation back to her. He parried with the first question that occurred to him. "Have you ever wanted to be married?"

"Occasionally. Not very often or for very long. I know about three unhappy couples for every happy one. Maybe five or six to one would be more accurate. Of course, they're mostly academics, so you could call them a skewed sample."

"How about your parents? Are they happy?"

She played with one of her chopsticks. "Oh yes, it always goes back to the parents, doesn't it? As best I can tell, they stay together from force of habit. That, and Germanic pigheadedness. My father has his infidelities, and my mother has her martyrdom. I supposed they've reached a kind of equilibrium."

"My wife had an affair once," he blurted. "We were separated for half a year." He was amazed to find himself telling her this. It was a piece of his life he'd shared with just one person, his closest friend, the man with whom he'd stayed when he and Sharon lived apart. Gottlieb had two brothers, in whom he confided almost everything, and he hadn't told *them*.

Cassandra took the disclosure in stride, as though it were something casual and slightly banal. *My wife took cello lessons once.* She looked straight into his eyes. "What was it like for you?"

As had been the case in the Italian restaurant, the night they met, he found himself unable to evade her. He fiddled with his napkin before answering. "Let me put it this way. I adored my father. I was a sophomore in college when he died, after a long illness. Multiple sclerosis. To this day, I miss him terribly. But Sharon's affair was more painful to me than his death."

"Well, that makes sense when you think about it. Nothing's more painful than a trust betrayed. Your father may have abandoned you by dying, but that's different from betraying your trust." She sipped iced tea. "Have you forgiven her?"

"Yes, I have. I *think* I have. Sometimes I'll think about it . . . them . . . late at night."

"One of those nights when you can't sleep," she broke in. "When you have the racing thoughts."

"Precisely."

"Forgiveness fascinates me, mainly because I'm so bad at it.

I suppose it's a legacy from my mother, who never forgave anyone for anything."

"A legacy you could do without. Take some free advice; get rid of it."

"I'm working on it," she replied dryly.

They turned their attention to the sushi. "What about you?" Cassandra resumed. "Have you ever been unfaithful to her?"

He shook his head. "Believe it or not, no."

"Why not? You've had opportunities, I imagine."

"In the course of my work, my own life too, I've seen the turmoil that it brings. There's enough turmoil in life under the best of circumstances. I'd just as soon not add to it." He rearranged the napkin on his lap. "But there's something else, something more personal and less noble. I'm a coward when it comes to rejection. I can't deal with it at all."

"What makes you so sure you'd be rejected?"

"From as far back as I can remember, I've always hated the way I look. I've always been heavy. I've always had unmanageable hair and bad skin. It seems as if I spent half my teenage years in a dermatologist's office because of acne."

She gave her head a quick shake. "That was then, this is now. You're a long way past adolescence, Hal."

"We often carry images of ourselves that have little to do with the present. Let me tell you about a patient I once had. She was one of the most beautiful women I've ever known. Shoulder-length jet-black hair, glorious blue eyes, lovely features. Twenty-six or twenty-seven, with a figure that stopped men in their tracks. But in her mind's eye she still saw herself as a skinny, gawky, flat-chested adolescent girl. An ugly duckling that no one would possibly want to be with."

He took a sip of iced tea and went on. "Now, in my own case, I no longer think of myself as the homeliest man in the world, but something of the old self-image lingers. At least to the point where I doubt a woman would find me the slightest bit attractive."

She regarded him carefully, at length, and then pronounced a verdict. "There's nothing wrong with how you look." Case closed.

"I had an affair with a married man once," she divulged a few minutes later. "It started shortly after I came here. I'd just turned thirty."

Gottlieb wasn't used to this much candor outside the confines of his office. It was making him feel lightheaded. A bit drunk, almost.

In his office, he would have known precisely how to follow up. But he wasn't in his office, and the follow-up came haltingly. "Was it important to you?" he asked finally.

"Important enough to last awhile. Nearly two years."

"What was he like?"

She looked just past his shoulder. "Older. He'd just turned forty-one when we started out. A professor. Of course he was; who else would I meet? His field was Romance languages. Very gifted linguist. Taught himself Basque for the hell of it. That's practically impossible. It's one of the toughest European languages in existence."

"But what was he *like?*"

She considered. "Agreeable. Funny, how it's the first word that comes to mind. Agreeable."

"You say that . . . I don't know, almost distastefully."

"Well, it makes me uneasy when people are too agreeable. I'm not used to them. He was also very gentle. I wasn't used to that either. I remember thinking, *his gentleness is like a language I don't understand.* Only now am I beginning to understand it. I'm a slow learner.*"* She continued to gaze just past his shoulder. "It's interesting. I haven't thought about him, or us, for years."

"What was the whole thing like for you?"

"To be brutally honest, it was a nice diversion."

An answer he hadn't expected, but his tone remained calm and neutral. "A diversion from what?"

"You know. From work. From all the day-in, day-out nonsense. Buying food, cooking, paying bills, cleaning the cat's box."

"You still had to do those things, of course."

"Yes, but they didn't seem so onerous." She tapped her chopsticks. "This may sound callous to you, Hal, but I liked that role. The other woman. I liked the control. I could see him or not as I chose. If I worked around the clock to finish up an article, if I needed to bury myself in the library for three or four days, I could put him on hold. I didn't have to see him, didn't even have to answer his phone calls. It's much harder to do that with a husband."

He'd heard other women say similar things but rarely with such bluntness.

"I had the best of him," she went on. "The lion's share of the warmth and charm. The small considerations, the bouquet of flowers or book of poetry sent for no special occasion except to let me know that he was thinking of me. And the gratitude, especially the gratitude. He was so grateful for whatever I gave him! Not just for the sex, which was never as important to him as he thought it was. No, he was terribly grateful for making him feel that he was still special. For listening to all the old jokes and stories that bored his wife silly. For the omelet I'd whip him up on a Saturday morning. For massaging his back when he overdid it playing squash."

"Grateful. I can see where he would be," said Gottlieb, more to himself than to her. "Why did it end?"

"He began to talk about leaving her for me. That scared me. I didn't want him on that basis. I didn't want *that much* of him. I also didn't want to hurt his wife. She'd never done a thing to me." She shook her head vigorously. "And I sure as hell didn't want to play stepmother to his children."

"You say that with a lot of vehemence."

"I've known several women who've married men with children. They come from different backgrounds, they have different careers, but they all agree on one thing. The hardest thing they ever tried to do was to be someone's stepmother. One of them described it in terms of a chronic illness. Not fatal but incurable, like psoriasis."

"How do you feel about having children yourself?"

She shrugged. "Sometimes it's very important to me, and sometimes it's the last thing in the world I want. Next year I'll turn forty. Unless I'm in a serious relationship, which strikes me as unlikely, I may start thinking about artificial insemination."

"The prospect of raising a child alone doesn't daunt you?"

"Why should it?"

They finished the sushi and sashimi, and lingered over another iced tea. Conversation skipped back and forth over a wide range of subjects. A review article he was writing on the treatment of chronic sex offenders. Preliminary research for a book she planned, on Joseph Goebbels. Concerns about their mothers' health. His had arthritis in her back and both knees, could only get around with a walker. Hers had quit smoking too late, and now she had emphysema. His plans to go to a psychiatric conference in Santa Fe the following October; hers to go to Germany in late September, for a sabbatical.

It feels like I've known her for longer than a week.

The waiter brought their check, and both of them reached for it simultaneously. For a moment his hand rested on top of hers. He felt his cheeks redden. One of her infrequent smiles crossed her face. "It's all right, Hal, you needn't blush." His blush deepened.

As they walked to the door, he turned to her. "Sometime I'd like to know about why you're so frightened of going into therapy."

Stopping dead in her tracks, she turned to him and shook her head. "Maybe next time." She spoke very slowly, very softly. "I suppose it has a great deal to do with my Uncle Franz."

CHAPTER IX

THAT SUNDAY, AS THE JULY SUN BORE down on them, the Gottliebs decided to spend the afternoon at Lake Michigan. Peter agreed to join them, to his parents' mild surprise. He seemed in good spirits, or so they dared to hope.

Sharon and Hal worked together in the kitchen, loading a cooler with sandwiches, coleslaw and carrot sticks, pears and nectarines, cans of iced tea and lemonade. A smaller box held potato chips and pretzels, paper plates and napkins, and plastic utensils.

Then they loaded up the trunk of Gottlieb's Saab. The crammed trunk also held a beach umbrella, towels and blankets, suntan lotion, a traveling Scrabble set, and a Frisbee. Gottlieb had spotted the Frisbee in a closet and decided to take it on an impulse, although he and Peter had neglected it for years. It reminded him of better days between them, when the simple ritual of tossing it back and forth had been among his principal pleasures.

Time passed quickly as they drove to the lake in air-conditioned comfort, oblivious to the ninety-one-degree heat outside. Gottlieb put on a jazz CD, a Count Basie. He could see Sarah in the rearview mirror, swaying back and forth in time to the music; he could hear her humming to herself. Peter liked the CD too, tapping his fingers on the door handle. As he drove, Gottlieb lay a hand on Sharon's knee. She answered by putting her own hand on top of his. *This will be a good day,* he made an optimistic prediction to himself. *The Lord knows we could use one.*

They headed to their favorite spot, Loyola Beach—a stretch of beach near the city's northern limit, rarely crowded despite the urban mass migration to the water. Stationing themselves a twenty-second stroll from the water's edge, they unfurled the umbrella and laid out the towels and blankets. As soon as they finished, they hurried to the water. The lake made them shiver, as always. The temperature might be 110 and the lake would still be cold, to Gottlieb's inevitable satisfaction.

Sarah, standing next to her father, was in her glory, jumping up and down in the water, laughing and cooing. Gottlieb turned to his son, a few yards away. "Come on, let's swing her around." Peter did as bidden; only briefly did he look put upon. He held on to her feet while Gottlieb held her hands, as they swung her in widening arcs.

"On three we'll let her go. Okay, one . . . two . . . three!" With that, she sailed a few feet over the surface of the water, shrieking happily as she landed with a splash. Even Peter deigned to smile. Gottlieb caught a glimpse of him as he'd been a couple of years ago. The doting brother, as smitten with her as everyone else, who liked to give her shoulder rides and read Dr. Seuss to her.

They swung her around a few more times, and then Sarah headed back to the beach, where she cajoled Peter into helping her build a sand castle. Alone now, Hal and Sharon ventured into deeper water, swimming side by side. Sharon, a strong swimmer, did the backstroke. He watched appreciatively as her legs propelled her with a steady rhythm, as her still-firm breasts bobbed along the water's surface.

The scene reminded him of the earliest days of their courtship, in which Lake Michigan had played a central role. They'd met in Chicago. She'd been a graduate student in clinical social work, and he'd been one of her supervisors. Their first date, dinner in a Thai restaurant, had ended with a moonlit walk along the lake. He kissed her for the first time a week later, as they lay on the beach, splayed out on one of his old blankets, no more than five miles from where they were right now. The day, in fact, had been much like this one. A sultry, lazy afternoon, not a cloud to be seen or a breeze to be felt. The lake had been witness to their first kisses and caresses, uncertain and tentative (at least on his part). It had been the backdrop to their first lovemaking (the bedroom window in his small apartment afforded them a view of it). They'd swum in its bracing water, walked along its shore as they probed each other's pasts, shared secrets, confided hopes, and devised dreams.

One of the many reasons why he loved the lake: in his mind it was closely linked to loving her, as he'd love no other woman, however warm her smile or quick her wit, or spectacular her face and figure. He might lust after other women; he might like them, he might even grow to love them, but not the way he'd loved Sharon.

These reveries broke off when she flipped over and disappeared into the gray-green water. Alarmed, wondering if she'd had a cramp, he started to go after her. At that point, having doubled back and swum under him, she grabbed his penis and gave it a spirited yank.

With a gasp, he inhaled equal parts air and water. When he finally stopped coughing, he opened his eyes and saw Sharon standing next to him, laughing. He could only talk in fits and starts. "Why did . . . you do . . . *that?*"

"I don't know. I guess I just felt playful." What went unsaid, *It's been so long since either of us felt that way.*

He stood next to her, put an arm around her. "I was watching you swim. It made me think about us. The early days, the way we'd come down here and swim and talk and so forth."

"I particularly liked the so forth."

His arm hidden by the water, he slipped it around her buttocks, resting his hand on the outer surface of her thigh. "Dear God, I was head over heels in love with you!"

"I was kind of fond of you myself."

"Do you remember how we'd come down here? How we'd talk for hours?"

She nodded. "I told you things I'd never told another soul."

"Same here."

"The future looked so bright." She smiled, a bit wistfully. "We couldn't conceive of anything bad happening to us! I remember what you said once. You said our future lay ahead of us like a highway paved with gold."

"I did?" He could scarcely believe he'd ever used so banal a phrase or been so upbeat.

"You did indeed, and I loved you for it." She shifted her stance, positioning herself in front of him, her back pressing tightly against his chest and belly. For an instant, he found himself transported back two decades earlier. They were twenty-eight and twenty-four, their ages when they met. He'd fallen in love for the first and only time. He knew their lives would be rife with pain and pitfalls. He knew they'd be lucky if a fraction of their dreams came true. He knew they'd get old and die, assuming that they didn't die when they were young. But this knowledge, sterile and unfelt, lay tucked away in some dark recess of his mind. The fact was, he felt immortal. He also felt unspeakably lucky. No ill wind would blow their way; they would always steer clear of the pitfalls. Of course they would. The future was a highway paved with gold. The phrase, however hokey, had been dead on.

⸙

They swam for another fifteen minutes and returned to shore. Peter and Sarah had given up on the sand castle. He now read a mystery beneath the umbrella while she waded in ankle-deep water.

Gottlieb asked Peter if he'd like to toss around the Frisbee, and he acquiesced with a sober nod. The windless afternoon allowed the Frisbee to carry straight and far. Both father and son were awkward and heavyfooted, but still they fell into an easy rhythm. Snap-throw-catch, snap-throw-catch. As his movements became surer after the long layoff, Peter's throws became longer and more ambitious, arching high and dropping precipitously, circling towards his father from the left and right. He also made a couple of diving catches.

They kept at it for nearly half an hour. "That was fun," the boy volunteered as they headed back to the blanket, both of them slightly out of breath.

"We should do it more often."

"Yeah." The *yeah* came out less flat than usual.

All four of them ate ravenously. It was close to two o'clock when they finished, the hot sun combining with the big meal to render Sarah listless and sleepy. She stretched out on one of the blankets and dozed off instantly.

Gottlieb faced his son. "How about keeping an eye on your sister while your mother and I take a walk?"

"Sure, go ahead." No *yeah* at all.

Hal and Sharon headed off, strolling just at the water's edge. He took her hand. "This has been the best family outing we've had in ages."

"It is," she agreed. "Not that there's been much competition. Peter seems—should I say it, *happy?* I'm almost afraid to talk about it. It's like jinxing a no-hitter."

"Do you remember how patient he was with her when she was little? How he used to read those Dr. Seuss books to her, over and over?"

"He was a good big brother when he wanted to be."

"He will be again, when he's ready. We saw hints of it today."

Her pace slowed and she turned towards him, regarding him quizzically. "You're an interesting man, Hal. Your optimism can be surprising, especially since you're usually so serious. Especially in light of what you do. That optimism of yours, I often wish I had it."

He shrugged. "It's easier to be optimistic than despairing."

"I'll have to take your word for it."

The conversation veered away from Peter, touching on

lighter topics. What movie should they rent next, and did she want to go to Wisconsin on Labor Day weekend, and did he want her to get tickets for a Cubs game late in the season? The afternoon rolled along like a slowly flowing river, and Gottlieb would have been quite happy for it to flow along like that indefinitely.

When they got back to Peter and Sarah, they were once more hot and sweaty. Enough time had passed since lunch for them to swim again, so all of them headed to the water. Gottlieb left the three of them near shore as he swam farther out alone. An enthusiastic swimmer since his grade school days, he rarely felt as free as he did in the water. He felt almost graceful as he glided along, notwithstanding his girth. Once he'd told Sharon that if he came back to earth as another life form, he'd choose to be a seal.

By the time he returned to the umbrella, Sharon and Peter had already set up the Scrabble game. Scrabble was the only board game Peter enjoyed, and he played it well. At the age of twelve he'd beaten both his parents, forming *xylem* on the next-to-last move. Despite his grunts and monosyllables, he'd always had a large vocabulary. His father waited eagerly for it to reemerge.

They played for just over half an hour while Sarah cavorted in the sand, digging a ditch with her plastic shovel. A close game: only fifteen points separated the three scores. Someone's dachshund puppy, loose on the beach, came over to them, but only Sarah paid much attention to it. "Mommy, Daddy, look at the doggie! He's soooo cute!"

"That's nice, honey," her parents chimed, almost in unison, scarcely taking their eyes away from the Scrabble board.

Sarah, meanwhile, had begun to rub the puppy's stomach. He responded by vigorously wagging his tail and licking the fingers of her free hand. Then he suddenly got up and began to run around in circles. Sarah, ecstatic, began to run after him. In hot pursuit, she came too close to the blanket and stumbled on the edge of it. The Scrabble board flipped over, its tiles flying in all directions.

"Oh, Sarah, just look at what you've done!" her mother scolded her.

"I'm sorry, Mommy, I didn't mean to." She looked close to tears.

"Between the three of us, we could probably reconstruct the board," Gottlieb suggested.

"Yeah, right," grunted Peter icily. He glared at his sister and kicked a heel into the sand.

"Peter, she didn't mean to do it," Sharon tried to calm him. "Besides, it's just a game."

But Peter was not to be calmed. "Brat! The shit she gets away with, when she bats those big brown eyes. It makes me wanna puke!"

"You're overreacting," said his father gently. "It's been a very nice day, up to now. Let's not ruin it, okay?"

"I'm gonna take a walk," he announced abruptly. "See ya later." He shuffled off, eyes downcast, shoulders slumped, and the pleasant day turned into history.

Hal and Sharon retrieved the tiles, and Sarah tried to help. None of them spoke for several minutes. Dejected, still contrite, Sarah headed off to the water's edge.

"God forgive me," confessed Sharon, "but I really can't abide him. Those miserable adolescent sulks of his, that self-absorption! *How many more years do we have to put up with this?*"

"Come on, Sharon, let's try to keep perspective here. All right, he's self-absorbed and moody. So is every adolescent who ever lived. So was I. So were you."

"Not like that, I wasn't. If I stormed off in a snit like that, my parents would have come down on me like a sledgehammer. If I'd secluded myself in my room the way he does, for hours— no, make that *days* at a time, living in squalor, they would have—"

"They would have what?"

"I don't know, but they would have done *something!*" Her tone hardened. *"You're* the hotshot shrink. Why don't *you* figure out what the fuck we should do with him?"

His voice stayed calm, but his own anger was mounting too. "Listen, Sharon, just because I do what I do, it doesn't mean I've got all the answers."

"You're goddamn right it doesn't!"

"I try to talk to him," he snapped, "to keep the lines of communication open. I try to be there for him, to the extent he wants me there, to the extent that he'll tolerate me there. I also try to let him know that I still love him. *I do the best I can."*

"So do I," she replied, more quietly. "But I guess our best efforts aren't good enough right now."

He reached for the bag of pretzels and munched distractedly on one. "As I said, let's try to keep perspective. He doesn't drink or use drugs."

"Not that we know of," she challenged him. "For all we know, he could be shooting up in that vile den of his. He could be smoking a dozen joints a day."

Gottlieb shook his head "His eyes aren't glazed. He doesn't smell of pot or booze. He has no tracks. Apart from all that, and this is what you keep forgetting, *he hasn't gotten into serious trouble yet.* His grades aren't what they used to be, but they're decent. More than decent. He's never had run-ins with the law. He's never shown the smallest hint of violence. For all he's going through right now, he's still a rather gentle soul."

"Jesus Christ, I get so sick of you defending him, no matter what!"

His voice rose. "Well, let me tell *you* something, Sharon. I get pretty sick myself, sick of your hysterics about him! Sick of how you blow up everything into some great calamity, sick of all your doom and gloom where he's concerned. By the way, don't you think he picks up on that? It would be nice if you tried to let him know that maybe, just *maybe*, you still believed in him!"

She faced the water, squinting into the horizon. "All right, tell you what, I'll turn over a new leaf. No matter what he does, I'll grin and bear it. Every chance he gives me, I'll praise him to the skies. And if he doesn't give me any chances, what the hell, I'll praise him anyway."

"Sharon, I'm not asking you to put on some big phony act with him! I'd just like you to stop being so judgmental, so critical. Not to mention, so blatantly pessimistic." More to himself than to her, he muttered, "Where's a Jewish mother when you need one?"

"Well, *that's* the answer," she lashed out. "Why didn't I think of it before? I'll become the perfect Jewish mother, and we'll all live happily ever after. I'll make chicken soup with matzo balls three times a week. From scratch, no less. I won't get angry, even if he burns the house down, I'll just sigh a little. I'll quit work, the better to be on call for him. I'll bend to his every passing fancy."

He stood up and began to walk off. "Where are *you* going?" Sharon said.

"Anywhere, to get away from *you.*"

"Well, *that's* helpful . . . " But people were talking and laughing all around him, and radios were playing, against the background music of the breaking waves, and he couldn't hear her.

⸎

He walked along the beach, alone, for more than half an hour. By the time he came back, Peter had returned as well. Without ado, they packed up their belongings and headed for the car.

They traveled home sullenly. No conversation, no CDs. Sarah slept in the backseat, but the other three sat up, barely moving, their eyes straight ahead, like soldiers en route to a dangerous posting.

Gottlieb spent the evening by himself. He paid bills, sorted through accumulated mail, glanced at the Sunday paper. Around nine, dimly aware that he was hungry, he fixed himself a peanut butter and jelly sandwich. Then he retreated to the dining room table with a couple of psychiatric journals. But his concentration faltered, and he might as well have been trying to read hieroglyphics. Peter kept intruding on his thoughts. Peter, briefly happy as they'd swung Sarah through the water, as they'd tossed around the Frisbee. Peter, storming off in a sulk. Sharon's taunt came back to him. *You're the hotshot shrink. Why don't you figure out what the fuck we should do with him?*

Abruptly tired of pretending to read, he stood up and walked into the family room, where Sharon watched TV alone. "Where's Sarah?"

"In bed, out like a light. She could barely stay awake while I bathed her."

"I think I'll head upstairs myself, make it an early evening."

She nodded briskly. "I'll be up in a while. "'Night, Hal."

"Goodnight."

He went upstairs, undressed and showered, brushed his teeth with exaggerated concentration, put on his pajamas. It was an hour before he usually went to bed, and he wasn't very tired. But he didn't want to prolong the day. It had dragged on much too long already.

He turned off the light, tried to sleep but couldn't. Instead, he found himself thinking about Cassandra Wirth. What had her relationships with men been like, the men before and after her professor? He imagined them as intense, passionate but unromantic, often brief. Had she been as blunt with other men as she'd been with him? Did she use bluntness to ward off vulnerability? Was she looking for a friend, or a lover, or both, or neither? What demons made therapy so terrifying to her, this self-assured woman who seemed to fear so little? And who was Uncle Franz, and what had he done to her?

He looked forward to seeing her again. To talking, at length, although the other possibilities weren't lost on him. He thought of the scrap of paper with her number on it, tucked in his wallet, folded carefully between his Texaco and Discover cards. He really didn't need it, since he'd already memorized the number, but he kept it there anyway.

About to fall asleep at last, his defenses down, he couldn't shield himself from an unsolicited blast of insight. *Part of my interest in her stems from my anger with Sharon. Pursuing her would not be a constructive way of dealing with that anger.*

The insight failed to dampen his curiosity about her in the slightest.

CHAPTER X.

"SHANNON'S SETTLING IN OKAY," reported Norma, as Gottlieb sat with her and Dwight in the GCFI canteen. "He kind of fades into the background." The Friday morning was already warm and muggy; the ancient wheezing air conditioner waged a losing battle against the heat.

"He's been eatin' in the dining hall for a couple of days," Dwight added. "No one's hasslin' him, so far."

"That's nice, but let's not get complacent." Gottlieb knew, they all knew, that defendants charged with crimes against minors were always at risk in correctional settings. Dining rooms, moreover, are particularly dangerous places. An ordinary knife or fork might turn into a deadly weapon in an eye blink, a tray or plate might turn into a missile. No coincidence that a disproportionate number of fights and riots started there.

"He's talking, at least from time to time, but he's still not saying very much," resumed Norma. "Still spends most of his time reading. His brother and sister brought him some books on Irish history, but most of the time he sticks with the Bible."

Gottlieb took a bite from a cinnamon cruller and turned to Dwight. "Do you hold to your theory about their having sex and her threatening to turn him in?"

"Well, it makes 'bout as much sense to me as anything else. Call me cynical, but I have trouble believin' he was tryin' to save the world from her."

Dwight reached suddenly for an envelope in the pocket of his white jacket. "Almost forgot to give this to you. Results of the neuro consult. Physical exam, EEG, CT scan, blood work. Everything came out fine. Sumbitch doesn't even have high cholesterol! Gonna make it to a hundred if they don't give him the needle."

Gottlieb took the last bite of cruller, finished his coffee, and wiped his mouth with the corner of a paper napkin. "I think I'll start with him today. Maybe I'll run your theory by him."

When he entered Shannon's room, his patient lay on the bed, a paperback resting against his drawn-up knees. His half-glasses combined with his serious face to give him a scholarly air despite the unscholarly prison khakis. He greeted Gottlieb in a friendly but subdued manner, without smiling.

"What's the book?" asked Gottlieb.

"Something Tim brought me. *How the Irish Saved Civilization*. Did you read it?" Gottlieb shook his head.

"It's interesting. It's about how the Irish kept some of the classical traditions alive during the Dark Ages. I'll lend it to you when I've finished, if you want."

Gottlieb made an equivocal sound, a kind of *uhmm*. On the one hand, he didn't want to start a precedent of exchanging gifts. But it was also the first overture Shannon made to him, and he didn't want to trample it.

He issued his customary invitation. "Shall we go to my office?" Shannon accepted with his customary nod. He got off the bed, rather stiffly, donned slippers, and they headed down the corridor together.

"We got back the neurologist's report—" began Gottlieb.

"And everything checked out okay," his patient interrupted. Gottlieb nodded.

"I'm not surprised. Brendan will be disappointed, though. He'd have an easier job defending me if they found something physical. A brain tumor or something."

"How do you feel about him?"

"Brendan? He's a good man, a good friend. I know most people don't care much for lawyers. They think they'd sell their grandmother's soul to win a case. But Brendan isn't like that. He fights hard, but he still holds on to his moral standards." Shannon shifted his weight in the chair in front of Gottlieb's desk. "You met with him the other day, I understand. He probably mentioned that we've known each other a long time."

"Yes, he did."

"This may sound funny to you, but I feel sorry for him."

A siren's blare broke into the quiet morning. "Why is that?" asked Gottlieb, as it faded.

"Because he's defending a man everyone hates. They'd like to lynch me, and a lot of people would like to lynch the lawyer who's defending me, for good measure. Besides, what kind of a case does he have? I can't even help him out by being crazy."

"He told me that he'd recommended you get another someone with more experience in these cases, but you turned him down."

Shannon nodded. "Brendan may not be a criminal lawyer, but he's smart. More important, he's familiar. That's what I need now, above all else. A familiar, trusted face."

"He told me this will almost certainly be a capital case," said Gottlieb carefully.

"I knew that from the beginning." He paused. "It's still very strange to find myself facing the death penalty. Not something I ever thought too much about, but I never saw myself as a candidate for it."

"Is that what you want? To be executed?" Gottlieb had worked with Death Row inmates. He knew they sought execution more commonly than generally imagined—as a last-ditch bid for the world's attention, as a fate preferable to life in prison, or as a de facto suicide.

Shannon made no reply. "Is that what you want?" Gottlieb asked again.

"If that's God's will, I accept it."

"But is it what you want?"

"Occasionally. Death holds no terror for me. Sometimes I think it would be a great relief. And sometimes I'd just as soon live." His tone conveyed a staggering indifference.

"Prison doesn't have to be a waste of time," he went on. "A

prisoner can still read, he can write. He can pray. He can even be useful, helping other inmates and tutoring them and so forth. He can take part in one of those programs where they talk to kids in trouble with the law and teach them what it's like to be locked up. That's always mattered a great deal to me. Being useful."

"There's also the possibility you'll get out someday."

"I suppose so." The prospect seemed not to impress him very much.

"I'm interested in the period between your wife's death and your arrest," Gottlieb changed the subject.

"I thought we already talked about that."

"We did, but some things still aren't clear to me. For instance, the effect her death had on your relationship with your daughter."

"Well, I won't say it brought us closer," he answered warily. His answers often had a wary edge when they talked about Christina.

"That was as much my fault as hers," continued Shannon. "My grief turned into a wall between myself and the rest of the world. But even if I had been more open and available, I've no illusions Christina would have met me halfway. None at all."

"How *did* she react when her mother died?" Gottlieb recalled what the girl's aunt said: *I didn't think her mother's death was too important to her.*

Shannon's answer jibed with his sister's view. "At first I thought she was shell-shocked, the way I was. Then, over the next few months, I decided she simply didn't give a damn." Gottlieb had never heard him utter the smallest profanity before.

"Her mother dies and she shows *no* reaction, none at all?"

"Oh, I suppose it was inconvenient to her. Margaret stayed active until the end. She drove Christina around, took her shopping, bought her clothes. Christina might have missed those things." He reached over, picked up a rubber band from

Gottlieb's desk and played idly with it. "But did she miss Margaret? Miss her as a person—as a person who happened to be her mother? I saw no sign of it. I wish I had."

"Were you lonely after Margaret died?"

"Yes and no. I missed her terribly. Her death was like an open wound that wouldn't heal. But I didn't want to be with other people any more than I had to be. A number of them reached out to me. My family, my neighbors, some of the ones I worked with. I kept them at a distance, most of them. I wasn't trying to be rude. It's just that I needed to be alone."

"Did you miss the company of women?" asked Gottlieb, as offhandedly as possible.

"Once in a great while. That part of life has never been too important to me."

"Did you go out with other women?"

"No. Definitely not." The question provoked a flash of indignation, but it disappeared in an instant. "Perhaps I might have, a couple of years down the road, but I wasn't anywhere near ready for that kind of business."

Gottlieb paused and quietly drew in a breath, as he sought to choose his words carefully. "Mr. Shannon, I need to ask some personal questions about you and Christina. Sometimes, when we're going through a painful, stressful time, we're not ourselves. We do things we ordinarily wouldn't do in a million years."

His patient's expression mixed annoyance and bewilderment. "I don't understand what you're driving at."

There's no easy way to ask him, so I might as well stop tap-dancing, thought Gottlieb. "When your wife died, did you ever have an inappropriate relationship with your daughter?"

Shannon's pallor gave way to a violent blush, and his pale blue eyes filled with fire. For a moment he was too angry to speak. "Never!" he replied finally. The blush persisted. "I'd have killed myself before it came to that! Never!" He glared at Gottlieb. "Is *that* what you think this is all about?"

"No, but I needed to ask you anyway."

"Why?"

"Because," Gottlieb answered neutrally, "these things occur more commonly than we like to think. Because, if something like that *had* occurred, it might have had a bearing on what happened later."

The anger ebbed, and Shannon looked abruptly drained. When he spoke, he sounded exhausted. "I didn't kill Christina because there was anything improper going on. In my whole life, I've been intimate with Margaret, and no one else. That must be hard for you to believe, but it's true. I know how everything's free and easy now, and everyone's supposed to be sleeping with everyone else, but we aren't like that in my family."

If he's putting on a show of outraged innocence for my benefit, thought Gottlieb, *it's the best I've ever seen.*

The session turned to more mundane matters. Gottlieb asked him about his eating and sleeping (so-so), and did he have recurrent nightmares (he hadn't), and how were his attention and concentration (okay, all things considered). He asked if at times he still felt that things weren't real, the way he felt the night of his arrest (he didn't). He asked him questions calculated to tease out subtle threads of paranoia, or grandiosity, or bizarre ideas about religion. None emerged. Gottlieb wondered, *Can he really be this unremarkable?*

"By the way," mentioned Gottlieb as he prepared to end their meeting, "your brother and sister told me you'd once taken Christina to see a therapist. It would have been when she was twelve or so."

"They told you that?" He sounded as if the disclosure was a small betrayal.

Gottlieb nodded. "Why did you?"

He folded his arms in front of his chest. Gottlieb thought he was considering how much to divulge. "It was that summer she went to camp," he said finally. "She didn't last long there, remember? I may have mentioned this already, but at first the lady from the camp said Christina had been homesick. That didn't sound like her at all, and I said so. Well, then the lady, I forget her name, suggested that Christina should get professional help. She said Christina had no idea how to relate to other children, and there'd be a lot of trouble down the road if she didn't change."

"Did she get into specifics?"

"No. I had the feeling that she wasn't being open with me. In fact, I remember telling Margaret that I thought she was being kind of slippery."

Gottlieb made a row of doodles on his notepad. "How long was Christina in treatment?"

"Not long. A month, six weeks at most. Christina hated going. We practically had to drag her there. A waste of time and money, she kept telling us. Looking back, I think she was right. As best we could tell, she got nothing out of it. And even with insurance, we had to pay a fair bit out of pocket. I made a decent living, but we didn't have money to throw away like that. After a while, we just stopped."

"Do you remember the name of the therapist?"

"Let me think. It's been a while." Shannon threw his head back, shut his eyes. "He was a child psychologist named Kendall, Kenton, something like that. Kenyon, that was it. Malcolm Kenyon. He had an office near Lincoln Park."

"How would you feel about my talking with him?"

He shrugged. "I wouldn't much care one way or the other."

CHAPTER XI

GOTTLIEB SLEPT LATE ON SATURDAY MORNING; eight thirty found him still in bed. He almost always rose at least an hour earlier, no matter how poorly he'd slept the night before.

Sharon was already up. By the time he roused himself from the bed and went downstairs, she sat in the kitchen drinking coffee and reading the paper. Her favorite CD was on, Nadja Salerno-Sonnenberg's performance of *The Four Seasons*.

He walked over to her, put a hand on her shoulder. "Hi. How long have you been up?"

"I don't know, half an hour or so." She looked him over carefully. "Are you all right?"

"Yes, of course I am. Why do you ask?"

"Because you almost never sleep this late. You must have been exhausted."

He shrugged. "Busy week, for a change."

"Think we'll ever be able to take it any easier? Before we keel over and drop dead, I mean."

"I hope so." He poured himself a cup of coffee and sat down next to her.

She passed him milk and Equal. "I was about fix myself scrambled eggs. Want me to make you something?"

"That would be nice. I'm kind of hungry." He found himself thinking of Cassandra and the conversation during their recent lunch. "An omelet, maybe?"

"Well, *there's* a switch from the usual Special-K." She sauntered to the fridge. "Hmm, not much in the way of ingredients. How about onion, green pepper, and feta?"

"Sounds fine."

He glanced at the paper while she chopped onions and peppers and crumpled feta. "Will you be going out today?"

"I may go to the mall. I need summer outfits, and a couple of the dress shops are having a sale. How about you?"

"I want to read awhile, maybe work on the new article. After that I'll run a few errands. Pick up the cleaning, go to a car wash, stop at Barnes & Noble." He stirred the coffee, his mind half elsewhere. "Maybe I can interest Peter into going with me."

"Don't count on it." The mention of Peter's name caused her voice to chill, her face to tighten.

"Would you like to take a walk when we get back?"

"Sure, if it's not too hot. Don't forget, we're going out tonight."

"We are?"

She rolled her eyes back. "Honestly, Hal, sometimes I think you could use a brain scan. We're having dinner with Ted and Sue Edelstein at that new Spanish place they've been raving about."

"I remember now." They had, in fact, discussed it only two days ago. Ted Edelstein, a cardiologist, had an office down the hall from Hal's. His wife, Sue, was a stockbroker. Gottlieb enjoyed them, more or less, notwithstanding Ted's adenoidal New Jersey accent and Sue's tendency to drone on about things like the merits of closed-end mutual funds.

The Gottliebs' social circle consisted of six or seven other couples whom they saw with a varying frequency, every three or four weeks to every three or four months. Their friends were people like themselves. Professionals, many of them doctors and lawyers, but they also included an art dealer, a vice president of one of Chicago's largest department stores, and their rabbi. The men had solid, prestigious careers, as did most of their wives. They lived comfortably but not lavishly. Despite their high incomes, they struggled to pay college tuition, first and second mortgages, and often alimony and child support from earlier marriages. Meanwhile they tried to fund their

SEP/IRAs and Keoghs, lest they become old and poor instead of merely old. Their eight-and ten-room homes, their Infinitis and Lexuses, and their not-infrequent trips abroad were nice enough but provided no sense of security.

Gottlieb thought of Cassandra's verdict: *I know about three unhappy couples for every happy one.* Were the couples of their circle happy? They got along, by outward appearances. Hal witnessed little overt warfare, no *Virginia Woolf* routines. Not uncommonly, they seemed vaguely bored with one another, as if neither one could say anything of more than fleeting interest to the other. Perhaps he meted out too harsh a judgment; perhaps it was just that everyone always seemed so tired. No matter how good the restaurant, or the movie or play or concert, they and their friends often fought to stay awake. They came by their exhaustion honestly. Husband and wife routinely worked ninety hours a week between the two of them. By the time they did the other things—raised children, ran errands, worked out, maintained some semblance of a social life—most of them ran on empty.

In the half a decade since returning to Chicago, Gottlieb had gotten close to no one in their circle. He knew their tastes in food and movies, he knew the names and approximate ages of their children, he knew odd bits of trivia about them (Sue Edelstein had an identical twin sister who ran a fishing lodge in Alaska with her husband. Sam Roth flew helicopters in Vietnam before entering the rabbinate). But he knew none of their important secrets, and they knew none of his. If he met with a real catastrophe, if one of his children were seriously ill or if his marriage foundered, he wouldn't turn to them.

If he never saw any of them again, he would scarcely miss them. An unpleasant thought, disturbing, which made him feel somehow defective.

⸎

As Gottlieb attacked the omelet with gusto, Sarah came into

the kitchen and stood next to him. "Hi, Daddy. We wondered if you were *ever* getting up!"

He looked at her with mock indignation. "Can't I can't sleep late once in a while?"

"Well, I *suppose* so." She lay on arm on him, her tiny hand almost lost in the crook of his elbow. "Will you play with me after you have breakfast?"

"Maybe later, honey. There are some things I have to do this morning."

"You could take her on your errands," suggested Sharon.

"Hmm. Yes, I could." He turned to her. "Maybe we could even stop at Baskin-Robbins."

She clapped her hands together. "*Yesss!*" Sarah loved Baskin-Robbins ice cream above all other treats. She loved to deliberate over picking out a flavor, a choice usually based on color. The more exotic, the better. A frequent favorite, therefore, was rainbow sherbet.

He resolved to ask Peter to join them but guiltily hoped the boy would turn them down. He didn't get to spend much time alone with his daughter, and he didn't want Peter to wreck it with his moodiness, his leaden silences.

⸎

Gottlieb secluded himself in the study as soon as he showered and dressed. He carried with him several computer printouts, abstracts of articles he'd gleaned from *Physicians On-line.* He also carried psychiatric publications brought from his office, intending to skim through them. A *Clinical Psychiatry News,* recent issues of *The American Journal of Psychiatry* and *Psychiatric Annals.* The *Psychiatric Annals* seized his interest more than the others. This issue featured several articles on aggression in the workplace, a phenomenon which disturbed him greatly. It disturbed him that any cretin with a grudge and a credit card could walk into a gun shop and buy enough weapons and ammo to turn his factory or office into a slaughterhouse.

Reading took more effort than usual; his mind wandered. Mainly it wandered in the direction of James Shannon.

Gottlieb, to his surprise, had begun to like him. The media accounts of his patient's offense hadn't led him to expect that. Like most people, he despised the perpetrators of crimes against children. But he did like James Shannon. He liked the simple, unpretentious nature of the man. He also liked his honesty; he found it difficult to imagine Shannon lying. He was touched by his devotion, his submission to God's will, and what seemed to be his disinclination to feel sorry for himself. Many of Gottlieb's forensic patients wallowed in self-pity.

He'd known Shannon for about a month now, had met with him on five or six occasions. He'd also met with his brother and sister, and the lawyer who happened to be a lifelong friend. These meetings had led him to the tentative conclusion that James Patrick Shannon had never committed a significant illegal or immoral act. That is, until one summer evening when he bludgeoned and strangled his sleeping daughter.

The late Christina Shannon: now *there* was a mystery. Her striking looks—the blonde ringlets, the flawless face, the wide-set dark blue eyes—were etched in Gottlieb's memory. He'd never seen her in the flesh, of course, but dozens of newscasts and articles had made no secret of her attractiveness. But what had she been like? Who *was* she? A bright child, well behaved but distant. An unpleasant aura had clung to her, had made her difficult for others to relate to. *I would have liked to like her*, her aunt said. *She was my only niece.*

What had she been like? Extremely spoiled, Gottlieb hazarded, especially by a sickly mother who gave birth to her late in life. A mother who gave birth to her at a point when both parents had almost given up having children. Spoiled, and with a mean streak. He recalled her father's anecdotes about the goldfish, and her reaction to her mother's spilling hot coffee on herself. But did spoiled and mean make her evil, whatever the word meant?

Despite his work with evildoers, despite having read at length about them, Gottlieb had paid small attention to the concept of evil per se. He relegated it to philosophy, not medicine, and philosophy had never sparked his interest. His only exposure to it had been a single introductory course, a survey. Some of it he'd found vaguely interesting: Socrates's use of the dialectic; Augustine's musings on the City of God; Rousseau's notion of the noble savage. Some of it—Hegel, Kant, and Schopenhauer, in particular—he found impenetrable, and wading through it had been excruciating. Much of it he regarded as *pilpul*, erudite nonsense, the Yiddish equivalent of agonizing over how many angels can dance on the head of a pin. Philosophic discussions of good and evil struck him as much ado about nothing, a needless muddying of the obvious. Good was when you helped people, when you tried to leave the world in better shape than you found it, when you showed reverence for life and living creatures. Evil was when you did the opposite. To the limited extent that Gottlieb considered it at all, he believed it resulted from ignorance, faulty parental and cultural influences, and bad biochemistry in one's central nervous system. It was pretty much the view he'd put forth on *Roundtable.* He did not believe in a discrete embodiment of evil, or a central agent of it – in other words, he did not believe in Satan. His interest in Satan began and ended with *Paradise Lost*, a work he admired but saw as a product of poetic license. He regarded the notion of a horned devil with cloven hooves as similar to the notion of Venus springing to life fully formed from ocean foam.

None of which shed much light upon Christina Shannon. The more he learned of her, the more questions occurred to him. Why had no one liked her? (Perhaps some people did, although he hadn't found them yet). Why had they asked her to leave that camp? Why had she shown no grief when her mother died?

How had things *really* been between her father and herself when the two of them were suddenly thrust together, without her mother as a buffer? Why didn't her aunt and uncle give the tiniest hint that they mourned her passing? As the story of the Shannons came to light, Gottlieb knew that crucial parts of it were still missing.

He remembered that James Shannon had given him the name of Christina's therapist. He took out the Chicago *Yellow Pages* and flipped through them quickly. A few moments later he found what he was looking for: *Malcolm Kenyon, Ph.D., Clinical Psychologist, Practice Limited to Children and Adolescents.*

He would call Dr. Kenyon the first thing Monday morning.

⚬

Gottlieb tried to force himself to read, to jot down some notes for his article, but half an hour later he gave up. Just as he left the study, Peter came downstairs. The boy wore a pair of rumpled khakis and an orange T-shirt emblazoned with *DAZED AND CONFUSED*. The outfit looked as though he'd slept in it.

It was a few minutes before eleven, but his heavy-lidded eyes were barely open. He hadn't washed or combed his hair. His father's first thought: *He looks homeless.*

"Good morning, Peter."

The dull eyes remained downcast. "Hi."

Gottlieb glanced at his watch. "You're sleeping late today."

"Yeah, well, it's not like I have a lot to get up for."

"I'm going out with Sarah later, run a few errands, stop at Barnes & Noble. Want to come along?" He tried to make the invitation sound as though he meant it.

"Uh-uh."

"Well, what are you going to do with yourself?"

Peter's eyes stayed glued to the floor. "I don't know, just hang around. Maybe call Gordy."

Gottlieb fought off despair as he tried to imagine the stultifying emptiness of his son's day. He recalled a quote from one of his old textbooks on adolescent psychiatry: "Idleness is particularly demoralizing to young people."

Just what he needs, Gottlieb fretted, *to become even more demoralized than he is already.*

✢

The afternoon passed quickly as he and Sarah picked up the dry cleaning, went to a drive-through car wash. and stopped at Blockbusters to rent *The Little Mermaid.* She'd already seen it twice, her father reminded her, but no matter. She deemed it the best movie in the world.

Then they went to Barnes & Noble. He left her in the children's department while he headed towards the history section, seeking out books on the Holocaust and World War II. Since meeting Cassandra, he found himself with heightened interest in the Holocaust, the rise and fall of the Third Reich, and the lives of its leaders. The next time he saw her, he'd ask her for a reading list. *The next time he saw her.* He looked forward to it with an unaccustomed eagerness, an eagerness tinged with no small measure of anxiety.

He wondered what she'd be doing tonight. A bike ride in the early evening, and then she'd read or work on the computer? Or, maybe she'd go out to a movie? Perhaps she had a date. But he guessed she'd be alone, and altogether comfortable in her solitude.

It occurred to him that he'd rather be spending the evening with her than with his wife and the Edelsteins.

He met Sarah, bought *Hitler's Willing Executioners* for himself and a Dr. Seuss for her, and they drove straightway to the Baskin-Robbins. She asked him to hold her up so she could get a better look at the row of flavors. A swirly purple-and-white one caught her fancy. Blueberry ripple.

He opted for lemon sorbet, and they took their selections to a table. Between the licks of ice cream, she kept up a constant line of patter, mainly questions. One of her friends, Ellie McFarland, had just gotten an orange-and-white tabby kitten, and maybe *they* could get a kitten too, and what did *he* think of *The Little Mermaid,* and are mermaids real, and why does ice cream make your teeth hurt, and why doesn't Peter like her, and what happens to the moon when the sun comes up?

Half-listening to her, his thoughts drifting here and there, he recalled his own grave doubts about their decision to have a second child. He was already forty-three, Sharon almost thirty-nine. Wouldn't they be too old? They'd be raising another adolescent when they were in their late fifties, paying for college in their sixties. Furthermore, their lives were still much too unsettled for his liking. They'd reconciled just a short time before, after a wrenching separation precipitated by her affair. An affair with his former partner and putative best friend, no less.

Newly reconciled, still tense and wary with each other, they had just decided to move from the Deep South back to Chicago. To uproot themselves, again, for the third time in their marriage. He knew some couples moved more often. Executives who were transferred every three or four years as a matter of course, and military and diplomatic types. Knowing this made the process no easier, no less formidable.

All of which made him deeply skeptical about another child. But Sharon had been adamant. An only child herself, she didn't want the same fate to fall on Peter. It was more than that, though. A woman not given to melodramatic outbursts, she told him the desire for another child was like a hunger that gnawed at her day and night. A woman not given to imploring, she implored him.

Grudgingly and full of qualms, he'd acquiesced. The result had been Sarah, born two weeks before his forty-fourth birthday. He shuddered at the thought that they might not have had her. And he felt an abiding gratitude to Sharon, for her insistence that they have another child, grateful for her rock-solid stubbornness.

CHAPTER XII

THAT MONDAY, AT 9:00 A.M. SHARP, Dr. Stanley Celinsky convened the monthly staff meeting at GCFI. Dr. Celinsky, a heavyset man of sixty-eight, served as the facility's only full-time psychiatrist (Gottlieb and the three others were part-timers). He'd attained a measure of local prominence as a forensic psychiatrist after serving as an expert witness in several well-publicized cases of twenty-five years ago. Around the same time, he'd written a few professional articles. But he held his present job mainly through the vagaries of local politics. A sister had married an alderman, a nephew served a third term as state senator. The Cook County machine was less than it had been in the heyday of the first Mayor Daley, but Chicago remained a city where clout spoke with a booming voice. Stanley Celinsky, a burnt-out case who still smoked a daily pack of Camels despite two heart attacks, whose mouthful of Tic-Tacs failed to hide his breakfast double vodka, held an iron grip on his sinecure.

Gottlieb glanced around at his fellow attendees. Besides Celinsky and him, the only other psychiatrist there was Regina Cruz, a woman in her early forties but looking a good deal younger, with dark flashing eyes and black hair barely flecked with gray. She chatted with Marie Donatello, the director of nursing. A sad-eyed brunette, Marie was two or three years Regina's junior. Dwight Sanderson had parked himself across from her. Two other RNs flanked him on either side. Behind them, in a row against the wall, sat the secretaries, aides, and ward clerks.

On Gottlieb's immediate left was Norma Caldwell. Next to her sat another social worker, Ezra Hill, an African American in his early forties, professorial and bespectacled, as sedate as Sanderson was flamboyant. On Gottlieb's right, a bit removed from the others, was Howard Pincus, a smarmy man with a bad toupee and a glistening mustache. Pincus held two masters, one in psychology, another in public administration. His official position was Associate Director for Medical and Legal Affairs, but he referred to himself, with folksy self-disparagement, as "the liaison guy." He made frequent calls to the police department and the DA's office but his real job, suspected Gottlieb, consisted of reporting back to the Mayor. Dwight harbored the same suspicion. "He's supposed to tell Hizzoner when that mo'-fo' Celinsky finally goes into DTs."

If you watched the principals file into the conference room, smiling at each other and drinking coffee and exchanging banalities about the weather, you'd be unlikely to pick up on their jockeying for position, their tendency to backstab, and their abiding dislike and distrust for one another. For Gottlieb, whose professional background consisted mainly of private practice and who wasn't much of a political animal to begin with, it had taken him time to learn the new terrain. To learn, for instance, that Marie Donatello and Ezra Hill could barely stand being in the same room together as a result of an affair that ended badly when Hill went back to his wife after a year-long hiatus. To learn that Howard Pincus had tried to get Dr. Cruz fired because she hadn't testified to the DA's liking in a murder case, and that she had tried to get *him* fired because of unwelcome sexual advances. To learn that everyone took potshots at Dr. Celinsky behind his back, writing him off as a drunken toady has-been.

The meeting's format never varied. A summary of recent admissions and discharges. Noteworthy incidents, especially patients' attacks on staff and each other, and their destruction of property. Reports from committees and subcommittees. Finally, a discussion of matters of general interest. In theory this provided an open forum, a chance for anyone to bring up anything. In practice it was used to keep underlings apprised of dictates from above.

Gottlieb made it through these gatherings on autopilot. He'd perfected the technique of keeping part of an ear tuned to subjects of possible interest to him while the rest of his mind went off on fifty tangents. This particular meeting promised to be no better or worse than usual, but attendance was down because of summer vacations. He hoped it augured well for brevity.

Marie Donatello gave the opening statement "There've been thirteen admissions and nine discharges since our last meeting," she summarized. One of the discharged patients, HIV-positive with AIDS dementia, had been referred to Cook County Neurology. They'd remanded another discharged patient to federal court after he'd been restored to competence. The youngest admission was seventeen, the oldest sixty-six. Gottlieb found himself caught up in the plight of the seventeen-year-old. What must it be like, he wondered, to come here at such an age, still more boy than man? What must it be like to find yourself amidst the hearers of voices who ordered them to rape and kill, and the viewers of apocalyptic visions, and the eaters of their own shit? To find yourself among the worst permutations of the insane, the perverse and the predatory.

Marie handed the meeting over to Dwight Sanderson and another nursing supervisor, Wanda Jaworski, whose tiny pale blue eyes were almost lost behind her huge thick granny glasses. They split up the reading of the incident reports. Among the highlights: one patient tried to carve a verse of Scripture on his forearm with the sharpened end of a toothbrush. Another kicked a fellow patient in the instep, full force, for no obvious reason or provocation. (The victim's X-rays came back negative; his wound had been dressed and his ankle wrapped, no need for an outside orthopedic consult.) Another, apparently bored, dismantled the head of the overhead sprinkler in his room. The architects and security experts who'd designed the place had assured them that this was impossible, but patients accomplished it at least once every few months.

In fact, it had been a quiet couple of weeks by GCFI standards. No serious suicide attempts, no assaults on staff, no fights among the patients, at least no fights that threatened life or limb. No escape attempts. *Almost like a real hospital*, mused Gottlieb.

Only three brief reports from the committees, one of them delivered by Norma, who chaired the social subcommittee. They'd arranged an outing for September, a White Sox game. Family members and friends welcome, formal posting to follow, deadline for signing up was August 5. Gottlieb checked his watch furtively. They were sailing right along; it was only 9:25 a.m. With luck they'd be finished in another twenty minutes, maybe even fifteen.

Celinsky brought up matters of general interest. Item one: someone from Personnel would host a forum on health-care benefits for salaried employees the week after next, explaining a new managed-care plan. ("Is it true we gonna get a whole overnight stay for a heart transplant?" Dwight broke in.) Item two: because of vacations, and fewer staff to bring patients to and from the visiting rooms, there'd be a cutback in visiting hours until Labor Day. Visits would also be staggered, depending on the housing units. Celinsky spoke in a droning mumble. Hard enough for Gottlieb to pay attention to him most of the time. Today it was out of the question.

His mind wandered to *Hitler's Willing Executioners*, as fascinating as it was horrific. After dinner with the Edelsteins, he'd read it until two in the morning. He recalled an incident: seven hundred Polish Jews were forced into a barricaded synagogue, subsequently set ablaze. A cordon of Germans with machine guns prevented escapees. "It's a nice little fire. It's great fun," proclaimed one of them. The book made him think of Cassandra, whom he'd begun to regard with something close to awe. How could she give over her professional life to the study of such material and keep sane? He realized, though, that she might ask him the same question.

Celinsky pushed his chair back from the table and folded his arms on his broad lap, his signal that the meeting neared its end. "All right, does anyone have anything else?"

Howard Pincus flashed his trademark smarmy smile and spoke for the first time. "Well, yes, there's something I'd like to bring up, concerning James Shannon." Gottlieb became attentive in a flash.

"Yeah, what about him?" asked Celinsky.

"There's a lot of interest in him downtown. There's a lot of public pressure to, uh, send him back to jail and get on with the case."

"Correct me if I'm wrong," said Gottlieb, "but they had no idea what to do with him in jail. He didn't talk, he responded to no one, he gave every indication of having a serious mental illness. Which is why they sent him to us in the first place."

"Well, yes, of course, but that was a month ago—"

"Shee-it!" Dwight interrupted, making use of his status as the resident free spirit. He was like the court jesters of five hundred or a thousand years ago; he could say what he pleased, and what most of the others thought, with impunity. To a point.

"Crazy bastard kills his daughter for no apparent reason, and then he don't say a word for two weeks," Dwight went on, "and now they're all over us like fleas on a hound dawg 'cause it's been a *whole month*, and we don't have him back in tiptop shape yet!"

Pincus's face reddened. "No one's all over us, Mr. Sanderson. But this is an important case, as I'm sure you're aware, and passions are running high and all that. There's some, uh, concern that he's using his stay here to avoid a correctional setting."

"This *is* a correctional setting," Regina Cruz informed him frostily. "It just happens to be a hospital as well."

"You know that, I know that, but the public doesn't. There

are people who think this place is a Club Med, compared to jail or prison."

Dwight again: "Never heard of no Club Med where they lock the guests up twenty-two hours a day. Where they put 'em in four-point restraints if they get outta hand."

Pincus fought to keep an even tone. "I'm not saying that's an *accurate* impression, but it's the impression nonetheless."

"Let's review the facts, Mr. Pincus," said Gottlieb softly. "First, his behavior after his arrest led police and correctional authorities to suspect that he was seriously ill. Second, he gave every indication that he was incompetent to stand trial in what's apt to be a capital case. Given his offense, and its possible consequences, it would seem to everyone's advantage that he receives as thorough a workup as possible. Furthermore, I think we could agree that he's entitled to it. "

Pincus played with his mustache. "Just out of curiosity, Dr. Gottlieb, do you think he's still incompetent? That is, assuming he was incompetent in the first place."

"I'd rather not comment until our workup has been completed."

"I understand, but, uh, which way do you think the evidence is pointing now?" Pincus's tone had a raspy insistence to it. The rasp belied his fake-diffidence and too-frequent smiles.

Gottlieb had played this game before. He'd found the broken record ploy most useful. "I'd rather not comment until our workup has been completed," he said again. Celinsky's cue to mediate.

"I think Hal's right to hold off on an opinion while the workup's still in progress." He turned to Gottlieb. "But of course you'll keep us informed about any important new developments?" Unclear just whom he meant by *us*.

"Of course."

"All right. Anything else?" No one responded. "Meeting's adjourned then."

Gottlieb checked his watch again—9:42 a.m. Not bad; these

meetings could drag on for well over an hour. Not bad at all.

He spent the rest of the morning seeing patients, writing orders, dictating progress notes, and conferring with Dwight and Norma. From time to time, he retrieved and answered messages from his office. It was nearly one, after lunch, before he had an iota of free time. Not much, but time enough to make the two phone calls on his mind.

"Hello?" Cassandra's tone was brisk but pleasant. The sound of it caused the beginning of a lump in Gottlieb's throat. He wondered why. He wasn't her lover; he wasn't even her suitor. Not yet, at least. Strictly speaking, they hadn't known each other long enough to become friends, although he thought of her as one, in spite of himself.

He tried to speak in as natural a voice as he could muster. "Hello, Cassandra. It's Hal Gottlieb."

"Oh, hi, Hal!" The briskness went away in an instant. "I was hoping you'd call today."

"You were?" he asked, instantly regretting it. *I must sound like a smitten schoolboy.*

"I can't tell you what a treat it is to talk to someone who's not an academic."

"Are they really that oppressive?"

"In the aggregate, yes. But I suppose that's true of any group. How would you find a steady diet of psychiatrists?"

"Deadly." He paused. "I wondered if you might be interested in having lunch sometime this week."

No hesitation whatsoever. "I'd like that. Any day but Wednesday should be good."

Gottlieb glanced at his appointment book. Notwithstanding a tight schedule, he figured he could move things around to create a wedge of time for her. "How about Thursday, twelve thirty?"

"Sounds fine. Why don't you come to my place? I'll fix us something."

"I'd love to."

She reverted to her brisk, efficient voice as she gave directions to her apartment. Gottlieb wrote down the directions carefully. The lump in his throat had disappeared, replaced by damp palms and a racing pulse as the call ended.

He waited for his pulse to slow, his focus to return, before he picked up the phone again. Then he dialed the number he'd been carrying on a scrap of paper since Saturday morning. Expecting to get an answering machine or service, he was caught off guard by the voice of a living, breathing man.

"Hello, Dr. Kenyon speaking."

"Good afternoon, Dr. Kenyon. My name is Dr. Harold Gottlieb. I'm a psychiatrist at the Greater Chicago Forensic Institute."

"Yes?" His tone, polite but noncommittal.

"One of my patients here is a man named James Shannon. I believe you treated his daughter, a patient of yours, a few years ago—"

"Christina," he interrupted. "I remember her quite well." He spoke with unnatural deliberation. "One doesn't forget a patient like Christina Shannon."

"I assume you know what happened to her."

"Yes, of course. I've been following the case with great interest, as you might imagine."

Gottlieb hesitated slightly. "Dr. Kenyon, I know this is an unusual request, but I wonder if you'd meet with me. There are some things about Christina, and what happened to her, that I'm trying to sort out. I'm hoping you might be able to shed some light on them."

"I'm leaving town for ten days, beginning Thursday morning. If you'd like to meet before then, I could see you around six thirty Wednesday evening, in my office." Gottlieb thought he heard a muted sigh. "The truth is, Doctor, I've been waiting for someone like you to call."

CHAPTER XIII

MALCOLM KENYON, A MAN OF INDETERMINATE middle age, was about five nine with short-cropped graying hair and a slightly triangular, elongated face. His most note-worthy feature: hazel eyes, more green than brown, warm but a bit wary, inquiring but unthreatening. The eyes of a man suited to bring solace to an abused third grader, or to tease out the burdensome secrets of a sullen adolescent. The eyes of a man who invited openness but did not demand it. *Whatever you choose to tell me, I will listen. You won't shock me, and I won't pass judgment on you. But if you want to wait awhile, to talk about MTV or baseball, or merely to sit and say nothing while you feel me out, that's all right too.*

His neat appearance bordered on the fussy. A hot summer day was coming to an end, but his outfit didn't show it. His white cotton shirt remained tucked tightly into the front of his gray trousers, his blue blazer showed scarcely a wrinkle, his red bow tie remained perfectly in place. By contrast, Gottlieb's tie was loosened and askew, his top shirt button was unbuttoned, and his seersucker sports coat looked as though he'd played handball in it.

As Gottlieb sat across from him, he was struck by the minimalist order of the large walnut desk between them. The desk held a phone, an appointment book, a few letters, a stapler, and a fountain pen, and that was it. Gottlieb's own desk tended to be awash in journals, notepads, prescription pads, mail opened and unopened, pictures of his wife and children, pens, pencils, and erasers. Every two or three weeks, he'd take an hour and wade through all of it. Two or three days later, his desk would look the way it had before.

"I remember when her mother phoned," said Dr. Kenyon. "It was about this time of year, July. Christina had just come back from camp. Something happened there, and they sent her home early. Her mother sounded terribly embarrassed. My guess is, it was the first time anyone in the family made contact with a mental health professional. She phoned late on a Friday afternoon, pleading with me to see Christina as soon as I could. I gave her an appointment for the following Monday."

"What was your first impression of Christina?" Gottlieb asked.

"Well-mannered," he answered quickly. "That's the main thing that comes to mind. Almost *too* well-mannered. Chillingly polite." Gottlieb remembered her uncle's comment, that Christina was polite because you weren't important enough to be rude to.

"She was controlled and self-contained," Dr. Kenyon went on, "and altogether lacking in spontaneity. And her eyes! I'll never forget those eyes of hers. Very blue, very pretty, but with no real warmth to them. She never took them off me. Children often take their time before making eye contact, but not her. Those eyes bore into me from the moment she walked in until she left. She didn't take them off me for a second. It was"—he stopped as he sought the right word—"disconcerting."

"I can imagine."

"She didn't want to be here," the psychologist continued, "and she made no bones about it. 'I'm doing this to get them off my back' is how she put it. I saw her about ten times, and she never showed the tiniest bit of interest in our meetings, never saw a need for them."

"Did she talk about what happened at the camp?"

"Only in generalities. She said the other campers hadn't liked her, and neither had the counselors. And she couldn't stand the scheduling. Having to do things at certain times, having to go to bed early. I gathered she liked to stay up late. She didn't seem to need much sleep."

"Did it bother her that no one liked her?"

"Not in the least. As best I could tell, she was absolutely indifferent to how others felt about her. Not just her fellow campers and counselors, but everyone."

"Including her parents? Gottlieb asked. Kenyon nodded.

"Did she talk about any particular incidents up there? Getting into fights, leaving camp without permission?"

"I asked her about those things, at different times and in different ways. She always denied them."

Gottlieb stole a glance out of Dr. Kenyon's window. His office faced the east, and the sky was already darkening. He had a sudden urge to be outside. Kenyon's office was pleasant enough with its gray and mint-green wallpaper, its nicely framed degrees, and its photos of marine mammals (harp seal, dolphin, gray whale, walrus). The office was pleasant enough, but Gottlieb found it confining and oppressive. *Perhaps,* he thought, *it's not the office. It's the subject.*

"A lot of campers aren't very happy or very popular," commented Gottlieb, "but they don't get sent home the way she did. How did she explain that?"

"She didn't. Whenever I brought it up, she simply dodged it. She said everyone thought it was for the best, and that's as far as she would go."

Gottlieb made a few random scratches on his notepad, on which were fewer notes than doodles. "You met with her parents too, I take it?"

Kenyon nodded and briefly checked Christina's manila file. "I met twice with her mother alone, with both parents once, and twice with all three of them."

"What were your impressions of them?"

"Ordinary, decent people. Hard-working, devoted to each other. Christina threw them for a loop. They had no idea what to make of her or how to deal with her. They knew there was something wrong with her, but they didn't know what. I could empathize with them. It wasn't something *obvious*."

Kenyon paused to sort through his thoughts. "In many ways, you see, Christina was a model child. She obeyed her parents, for the most part. She made good grades. She caused no problems in the classroom. She kept her room neat and clean. She did her chores without a fuss. Loading the dishwasher, taking out the garbage, and so forth. She never showed the smallest hint of depression or anxiety. She didn't throw tantrums; she wasn't violent; she didn't try to run away from home. In fact, she did none of the things which ordinarily prompt parents to bring a child to me."

"What *were* their concerns?"

"That she had no friends, and appeared to have no need for friends. That she didn't seem to care about anything or anyone." He paused. "And they were terribly concerned about her cruelty. From the time she was a toddler, she seems to have been fascinated by the sufferings of others. People or animals, friends or strangers, it didn't matter. A neighbor's cat or dog would get killed by a car, and she'd seem happy about it. She never cared much about television, but TV news of some catastrophe—a famine, an earthquake, or a plane crash, say—would captivate her. She was always singularly lacking in compassion."

"Did she like to inflict pain herself, or was her fascination with it strictly passive?"

"Are you asking me if she was actively sadistic?" The psychologist rubbed his forehead. "No. At least, not to my knowledge. But of course she would have denied it."

"What were they like when you met with all three of them together?"

"They were like . . . it was as if Christina and her parents belonged to different species. You got a sense that they had nothing in common. Nothing. The Shannons were unlike any family I've ever worked with. It was all the more striking because the sessions were so calm. No yelling, no histrionics, no overt displays of anger. Mr. or Mrs. Shannon would introduce a topic, an area of concern to them, and Christina would pooh-pooh it. That's pretty much how the sessions went. If you videotaped the three of them and showed the tapes to someone who didn't know English, he'd never guess that this family had serious problems."

Kenyon lightly tapped the cover of Christina's file, then resumed. "I found myself with a strange reaction to her parents. I felt sorry for them, but it went beyond that. I was worried about them."

Gottlieb's head jerked up. "Why?"

"Nothing I could pinpoint. I wasn't afraid she'd burn the house down, or take an ax to them like Lizzy Borden. It wasn't like that. But—I don't mean to sound melodramatic—the feeling was real, and very strong."

Gottlieb wanted to shift the discussion around to James Shannon. "About her murder: there's no question that he did it, but we still don't know why. There's no pattern of recurrent violence that we know of, no drug or alcohol abuse, no evidence of an underlying physical disorder. By all accounts, he's the most unlikely man in the world to commit a violent act."

"But you must have theories."

Gottlieb nodded. "Two main ones. First, that he did it in the course of a psychotic depression triggered by his wife's demise. Second, that he had an illicit sexual relationship with her, which was about to blow up in his face. Frankly, I don't much care for either of them, especially the latter."

"Has he said anything himself about a motive?"

"Just one thing, shortly after we admitted him. He said he did it, and I quote, 'to save the world from her.'" He thought he saw Kenyon shudder, barely noticeably.

"That's all he'd say," went on Gottlieb. "He hasn't talked about it since. Whenever we've brought up the subject, he says he can't talk about it yet. Or else he won't say anything at all."

"'To save the world from her.' Do you think he meant it?"

"There's been no indication that he didn't." Gottlieb made another row of doodles in his notepad. "How about you? Based on your knowledge of Christina and her family, do you have any theories of your own?"

Kenyon shook his head. "Not really. But I'll tell you my first thought, as soon as I heard about it on TV. I thought, *What in God's name did she do to provoke him?*"

"Interesting reaction."

"I thought so myself." He raised his head, looked directly at Gottlieb with his warm hazel eyes. "According to the press accounts, he's at your facility to find out if he's competent to stand trial. Do you think he is?"

Gottlieb wondered how much he should reveal. "Off the record, yes."

"So he'll almost certainly be found guilty, and he'll end up on death row, or serving life without parole."

"I don't want to speculate, but . . ." His voice trailed off.

"God help him," said Kenyon quietly.

They fell silent. "I'd like to know what really happened at that camp," muttered Gottlieb. "By any chance, do you have the name of it?"

"I might." He flipped through Christina's file. "Here it is. Green Lake Camp for Girls. As I recall, her parents said it was about an hour from Milwaukee."

Gottlieb jotted down the name. He checked his watch. The psychologist had given him almost a full hour, and he didn't want to overstay his welcome. "I've asked a lot of questions," he said as he prepared to leave. "Is there anything I haven't asked that you think would be important for me to know?"

Kenyon mulled over the question. "Only this," he answered finally. "I've been in practice for more than twenty years. I've worked with all kinds of children and adolescents, including youthful offenders who've committed absolutely heinous acts. Murders, sexual offenses, cruelty to animals, the whole gamut. But I disliked Christina Shannon more than any other patient

I've ever had."

※

The next day, as Gottlieb sat behind the wheel of his Saab in heavy traffic en route to Cassandra's, he tried to calm himself. To remind himself, *It's just for lunch. Nothing will happen unless we allow it to happen, unless we make it happen. Nothing* needs *to happen. Ridiculous, my getting all worked up like this! Nothing need happen.* These reminders failed to focus his attention or curb his bounding imagination.

Eager to distract himself, he rifled through the CD case on the passenger seat next to him. Gottlieb loved to listen to the Saab's CD player. It restored him as he drove the long stretches between office, home, and hospital; it gave him a respite from the grinding days. He glanced through the available CDs, his usual fifty-fifty mix of jazz and classical, the only kinds of music he really cared about. His eye caught sight of a Jobim, the great master of Brazilian jazz, easy and rhythmic, as seductive as a girl sauntering along the Ipanema beach. Perfect.

Caught up in the CD, drawn into it, he felt himself start to relax. His mind slowed, and he could think in his usual fashion. Careful, thorough, linear. Used to exploring the feelings of his clientele, he tried to delve into his own. How, precisely, did he feel about this afternoon's engagement? It undeniably excited him, but it wasn't the usual sexual excitement. Or if so, that made up only part of it. He decided it was something subtler. The excitement that comes from making a sharp break with one's set routine. More than that: the excitement that comes from embarking on a voyage across uncharted waters.

He had no idea of where this relationship—if that's what it was—would go, or where he wanted it to go. Of course he found himself powerfully drawn to her. Through the years, he'd known a number of attractive women, some of them more attractive than she was, but their pull had been nowhere near this strong. To occupy himself, he made as objective an assessment of her appearance as he could. A large woman, big-boned, not fat but extremely muscular, oak-solid. Square face, unimaginatively framed by long blonde bangs; not one, she, to waste money on a top-dollar hair stylist. A crop of freckles lent her face a girlishness it might otherwise have lacked. Bright eyes—penetrating, quizzical, a bit bemused by things. A pretty mouth with heart-shaped lips, warmer than the rest of her face (her most attractive feature, in his view). A strong chin, which hinted at a stubbornness he found oddly appealing.

Not his type. He'd always been drawn to more petite women. Slenderer women, more finely featured. It didn't matter. He hadn't felt this way about another woman since the day he met Sharon.

The thought came to him, not for the first time. *Is this a delayed reaction to Sharon and Gary? Is this a manner of revenge?* The possibility disturbed him. To seek revenge had always struck him as singularly distasteful, a pursuit as demeaning to the seeker as the target.

He allowed himself to think about Gary Nuland, something he did rarely. The same Gary Nuland he'd known since they started medical school, where they'd been partners in the freshman biochemistry lab . . . whom he met again by chance at a psychiatric convention, many years after they lost contact . . . who pulled out all the stops as he wined and dined them, and who invited him to join a thriving practice at a time when Gottlieb's own practice faltered. The same Gary Nuland who took Gottlieb under his wing, introduced him to a slew of new colleagues, referred him patients by the dozen, and had made him a full partner after just a year together. The same Gary Nuland who'd been, in fact, the perfect friend—generous, hospitable, supportive—except for the bad habit of sleeping with his wife.

Gottlieb was not an especially imaginative man, but fleeting images of them together haunted him. The images came rarely now, no more than once every three or four months. They mainly came when he was on the verge of sleep. He'd see their heads together on a pillow, their bodies tangled in sheets. He'd see Gary's thick brown hair, as straight as his own was kinky, his deep brown soulful eyes and unblemished skin. Gottlieb had always been struck by Nuland's looks. When he compared the way they looked, it made him feel like Caliban.

The images never lasted long, a few seconds at the most. Just long enough to bring a softball-sized lump to his throat, to turn his stomach into a trampoline. Just long enough to ensure he'd scarcely sleep that night.

He remembered Cassandra's question about whether he'd forgiven her. He thought so, he was almost sure of it. Almost. But he would never forgive Gary Nuland, not if he lived to be a hundred. Never.

Gottlieb forced the thoughts of Gary from his mind. They led nowhere; they merely wrecked his sleep and filled his waking hours with a subtle poison. They went in circles, as endless as a Mobius strip. He found no profit in them.

Cassandra greeted him with a smile that was almost diffident, but without a hug or handshake, just a quick patting of his elbow. Another steamy summer day, but her appearance belied the heat and humidity. She wore a pink cotton blouse, powder blue Bermuda shorts, and tan sandals. No jewelry, apart from a simple gold necklace. No makeup, apart from flesh-colored lipstick and the smallest hint of eyeliner.

"Come in and make yourself at home."

He entered a spacious living/dining room, and was struck by her emphasis on white. White on white wallpaper, white sofa and love seat, white bookcases. Only a pair of green-and-taupe armchairs broke up the white motif. The armchairs, and a scattering of hanging art, mainly Dürer reproductions. As he ambled around the room, one of the Dürers caught his eye: the drawing of a young man with long flowing hair and an exquisite sensitive face, done in reddish-brown pencil.

Cassandra came to his side, and they studied the print together. "I've always liked Dürer," Cassandra said, "and that's one of the ones I like the most. It's a self-portrait and—"

A subdued meowing interrupted her. Gottlieb felt something rub against his leg. He looked down and saw a large cat with luxuriant gray fur and bright golden eyes bidding for his attention. The long gray fur had a bluish tint. "And this useless oaf is Freitag." She picked him up and draped him over her right shoulder, like a stole.

Gottlieb stroked him beneath his chin, which brought forth enthusiastic purring. "It looks like you've made a friend for life. Funny, as a rule he's standoffish with strangers."

"Freitag. That's the German word for Friday, isn't it?"

She nodded. "I brought him home on a Friday, and the name seemed right for him." Reaching over with her free hand, she ran a finger down his spine. The volume of purring increased. "He's spoiled and lazy. He wouldn't chase a mouse if one bit him on the nose. He wrecks my furniture and leaves hair everywhere—if his hairballs were any bigger, you might trip over them. If I had a dime for every time he scratched me, I'd be rich. It doesn't matter, I'm still crazy about him. Sometimes I think we were lovers in a previous life."

"What did you do wrong to come back as a person?"

She set Freitag down on the floor. Gottlieb took a few steps towards an open door on his left and peered into a book-lined den. She moved ahead of him and beckoned him to join her. "My study. It's my favorite room."

He looked around approvingly. "I can see why." It was spacious, almost as big as the living/dining room but more welcoming. Light poured in from windows on two sides. She'd had the walls painted a light blue. The chairs were a darker blue, close to violet. The decorations were more colorful as well, featuring a pair of abstract paintings with exuberant swirls of red and orange. Against one wall sat a long oak desk with a computer and cordless phone on one side of it and several open books and journals on the other.

He walked over to one of the two large bookcases which filled most of a wall. There were books in English, German, and French on European history, from the Middle Ages to the splintering of the Soviet Union. Biographies of European movers and shakers from Charlemagne to Henry VIII to Lenin to Gorbachev. A generous sampling of European literary figures, from Chaucer and Shakespeare to Günter Grass. A scattering of works on other subjects, as diverse as *The Photographs of Ansel Adams*, *501 Must-See Movies*, and *The British Museum Book of Cats*.

Books on twentieth-century Germany filled an entire shelf and spilled over into another one. They included Goebbels's diaries, Speer's autobiography, a half a dozen biographies of Hitler himself, and studies of everyday life in the Third Reich. There were accounts of World War II, the Occupation, and the Nuremberg Trials. Books on the neo-Nazi resurgence of recent years.

"It's just part of them," she said. "I have more than that in my office at the university. There are times when I think I'll go stark raving mad if I read another word about the Holocaust." The bright blue eyes conveyed, for once, a vulnerability instead of her usual self-assurance.

"What do you do when that happens?"

She shrugged. "I get on the floor with Freitag and brush his coat. Or I take a walk or ride the bike. Or I have a glass of wine and put on a CD. Classical guitar works particularly well for me, I don't know why. And the feeling passes."

"And then you go right back to where you were?"

"Of course. Just as you go right back to your patients when you reach the end of *your* rope."

Gottlieb took a step towards the bookcase and picked up a thin paperback, Elie Wiesel's *Night*. "This is the most powerful book I've ever read about the Holocaust. The way he writes about the night he arrived at Auschwitz. That first night."

He thumbed through a few pages in search of the exact quote. Cassandra beat him to the punch, reciting from memory, her eyes closed. "'Never shall I forget that night, the first night in camp, which has turned my life into one long night, seven times cursed and seven times sealed.'"

♦

In a flash she reverted to the efficient hostess. "Enough. How about giving it a rest and having lunch?" Gottlieb nodded, replaced the book, and followed Cassandra into the kitchen.

She handed him a bottle of *Vinho Verde* and a corkscrew. "Do me a favor and open this while I get things ready, okay?" He did as asked while she took deviled eggs, whitefish salad, and a plate of sliced tomatoes and provolone from the fridge. Quickly, smoothly, she added finishing touches, a twist of fresh ground pepper here and a dollop of fresh parsley there, humming to herself while she worked. At times he thought he saw her pretty mouth begin to form a smile. He wasn't sure.

He helped her bring the food to a table already set. After she made one last trip to the kitchen, for a basket of sliced marble rye, they were ready to eat. Despite his earlier high school angst, he felt almost relaxed now. Relaxed in the company of this woman whom he'd known for a matter of weeks, a woman whom he'd seen exactly twice and phoned on perhaps three more occasions, but a woman with whom he sensed a powerful, unnerving kinship.

I feel like I'm on vacation, it dawned on him. He felt far away, a willing exile on an island of calm where people didn't clamor for his attention, where they made no demands on him at all, in fact. It also dawned on him that no one knew where he was now. Not his patients, not his coworkers at GCFI, not his wife. Especially not his wife. A rare, exhilarating state for him. He usually kept compulsively in touch.

Lunch passed easily and leisurely. A simple meal, flawlessly prepared. Deviled eggs tart and crunchy with finely minced celery, whitefish salad accented with capers, sliced hothouse tomatoes doused in a citrus vinaigrette. Gottlieb drank the white wine slowly. Nonetheless, he found himself fighting off lightheadedness. Once in a while he found himself feeling close to giddy.

Conversation glided back and forth among a dozen topics. An upcoming trial in which he'd testify as an expert witness for a schizophrenic pedophile. A graduate seminar she was teaching on European Colonialism ("At least it's giving me a break from the Holocaust"). Movies—*The Horse Whisperer* ("Good enough but too long," she decreed. "A *Titanic* with oats.") The end of the Cold War, and what would replace the Evil Empire, and would we someday yearn nostalgically for the USSR? The series finale of *Seinfeld*.

He was hard-pressed to remember the last time he'd enjoyed a meal so much.

When she went to the kitchen, he found himself thinking of the end of their second meeting. "Who was Franz?" he asked, after he'd returned with their mugs of coffee. At first she looked at him blankly. "The last time we met, you were talking about why you dreaded going into therapy. You said, 'I suppose it has a lot to do with my Uncle Franz.'"

Her head flew back sharply. For a few moments she said nothing. When she spoke again, it was in a tone he hadn't heard before, soft and tentative. At times she almost mumbled.

"My father's family was upper middle class," she began. "Doctors and lawyers and professors. My mother's family was different. Skilled tradesmen, mechanics, a few small businessmen. Not so high up the ladder. One of her uncles, my great uncle, was a man named Franz Blau."

She sipped coffee, clutching the mug with both hands. "Franz had always been something of a black sheep. Bright enough, according to the family folklore, but he didn't do much with his brains. Bored in school, restless and distracted. He came of age just after World War I, just in time for the economic chaos of the Weimar Republic. He worked at this and that, mainly as a waiter or hotel clerk. Once he tried to start a business of his own, selling cigarettes and candy from a kiosk in a Berlin railway station. He didn't fail, not quite, but he certainly didn't prosper. Most of the time he lived a hand-to-mouth existence. In the process he turned angry. Bitter. One of those angry embittered people who knew he should have done more with his life but who couldn't or wouldn't take responsibility for his failures. And then Hitler rose to power." She fell silent, stirring the coffee with a spoon, seeming to lose her train of thought. He began to throw in a question but decided to wait her out.

"Franz became enraptured, an instant convert. The Nazi party was tailor-made for a man like him. A man who was bright but undisciplined, full of all manner of resentments. Consumed with poorly focused anger. 'A man with a hunger for scapegoats,' my father said. 'A man who looked for easy answers.' And so he joined the party, and he loved it. He loved the medieval pageantry, the parades and the rallies and the bonfires. He loved learning of his innate superiority to the rest of the world, which he'd always suspected anyway."

Cassandra took a moment, as if she had to steel herself to go on. "He loved Hitler. It wasn't just that he became a passive follower, or saw him as the least of several evils, or had his fingers crossed behind his back. He *loved* him, he would have died for him. He, and tens of millions others."

Stopping to sip more coffee, she resumed. "And so he joined the party, and then he went beyond mere membership. He joined the *Schutzstaffel*, the SS. You probably know that the SS consisted solely of volunteers. To make a long story short, he enjoyed a huge success there. The first success he'd ever had in life. He became an officer, and his career took off like a rocket. He met Eichmann and Himmler. It's possible he met Hitler himself. Then he became involved in drawing up plans for the camps. It seems he had a talent for planning and administration. Eventually, he became second in command at a camp called Neuengamme."

"That's one I haven't heard of."

"No reason why you should have. It was small, relatively unimportant, tucked away near the Danish border. When most people think of concentration camps, they think of the big, notorious ones. Auschwitz, Buchenwald, Dachau, and such. There were actually hundreds of them, scattered all over occupied Europe, from the Baltic to the Balkans. Some were very small, with less than a thousand prisoners at any given time. Even a Holocaust historian would find it hard to name them all."

She pushed the coffee mug aside, poured herself the last of the Vinho Verde, drank half the glass in a single swallow and went on. "Neuengamme had no Zyklon-B, no crematoria, no Dr. Mengele performing ghastly medical experiments. It was nothing more than a tiny cog in the machinery of death. They used it primarily as a staging point for transport to the larger camps. From time to time they shot prisoners, or beat them to death with shovels, but they didn't kill them by the hundreds of thousands. Small potatoes, you might say."

"What exactly did your uncle do there?"

"He handled much of the day-to-day administration. Routine stuff. Making sure the camp had provisions and supplies. Making up the duty rosters, settling his underlings' disputes. Keeping tabs on the *kapos*."

"The who?" Gottlieb hadn't heard the word before.

"The kapos. Jew-bosses. Favored prisoners, semi-trusted by the Nazis, who kept the other prisoners in check. They were also informers. Prisoners hated them as much as the Nazis, maybe more. When the camps were liberated, a few of them were literally torn apart."

She took another moment before continuing. "Back to Franz," she said finally. "He also organized transports to the larger camps, especially to Auschwitz. He personally shot a few prisoners, and he hanged a few escapees, but he wasn't especially sadistic by SS standards. He didn't burn them alive or drown them in cisterns of human waste the way they did in other places. He didn't tie the pregnant women's legs together when they were ready to give birth. And then the war ended." She appeared to lose her train of thought again.

"He was arrested?"

She nodded. "He was tried for crimes against humanity . . . he wasn't important enough to be hanged. They gave him twenty years. He died in prison in 1958."

She finished the glass of wine. "And that's it, that's the story of my Uncle Franz. And yes, it has lots to do with why I've dreaded going into therapy, and why I became a Holocaust historian."

"How old were you when you found out about him?"

"Eleven."

"What was it like for you, finding out?"

Her eyes flashed angrily. *"What the hell do you think it was like?* It was devastating. More devastating than anything that's happened to me before or since." She stood up, began to pace. "Up to that point, I'd been proud of my family. I knew they had their faults, of course, but I was proud of them anyway. Despite the War and the Holocaust, I was proud of my German heritage. I grew up in a bilingual household, I always loved the language—even now I still dream in it half the time. My parents were people who cared about music and art and literature. They enjoyed respect in the community, my father's patients regarded him as a demigod of sorts. I remember telling you how my father had affairs and my mother could be the quintessential martyr, but they were basically good people. And then, to learn *that . . . "*

Her eyes took on a faraway look. "I used to lie in bed at night, trying to imagine what life was like in Neuengamme. Not just for the prisoners, but what it was like for the SS. What were they thinking, or did they manage not to think? Uncle Franz: what was *he* like? How did he feel sending women and children off to Auschwitz, or ordering someone shot or hanged? Presumably, he wasn't a born murderer. So, what *happened* to him? Were we alike, he and I? We couldn't be, but then again we had to be. We came from the same stock, we were products of the same culture."

"Not really," he interrupted. You're a native-born American. Apart from your education and your travels, you've lived here your whole life. Living here has shaped you in a hundred ways, a thousand."

The tempo of her pacing quickened. "Of course, it has. But that doesn't cancel out these other similarities. I was ten when I went to Germany for the first time. A little girl who'd never been outside the United States before, except for a weekend in Montreal with her family. Now here's the creepy thing, Hal. I felt *at home* there. It wasn't just that I spoke the language. How they lived, what they ate and drank, how they dressed . . . how they looked when they stood waiting for a bus or in a movie queue . . . it was all *familiar* to me, as though I'd been there before, even though I knew I hadn't been. Déjà vu, you call that? The point is, I knew that I was one of them, in some fundamental way I couldn't explain, just as I knew that I was indelibly American. It confused me then and it confuses me now."

Gottlieb took his time before responding. "The bad news," he said, "is I can't absolve you for what your uncle did. No one can. The good news is, you don't need absolution in the first place. You're not responsible for anyone's actions but your own—"

"I *know*," she broke in testily. "With due respect, that's pretty obvious."

His face reddened. "Well, a lot of psychiatry consists of stating and restating the obvious, which people have a way of overlooking. A supervisor of mine once described much of psychiatry as codified common sense. Take guilt, for instance."

"Do I have to?"

"Let's say a child is badly treated," he went on. "She's criticized at every turn. Her accomplishments may be considerable, but they're disregarded. She feels unwanted, unloved, and unlovable. She'd done nothing wrong, but she feels guilty. Why? Because she thinks it would all be different—better—if only *she* were better. Smarter, prettier, whatever. She asks herself, *What's wrong with me to make them treat me like that?* She doesn't ask the more valid question, *What's wrong with them for treating me like that in the first place?* Now this question may be obvious to you and me, but it may escape her altogether, even if she has an IQ of 150."

"I suppose." She sounded indifferent. She also sounded very tired, as though she'd talked for hours.

Her pacing brought her to his side of the table. She stood behind him, rested a hand on his shoulder. "I've never told anyone about him, never thought I would. Thanks for listening."

"You're welcome." Without facing her, still sitting, he placed his hand on top of hers. His hand, much larger, covered up hers like a baseball glove.

He stood up, very slowly, and turned around towards her. Their faces were close enough for him to discern the outline of every freckle, to see the fine striations around her blue eyes, infinitely sad now. The wish to kiss her, to kiss that splendid mouth he'd deemed her best and warmest feature, swelled up in him like a wave about to crash against the shore. At the same time, from some deep crevasse of his brain, a voice made itself undeniable. *No. Don't do this now.*

He touched her cheek with the back of his massive paw, with a touch lighter than the lightest feather. "Let's clear the table. I'll give you a hand."

CHAPTER XIV

GOTTLIEB SAT ALONE IN HIS OFFICE at GFCI savoring the quiet moment. It was Friday morning, about ten thirty. Only three more hours there, plus three more in his office, stood between himself and the weekend.

For once there were no plans, no social engagements. Unusual for him and Sharon. Spontaneity did not come easily to him, but he found the prospect of two unplanned days agreeable. He would read, walk, or swim as he saw fit, take Sarah to a playground if the heat was not oppressive. Sitting in his office, his feet on his desk, he even imagined himself doing nothing. Relaxing outside on the patio, iced tea in hand, watching the birds and squirrels and clouds. At the age of forty-eight, however gingerly and belatedly, Hal Gottlieb had begun to discover the joys of unstructured time.

So far, a light day. He'd met with James Shannon and three other patients, conferred with Dwight and Norma. Apart from the paperwork, ever uncompleted, not much remained for him to do.

He welcomed the lull, which would give him the chance to read the journal James Shannon handed him at the end of this morning's session, the journal begun right after his arrest. The same grade school composition book with a black-and-white speckled cover that sat on the desk in Shannon's cell, the day of Gottlieb's first encounter with him. Gottlieb had offered to read it at any time. Now, a month later, Shannon had finally felt ready to take him up on it.

"I don't know if you're still interested in taking a look at this," his patient had said, almost shyly. Gottlieb struggled to keep his eagerness in check.

Shannon wrote in a neat steady hand, careful and unadorned, the handwriting taught by generations of nuns. Gottlieb started reading:

June 7. It's finally sinking in. I no longer think of this whole thing as a bad dream I can't wake up from. What I've done & where I am & the fact that all the good parts of my life are over, these are the new realities. I look back on my life of a month ago or even just a week ago, and it might as well be someone else's life. It has nothing to do with me now.

God will give me strength to deal with these new realities, which I do not doubt, I cannot doubt. I will try to hold on to the passage in the book of Proverbs,

Trust in the Lord with all thy heart,
And lean not upon thine own understanding

From the beginning, my own understanding has been of no use at all.

I can best cope, I think, by taking things day by day, even hour by hour, & sometimes minute by minute. I will get through the next five minutes, & then I'll worry about the five minutes after that, & then the five minutes after that, & so on. As they say, 1 day at a time. I must have heard that said a million times before, but I never understood it, not fully, until now.

I speak to no one here & almost no one speaks to me, which is as I prefer it. What with the nature of my crime, and the way the media has had a field day with it, I expected a rough time from other inmates. It's a big relief to have them leave me alone. I guess they think anyone who'd do what I did must be very crazy, so they shy away from me, more than they would otherwise. It's as if they think I have something contagious. The guards too. My crime must be terribly frightening even to them. They wonder if what happened to me could happen to them, they wonder if they could go crazy and kill someone, God forbid one of their children. I can see it in their eyes.

June 9. I wouldn't have guessed it, but the hardest part of being locked up like this is the noise. I can get used to the confinement, the lack of privacy, although it's hard to wash and use the toilet when I know the camera's on me. I can even get used to the danger that is always present. You feel it in the air, it's as real as rain or snow. But I don't think I'll ever get used to the noise. Not even if I'm locked up for as long as I live, which will almost certainly be the case.

I'm finding that the only way to deal with this is to go very deep inside myself, to a safe and quiet place which has no connection to the rest of my life or even the rest of the world. I imagine this place as a quiet island in the tropics somewhere, the Caribbean maybe, with rough seas all around it. But the island itself is always safe and always peaceful.

I think of Margaret more, not less, as time goes on. Maybe that's just because I'm here and there's little else to do besides think, but I believe it's more than that. Memories of her sustain me, for instance when I lie on my bunk late at night, alone as I've never been alone, trying to drown out the clang of the doors and heavy footfalls, the yelling and screaming.

Earlier this week, maybe Mon. or Tues., I found myself remembering our honeymoon in San Francisco. 20 years ago it was, but it seems like yesterday, that's how clear it is to me. I remember the flight out, first time she'd flown, and the way she grabbed on to my arm when we took off, the way she tried to watch the movie but whenever the plane went through bumpy air she lost her concentration. She didn't like it one bit when they brought down the landing gear, she thought we were having engine trouble. Then before you knew it we were on the ground. She couldn't believe we'd gone so far in so short a time.

I recall every detail of our time there. Riding on the cable cars, up & down the steep hills. She loved them, she said she could ride on them all day. Taking the boat to Alcatraz while the gulls flew all around us, swooping down when anyone threw out popcorn or a piece of a hot dog bun. Holding hands as we walked through Chinatown. Having lunch there, something a bit peculiar, with purple vegetables I never saw before, but very tasty. I couldn't get the knack of using chopsticks, but she did all right with them right away.

We were there a week & I remember everything we saw, everything we ate and drank, everything she wore. Especially the frilly white lace nightgown she wore that first night.

I guess most people remember their honeymoons in detail, but I remember smaller things as well. The small things are just as clear and just as important. Like that night in Dec., the year we were married, the first cold night of the winter. I came home half frozen, & she made Irish lamb stew from a new recipe she wanted to try out. I remember how tasty it was, how it warmed me through and through. By then she'd started baking, and we had that soda bread I liked so much. After dinner I made a fire. There was nothing good on TV so we played gin rummy. A very simple evening, and I suppose most people would think it nothing special if not downright boring, but it made me feel like the luckiest man alive.

It's been so long since I've said a word to anyone, I sometimes wonder if I can still talk at all. Well, there are worse things than not talking. There are orders of nuns who don't talk, & some of the Brothers too, & I'm beginning to understand the appeal of that kind of life.

This morning I was reading the Gospel According to Matthew, and I was struck by Matthew's account of the Temptation. I wondered, as I've wondered before, just what it means. Did Jesus really fast for 40 days & 40 nights? If so, was it really the devil who came to

Him or was He just imagining it? Was He thinking all sorts of crazy things because of lack of food and sleep?

But if it really happened, why did God permit it in the first place? Since God knows everything, surely He knew that Jesus would resist temptation. So why would He subject his Son to it, why was that necessary? It seems cruel of God to test the faith of good people when He already knows they're good enough to pass His tests, but He keeps doing it, over & over. I don't want to think of God as cruel but there are times when it's hard not to. God forgive me for these thoughts.

Just who is the devil anyway? What does he want from us? Has he existed since the dawn of time or only since the dawn of man? Did God create him? He must have, since He created everything, but why? But if He didn't, then who did?

June 16. The meeting with Brendan didn't go too well this morning. I get the feeling he's very angry with me. Maybe not angry so much as frustrated. Who'd blame him? I can't bring myself to talk to him, not yet. Not to him, not to anyone. There are times when I want to, at least to say hello to someone or ask a guard for something, but I can't.

I can't talk to him, & at times it's hard to listen to him too. He tries to talk to me about the case, about motions and so forth, & suddenly, without warning, I'll lose my concentration. This is something new for me, as I've always been focused & attentive.

Well, it's very different now. I don't know where my mind goes off to. Wherever it is, it's far away. Sometimes it's as if people are suddenly not speaking English anymore, as if they're speaking a language I don't know at all.

But it's good to see Brendan anyway, not because he's my lawyer but because he's my friend. At one point this morning, when we were sitting across from each other, I had a sudden recollection of the two of us as boys. It would have been a long time ago, more than 40 years. I remembered the two of us playing baseball with Brian Cleary & the Becker twins & the rest of our crowd. Playing ball on one of those perfect summer days, a breeze coming off the Lake. The kind of day when a baseball diamond is the world's best place to be, nowhere else can hold a candle to it. After the game we'd go home, his home or mine, it didn't matter, & drink Coke & eat potato chips & maybe watch TV, which was still a novelty.

The future looked pretty bright. Not that we talked about it much, we just assumed the best. We lived in the present, mostly, & that was more than good enough.

Who'd have guessed that things would turn out the way they did?

June 15. First day at GCFI. I didn't know they planned to move me, but I guess I shouldn't have been surprised since I still haven't talked. Most of the time I don't much care where they send me or what they do with me, but this new place does seem better than the jail. At least it's quieter. And the ones who work here don't seem as tense & angry as the ones in the jail. Another plus. Sometimes they'll even look me in the eye, which no one has done since they arrested me.

Still can't bring myself to talk to anyone yet. Guess I'll have to sooner or later. Can't wrap myself in this cloak of silence forever.

One of their doctors, named Gottlieb, introduced himself. He seems like a decent sort, soft spoken & with a reassuring way about him. When I couldn't or wouldn't talk to him, whichever, I hope he didn't take it personally. He's the only mental doctor I've ever seen except for that one with bowties and the pictures of whales, Kenyon, the one we took Christina to. Waste of time & money, but that wasn't his fault. I'm sure he did the best he could. He was in over his head with her, like the rest of us. There's no Doctor in the world who could have helped her, I don't care how good he was.

Sometimes, in fact a lot of the time, I feel completely divorced from the rest of humanity. It's not just that I'm an outcast, although of course I am. Even if I did get out through some miracle, even if I went to another state or another country, I would still remain an outcast. But it's more than that. If I do have contact with other people I'm afraid I'd contaminate them in some way, the same way she contaminated me. I know this isn't logical, but it's how I feel.

June 17. I finally talked to someone, namely Dr. Gottlieb. I guess I was relieved to find out that I still could. I wondered if I'd weakened my throat to the point of becoming permanently mute, same way you weaken a limb when you don't use it & eventually you're paralyzed.

My own voice is unfamiliar to me, and very startling. I sound older than I did before, like a man who should be in a nursing home. If a scarecrow could talk, he'd sound like me.

Gottlieb is an easy man to talk to. For one thing he's very patient, more patient than I'd be if I were him. For another he doesn't seem to hate me for what I've done. Maybe he does, maybe he's just good at not showing it.

Mainly we talked about my background, my family and whatnot. It must have sounded strange to him, hearing about such an ordinary man in such an unlikely situation. Or, maybe it wasn't strange at all, maybe it's just another day's work for him. Maybe nothing surprises him anymore. He must hear it all, like a priest.

Of course he wants to know about Christina. I can only talk about her for short times, in bits and pieces, and that seems to be okay with him. He doesn't push. Another thing I like about him.

After he left, I found myself wishing that I'd met with him several years ago. This surprised me since I've always been so private & self-contained, like the rest of my family. I'm beginning to realize what a heavy burden that has been, to be so self-contained. A burden for all of us, I think. A family curse, almost. Why are we like that, *how did we get to be that way?* I guess because our parents were like that too, and their parents before them, & so on, back through the ages. Because none of us thought we had a choice.

Who knows, if I could have talked to Gottlieb about her, maybe things could have been different. Of course there was nothing he could have said or done to change her, but maybe he could have told me what to do about her. Well, I guess we'll never know.

June 23. Another meeting with Brendan. I'm talking to him, finally, although I still can't be as open as I should be. Like Gottlieb, he wants me to talk about Christina. They've no idea how hard that is. Not hard, impossible. It's hard enough just to think about her. Most of the time I try not to.

Again, I found myself feeling sorry for him. Here he is, stuck with a guilty defendant who made a full confession & who can only pay him a fraction of what he'd ordinarily make on a case like mine. I suppose I must be the worst client he ever had.

After he left my sister came. A big day for visits. Even though I know she hates coming here, not that I blame her, it was good to see her. We chatted about her family, her daughter's college applications, her son's new job as an X-ray technician. She did most of the talking. To hear about such ordinary matters is comforting. It's comforting to know that life goes on, even though my own is pretty much over.

Small things become very important here, a visit from a brother or sister, a piece of mail (except for the hate mail I still get), even a meal that's a cut above average. Last night dinner included potato salad made the way Margaret used to make it, with crumbled hard-boiled eggs & sprinkled with paprika. I never would have thought that something so simple could bring me such pleasure. I should make a point of requesting it as part of my last meal, before they give me the lethal injection.

July 1. Last night I dreamt about Christina. Strange, how infrequently I dream of her, considering. In this dream she was very young, no more than three. Pretty as a picture, with her blonde hair & big blue eyes. Such a pretty child she was, she could have been one of those child models. Her beauty was so misleading.

But what struck me most about this dream was what she did, not how she looked. It was late in the afternoon & I'd just come home from work & she ran to greet me, smiling & laughing, & she threw her arms around my leg & cried out Daddy, Daddy! She was absolutely overjoyed to see me.

Why did I dream this? Nothing like it ever happened. Whenever I came home she said hello, always in that cool polite way of hers, but she showed no joy, no gladness. When I came home it was okay but if I hadn't, if I'd had a heart attack at work and died, that would have been okay too.

Perhaps that's why I had the dream. I wish she'd really been that way, just once.

It puzzles me that after all that's happened, I still find myself protective of her. I want to hide the things she did, to hide the way she really was. I want to hide all of it from the world, just as I tried to hide all of it from myself.

Yes, I'm still protective of her, but I suppose there's more to it than that. If I told the truth about her, the whole story, people would never believe it. Who could blame them, why should they? I tried not to see the truth, nor did Margaret. It was easy to do this, at least at first. We told each other she'd change, we took turns reassuring each other. We said the same things in different ways, over and over. She'd outgrow the way she was, she'd snap out of it and turn over a new leaf. All children go through difficult periods. You don't understand them, and they don't understand you, the way things have always been between parents and children and the way they always will be. But in time it all works out, or so we tried to keep believing.

We kept waiting for that to happen, kept waiting, hoping against hope. Which was futile. After that summer when they sent her home from camp and we took her to Dr. Kenyon, I knew the truth about her. At least I had a pretty clear sense of it, whether I wanted to or not. So did Margaret. Christina was the way she was, and that was that. And then Margaret died, and it was too late.

†

Saturday evening, like the rest of the day, passed uneventfully for the Gottliebs. In part this was due to Peter's absence. He was spending the night at the home of Gordy Wilder, his one close friend. Gordy, a tall lanky youth with a triangular face, would have been reasonably handsome if not for his fixed scowl and scraggly goatee. He and Peter spent hours together, mumbling secretively, meandering through malls and listening to music Sharon dubbed satanic acid vomit rock.

Gordy's father worked as a cost analyst for United Airlines and his mother as a Realtor, but, like Peter, he looked unkempt and ill-clad. A typical outfit might be a stained T-shirt, baggy Bermudas, and battered sneakers. He also wore a baseball cap, its brim reversed. A fashion statement even Peter hadn't made, so far.

Gottlieb felt no good could come from this relationship. He might have felt better if he had an inkling of what his son's friend was all about. But Gordy remained a self-wrought enigma. Peter described him as "pretty smart." If so, he made no show of his intelligence. In fact, Gordy seemed to make a point of never saying more than four words at a clip to either Hal or Sharon. He said hello and good-bye, he answered questions with a flat yes or no, and that was that. While not overtly rude, he managed to convey the vague but unmistakable notion that he regarded them as the enemy.

In his most dour moments, Gottlieb likened them to Leopold and Loeb.

He tried to reassure himself: *At least Peter has a friend. Better one than none.* This provided little comfort.

Despite his qualms about the two of them together, Gottlieb had unabashedly enjoyed his son's absence. He'd relished a classic summer meal, light and simple — shrimp salad, corn on the cob, orange sherbet for dessert. He'd also relished the meal's calm ambiance. After dinner Sarah sat on her father's lap as they watched *The Lion King* for the third time while Sharon read upstairs, alone. Gottlieb furtively glanced through a few journals. Sarah chastised him if she caught him at it— "Daddy, you're not paying attention!" She took her Disney movies very seriously, had seen some of them so often that she knew whole segments of the dialog by heart.

When the movie was over, he brought her upstairs. Sharon came into her bedroom as they tucked her in and kissed her good night, and Gottlieb was soon in bed himself. Sharon went back to her Martha Grimes mystery. He tried to read a *Newsweek* but his mind wandered, and he fidgeted as he lay next to her.

She put the book down. "You're awfully restless, Hal. What's the matter?"

"Nothing important. I was thinking about James Shannon. Today he gave me some things he had written, a kind of journal he's kept since his arrest."

Her interest picked up, as it usually did when the conversation turned to Shannon. "Oh? What's it like?"

"It's like his speech. Simple, unpretentious. He writes a lot about his wife. Some of it's kind of touching, like when he goes on about their honeymoon. It's obvious how much he cared about her."

She shifted in the bed to bring herself nearer to him. He drew her in close, in the crook of his arm. "Did he care enough to go off the deep end when she died?"

"It's not the journal of a man who'd go off the deep end, period." He ran a finger along her side. "Do you know anything about the New Testament?"

She made a clicking sound against her hard palate. "Only that they crucified him, and they've blamed us for it ever since. Why?"

"At one point he writes about the Temptation, where Jesus and the devil are alone in the wilderness for forty days. He brings up an interesting question. Why does God test people's faith if He already knows they're faithful? Presumably, He already knows if they are or not, since He knows everything."

"Well, I'm not exactly a biblical authority, but don't you find that question in the Old Testament too? Isn't that what the book of Job is all about?"

"I suppose. Interesting that you should mention that. He was reading the book of Job the day I met him." Gottlieb drew a knee up, draped his free arm around it. "But this journal . . . I think he identifies with Jesus."

"And identifies his daughter as the devil?" she broke in.

"Something like that."

She snorted. "Isn't that just a tad grandiose, if not out-and-out delusional?"

"Not necessarily. If you identify with Jesus, it doesn't mean you *think* you're Jesus."

Her tone remained skeptical. "How about identifying his daughter as the devil? You can dislike your children, even hate them, but that's not the same as thinking they're the spawn of Satan."

She broke the ensuing silence. "This case is really getting under your skin."

He nodded. "I never had one like it. I've never had a patient like James Shannon. And the more I learn about his daughter, the more of a mystery she is."

"You're not getting caught up in this satanic nonsense, are

you?"

"No. I see Satan as a convenient projection of everything we hate about everyone else, and especially ourselves, and nothing more."

"Hmm." She turned to him, looked at him thoughtfully. "Okay, well . . . I don't think I've ever asked you this directly, but how *do* you account for evil?"

He took a moment before answering. "For starters, I don't think it's a single entity any more than cancer is. All kinds of things can cause it. Abusive parents, social injustice at the top of the list. Or peer pressure or mob sanction. Say you're at a Nuremburg Rally, and half a million of your kinsmen are telling you how heroic it is to kill Jews. And then there's bad brain chemistry. Some biochemical problems in the brain result in Alzheimer's, others in Parkinson's disease. Is it really so strange to think that others might result in terrible behavior?"

"Well, then, maybe Ms. Shannon doesn't have to be such a mystery after all. Maybe she was just an extremely unpleasant little girl, spoiled rotten by doting parents who'd almost given up on having children. A spoiled, unpleasant little girl with bad chemicals in her brain. Voilà."

"Maybe." He didn't sound convinced. "The thing is, Sharon, bad behavior tends to fall into certain patterns. And her pattern, at least the accounts I've had of it, fits nothing I've ever seen before."

"But you're not a child psychiatrist. And even if you were, you never met the girl, so how could you make a good assessment of her? Your information's secondhand." She pulled herself closer to him and rubbed her face against the coarse dark curls of his chest hair. "Mmph. I don't want to talk about the Shannons anymore, okay?"

"Okay." With his free hand he reached over to the bedside table and turned off the light. Her face still nestled against him, she ran her fingertips along the side of his neck, his cheeks, his lips. He kissed her fingers and then reached down, scooping her up from under her arms, bringing her head to the level of his own. He kissed her lips, her eyes. Their legs entwined.

With quick well-practiced motions, she slipped off her knee-length jersey, and he wriggled out of his pajama bottoms. Their hands roamed over the minutely known terrain of each other's bodies, his hands lingering on her breasts. Sharon's bosom, still firm, was larger now than when they'd gotten married, enhanced by nursing their two children. Her pregnancies had also resulted in stiffer, darker nipples, in which he still took inordinate pleasure.

In a few minutes they were making love, on their sides with her back against his chest. She lifted her upper leg and drew up her knees as he entered her, while his hand made figure eights along her back and the top of her buttocks. He heard her characteristic sound, a cross between a sigh and coo, as he thrust against her, as she met his thrusts with a scrunch and swivel of her own, as they joined together for the thousandth time, the five-thousandth time? He had no idea how many times they'd done it through the years; he couldn't even guess. Sometimes he divided his life into two phases, before and after he and Sharon became lovers. The first phase was getting harder to remember. He knew there was a stretch of more than twenty years when he'd lived without her, but most of the time it was empty knowledge, hazily remembered and devoid of feeling. He knew it the same way that he knew he'd been in kindergarten once.

The act was not extraordinary. A deep if simple pleasure, a comfort, a release and relief. As familiar as the advent of dawn or dusk, and no less valuable for its familiarity. The act was not extraordinary, except for Cassandra.

Turned towards his wife's back with his eyes tightly shut, still driving himself into her, Gottlieb found himself besieged by the unexpected jarring image of another woman next to him. He imagined the firm, broad expanse of Cassandra's compact body, the taste of her pretty mouth, the touch of her large high breasts, the pressure of her well-muscled thighs. He wondered, what would she be like in bed? What would be her quirks and tricks, her sounds, her smell, her rhythm? Would she buck and jolt, or bite and scratch? Or would she lie back and accept him with a calm passivity? Not likely, that. He could see her as many things, but never as a passive partner.

Unsettling. Gottlieb, the psychiatrist with two decades of experience, knew that men and women routinely fantasize about other partners when they're having sex. Apart from being commonplace, the phenomenon was potentially useful, a good safety valve. But Gottlieb, the steadfast husband, had never had such a fantasy come unbidden to his conjugal bed.

Afterwards, while he and Sharon lay together, she turned to him. "Well, now, Hal, I don't know what got into you just then, but I liked it."

"I'm glad. Me, too."

"You haven't been trying out Viagra samples, have you?"

He emitted a brief laugh. "Not yet."

She turned to her side and positioned his arm across her breasts. "'Night. I love you."

"I love you too." He wondered if he didn't sound a bit perfunctory.

⸙

Gottlieb couldn't sleep. Tossing and turning, trying not to wake the demurely snoring Sharon, he threw on a robe and went downstairs to the kitchen. He poured himself a glass of milk and opened a box of oatmeal cookies, more for lack of something else to do—he wasn't hungry, wasn't thirsty. Pacing, beset by an irrational claustrophobia, he felt his spacious kitchen to be as confining as a cell at GCFI.

His pacing took him to the study, where he retrieved James Shannon's journal from his briefcase. Splayed out on the couch, he read it again, slowly and carefully. Towards the end he came to the mention of Christina's abortive stay at camp. "After that summer when they sent her back from camp, I knew the truth about her."

He got his wallet and fished a scrap of paper from it, on which he'd jotted down a name. Green Lake Camp for Girls. About an hour from Milwaukee, Kenyon said. He checked a schematic map in the front of the phone book, trying to determine the right area code. Then he picked up the phone.

A chirping voice answered. "Directory Assistance for what city, please?"

"I'm, uhm, not certain. I'm trying to find the number for a summer camp, and I'm afraid I don't know the nearest town."

The voice chirped less perkily. "What's the name of the camp, sir?"

"Green Lake Camp for Girls. It's about an hour from Milwaukee."

"I'm afraid I don't see a listing . . . wait, just a moment." He heard the tapping of a few computer keys. "Yes, there is a Green Lake Camp . . ."

Gottlieb jotted down the number, unsure about what he planned to do with it.

CHAPTER XV

As HE WENDED HIS WAY THROUGH HEAVY Monday morning traffic on the Eisenhower Expressway, Gottlieb tapped the steering wheel impatiently with the fingers of his left hand. His right hand held a cell phone. He'd just called Cassandra and was waiting for her to answer.

"Hello." Strictly business, not a greeting or a question. The subtext, *I hope this is worth my time and trouble.* But the businesslike tone vanished as soon as she recognized his voice. "Oh, hi, Hal! I was wondering when I'd hear from you."

"I wanted to call sooner, to thank you for lunch, but . . . the thing is, Cassandra, I know how busy you are. I didn't want to call too often and make a pest of myself." While not glib, Gottlieb usually spoke in a clear, cogent manner. She, however, had a way of making his words sound tentative and sometimes close to jumbled.

"Call as often as you'd like. If you start to make a pest of yourself, I'll tell you."

"So I gather I haven't done it yet."

"Nowhere near it. Don't be so insecure."

"I'm not, for the most part." He struggled to keep from sounding hopelessly adolescent. "You see, this whole, uhm, thing, is still new to me. Seeing you, even calling you."

"You'll get used to it. I *hope* you do."

Caught up in the conversation, distracted, he found himself drifting towards the lane to his left. A woman in a green Toyota honked her horn and gave him the finger as she zoomed by. "Jesus!"

"Hal? Are you okay? What happened?"

"I'm fine, it was just a momentary lapse. I'm calling from

the car, and the traffic's heavy."

"You shouldn't be talking while you're driving," she admonished him, rather mildly. "Why don't you call me back later?"

"No, stay on the line. When can I see you again?" The question, he thought, contained a certain urgency.

"It's up to you. I've got a lot to do before I leave, and of course there's the seminar on colonialism, but apart from that, my schedule's pretty flexible."

"Before you leave?"

"I'm going to Germany in September. A sabbatical. The Goebbels book. I told you all about it in when we were eating at the Japanese place, remember?"

He had, in fact, forgotten. The prospect of not seeing her for six months hit him like a cloudburst in the middle of a sunny day.

"It must have slipped my mind," he said finally, "but I remember now." He hesitated. "I'll miss you."

"You could always fly over to see me," she bandied lightly.

"Wouldn't you be surprised if I did!"

"Beyond surprised, thunderstruck. But I'd like it."

Gottlieb had a brief, intensely pleasant fantasy of driving to O'Hare some ordinary night with nothing but a passport, a few credit cards, and a toothbrush, and heading off to Germany. A place he'd never visited, despite an abiding curiosity about it. Germany was part and parcel of his heritage, almost as much his as hers. His forebears on both sides were German Jews. Although born in the United States, his paternal grandparents spoke German before English. Germany might have been the birthplace of the Holocaust, but it was also his ancestral homeland. Cassandra wasn't the only one with mixed feelings about it.

He would see places he'd only read about. Berlin and Munich, the Black Forest and Bavarian Alps, the Rhine valley. He'd wander side streets of medieval cities, explore cathedrals, discover museums—Berlin alone had eighty-five of them, he'd read somewhere. He'd feast on wurst and Wiener schnitzel, red cabbage, and spätzle, washed down with a Pilsner or a good Riesling. And she, of course, would be his guide, his interpreter, his boon companion. Not to mention his lover.

He pondered the fantasy with a wry detachment. *Quite a scenario I'm dreaming up with someone I haven't so much as kissed yet.*

"Hal? Are you still there?"

"More or less. About this week: maybe we could get together for a few hours on Wednesday afternoon?"

"Sounds good to me. What exactly did you have in mind?" He couldn't decide if she said this teasingly; he still hadn't learned how to read her.

"What I have in mind isn't clear to me, as long as I see you."

She hesitated before replying. "Listen, Hal, I like you a lot. But I don't want you doing anything you don't want to do. Seduction's not my style. So, how about meeting somewhere other than my apartment? A place that's out of harm's way."

"That would probably be better." Equal parts of relief and disappointment swelled up in him.

"We should do something indoors, though. They're talking about another heat wave."

"Have you been to the Shedd lately?" The Shedd Aquarium was his favorite among Chicago's renowned attractions, even more so than the Art Institute.

"Not for years. I don't know why it's been so long. I've always loved it."

"Let's do it, then. We could meet at the main entrance. About 2:30?"

"That should be fine. Now, I think you should quit while you're ahead. Get off the phone before you kill yourself. Auf Wiedersehen."

"Good-bye, Cassandra."

Auf Wiedersehen. His German consisted of a few words and

phrases picked up here and there, and he'd rarely heard it spoken. Still, he conceived of it as a harsh, unlovely, rasping tongue. The language of endlessly compounded words and impossible sentences, as twisted as the roots of an old, gnarled tree. The language of SS men as they'd herded their victims to and from the cattle cars: *Schnell, schnell, schnell!* The language of Hitler himself. But when Cassandra said auf Wiedersehen, she made the words sound as gentle as light rain against a windowpane.

※

The forecasters proved right, and by Wednesday they found themselves in the grip of another heat wave. In the short walk from his air-conditioned car to the air-conditioned lobby, Gottlieb felt his face become hot and flushed, his undershirt sticky. The Shedd, magnificently perched at the edge of Lake Michigan, often receives the benefit of cooling breezes off the lake. Not today.

Despite the crowded lobby he spotted her right away, and his pace quickened as he headed toward her. She wore an off-white skirt, and a peach-and-plum-striped blouse, and her customary tan sandals. As he hugged her, she pressed her cool cheek against his overheated face. The heat wave had no obvious effect on her. It might have been a crisp October afternoon.

He moved a step back from her and touched her shoulder. "It's nice to see you."

Cassandra's lips curved into a hint of a smile. "You sounded so *solemn* when you said that. Funereal, almost." The heat-induced redness of his face was compounded by a blush. But she took him off the hook before he felt obliged to defend himself. "It's nice to see you too."

They bought tickets and made their way to the Aquarium's central exhibit, a huge tank holding ninety thousand gallons of water behind two and a quarter inches of laminated glass. The tank was made to replicate a coral reef. Hundreds of aquatic creatures inhabited it, from rainbow-hued tropical fish no larger than minnows to nurse sharks and sea turtles to bright green moray eels. Most of them swam around in lazy circles or darted in and out of rock formations; others hugged the sand and pebbles at the great tank's floor.

Cassandra stood transfixed, her blue eyes following their movements with rapt interest, saying nothing. "It really makes you wonder," she said finally.

"I beg your pardon?"

"It makes you wonder about the varieties of life, about evolution. About all these fantastic adaptations. Look at that one, with the spines, like a porcupine! Or that one, in front of the fan-shaped piece of coral. He looks as though he has an eye in the middle of his tail!"

Gottlieb nodded and said, "It's a great defense, that kind of marking. Makes a predator thinks he's bigger than he is. Besides, if he is attacked, he'll only lose a piece of his tail instead of his whole head."

She pointed to a small shark, only four or five feet long, circling the tank with easy grace. Its mouth was slightly open, just enough to expose a profusion of short triangular teeth. "I've always been fascinated by sharks, ever since *Jaws*."

"Me too. Some of their adaptations are incredible." His tone became a bit pontifical. "There are species that have up to three thousand teeth, arranged in twenty rows. Some sharks can detect blood in amounts as small as one drop in two dozen gallons. Others find their prey by detecting electrical charges of up to a millionth of a volt."

"You know a lot about them."

He shook his head. "Not really. I'll read an article, or I'll watch something on Public TV or the Discovery Channel."

They fell silent as they stood before the tank. "This is marvelous," she said at last. "I could spend all day here. So peaceful. By the way, how do they keep the local citizens from eating one another?"

"By keeping them extremely well fed, I imagine."

They took a few steps around the periphery of the tank. Gottlieb pointed to a huge sea turtle circling nearby. "I've always liked turtles. I used to have them when I was a boy. I like their eyes. They remind me of the eyes of kind old men."

She gave a short laugh. "That's a bit anthropomorphic, don't you think?"

"I suppose."

"I've read that some of the Galapagos tortoises are supposed to have lived for more than two hundred years. Now *there*'s a place I'd go to in a heartbeat. The Galapagos Islands."

"Some friends of ours went there last year. They travel a lot, this couple, and they said it was the most interesting trip they've ever taken." *I'd like to go there with you,* he almost added, the unspoken words roiling inside his head.

"It's fabulous here!" He stole a glance at her, and for an instant, he could see a carefree little girl, smitten with natural wonders, long hidden within the heavily burdened woman. "So dark and quiet, so *apart* from everything," she went on. "I should come here more often."

"You should. It's not that far from where you live."

She turned to him. "I especially like the fact that it has nothing to do with the Third Reich."

"God, you must get sick of it."

"More than you could know."

"I doubt that," he responded dryly. "But why not give it a break, then? There *are* other aspects of European history, presumably."

"So I keep trying to remind myself."

"I mean it. There's more to German history than the Holocaust, and there are other European countries besides Germany in the first place. Delve into something different for a while."

She bristled, "Do you think it's that easy to let go of an

obsession?"

"No, but it's easier if you try."

She looked up at him, surprised by his challenging edge. When she resumed, her tone had softened. "Once I start a book, I give myself over to it wholly. It was like that with the others, and it will be that way with the Goebbels book. But when it's done, I've been thinking of moving on to something else."

She went on, pensively. "It occurred to me that historians don't pay as much attention to Switzerland as they should. Now here's this confederation that has survived for nearly a thousand years. A place where they've built a multiethnic democracy on a continent where different ethnic groups, even very similar ones, habitually try to massacre each other. I'm aware the Swiss have their faults. Their actions during the Holocaust left a great deal to be desired, and their banking system protects the fortunes of some of the world's worst people, but that doesn't mean their history's not worth studying."

He nodded. "It sounds fascinating. Hard to imagine better use of a historian's time and energy."

"Maybe I will." She spoke thoughtfully. "Maybe I'll surprise us both, especially myself." In a flash her tone took on its customary briskness. "But first I'll write the Goebbels book."

They lapsed into another silence as they walked slowly around the tank. They walked past fish that looked like silver pencils and rocks and butterflies, past sea anemones and sea horses and sea cucumbers, past lumbering fat groupers and sleek fast eels, past skates and stingrays with their undulating leaf-like bodies. Past archer fish, sticklebacks, and puffers, past sharks and turtles. Gottlieb let his eyes wander, his thoughts wander, as he let himself be drawn into the intricate beauty of the world before him. He glanced at Cassandra, who seemed similarly enthralled. The last vestiges of his adolescent self-consciousness disappeared. He reached for her cool, smooth hand, which she offered without resistance.

In all, they spent half an hour strolling around the tank. Then they made their way to the smaller exhibits on its periphery, laid out like the spokes of a wheel. She laughed at the scallops, which she'd never seen before as living creatures in their natural habitat; she said they reminded her of swimming dentures. He pointed out the catfish, with their unkempt whiskers probing along the bottom of his tank: his candidates for the fish most in need of a cosmetic makeover. They walked past gar and walleyed pike and speckled trout.

He watched her recoil as they stopped in front of an octopus. "They're quite timid, even the larger ones," Gottlieb said.. "Usually they're more frightened of us than we are of them. They're actually very interesting creatures."

"How so?"

"Well, for one thing they're probably the smartest invertebrates. They're capable of learning and remembering. There've been experiments in which they're trained, so to speak, using food as rewards and electrical shocks as punishment. They also have considerable dexterity—they can unscrew a jar with their tentacles. And they have a complicated, highly developed eye."

"They're related to squid, right?"

He nodded. "They're both cephalopods. Beaked head and highly dexterous prehensile tentacles."

Her grip on his hand tightened. "When I was little, I read this story about a giant squid. I don't remember if it was fact or fiction, but that doesn't matter. It was about shipwrecked US sailors in the Pacific during World War II. They were in a lifeboat. A giant squid came up to the surface. It plucked several of them from the boat, one by one. That has to be one of the worst things I've ever read, as bad as anything about the Holocaust. I tried to imagine what it would have been like, trapped in that boat, waiting to find out if you're next."

She shuddered, paused a moment and went on. "I'm fascinated by how people find it in themselves to face horrific deaths. How they faced things like crucifixion, or being torn apart by wild animals in the Coliseum. In one of his novels, Kurt Vonnegut wrote about what the Southwestern Indians used to do sometimes. *They buried a man in the desert, poured honey over him, and then the ants would come.* How can someone face a death like that?"

"It's possible," he said slowly, "that the parts of the brain which deal with pain and fear are overwhelmed, so there's a kind of shutdown. *Dissociation*, it's called. It's what happens in conditions like post-traumatic stress disorder."

"Well, it's nice to think that something like that happens. I hope it does. *But what if it doesn't?*"

His hold on her hand tightened. "You have a terrible imagination."

She looked at him. Even in the dim light, he took note of her widened pupils. He imagined her as a little girl reading about the doomed sailors as they waited for the giant squid to pick one, her pupils widening in the same way. "Tell me, Doctor, is there a cure for that?"

"Yes and no. I believe that if you're blessed or cursed with it, take your choice, you're stuck with it. But you can get around it by learning to live in the here and now. You learn to allow yourself to take the good of life at face value and put the rest aside, at least temporarily."

"That works for you?" She sounded skeptical.

"Sometimes. To a point."

She looked at him with quizzical respect. "You must hear the worst things imaginable."

He turned his head away from her. "I've heard some things I'd never tell another person. No one else should have to hear them. *I* shouldn't have had to hear them."

"I want to hear them. Not now, but sometime."

"No, you don't. Trust me."

"Yes, I do."

He turned towards her again. "For God's sake, why?"

She weighed her words before answering. "Because I think

that's part of a historian's sacrament. To bear witness. To honor those who've suffered by remembering them, by passing on their stories."

"All right," he acknowledged, "but there has to be a balance. You have to remember the Sistine Chapel as well as Auschwitz. You have to remember Shakespeare and Mozart as well as Hitler and Goebbels. Otherwise you'll get lost in the darkness. You have to . . ."

"Shh." She cut him off in midsentence. Then she lifted up her head to his and kissed him, kissed him so softly that he could scarcely discern her mouth against his lips, kissed him in front of an octopus who watched them shyly, half-hidden behind a rock, an octopus who watched them with his extraordinary, almost-human eyes.

CHAPTER XVI

L ATER THAT AFTERNOON GOTTLIEB SAT in his office, his mind churning. He sank back into his desk chair, threw his feet onto a hassock, and prepared to focus on the patients who'd fill the balance of his day; the first one was due in fifteen minutes. Cassandra kept intruding. Cassandra, in her peach-and-plum blouse, standing before him whenever he shut his eyes. Cassandra's cool smooth hand in his. Cassandra, reaching up to kiss him.

He tried to distract himself with images of fish of every size and shape and hue as they glided around the coral fans and rock formations. The fish diverted his attention, but only for moments at a time. Cassandra crept back into his mind with a raw, insistent power.

He tried another tactic, forcing himself to wade through the inevitable pile of papers on his desk. Unopened mail, insurance forms he had to dictate, reprints of articles he meant to read. Amidst the clutter, he spotted James Shannon's journal. On the back of its front cover he'd jotted down the number of Christina's camp in Wisconsin.

He picked up the phone on an impulse and slowly dialed the number. Even as he listened to the dial tone, he still wasn't sure of what he'd say.

"Good afternoon, Green Lake Camp for Girls," a woman answered. Gottlieb discerned the friendly, slightly sing-song twang of the upper Midwest.

"Hello. I'd like to speak to the camp director."

"I'm sorry, she's off grounds until this evening. But Ms. Harvey, the assistant director, is here now if you want to talk to her."

"That would be fine."

"Who may I say is calling?"

"Dr. Harold Gottlieb." His twitchy legs bounced on the hassock while she put him on hold.

A few seconds later, another voice broke in. "This is Alice Harvey speaking."

"Hello, Ms. Harvey." He introduced himself again. "I'm calling about one of your campers."

"Are you her doctor?"

"No—"

"A relative?"

"No, but . . ."

Her tone remained polite, but a firm and not unduly friendly edge came into it. "I'm sorry, Doctor, but we don't divulge information about our campers over the phone. I'm sure you understand."

"Let me explain." His own tone became firmer, more authoritative. "She's not a camper now, and she hasn't been at Green Lake for several years. But she has recently been the victim of a violent crime, and we're wondering if anyone at the camp could help with our investigation." Gottlieb discovered long ago that *we* and *our* carry much more weight than *I* and *mine*.

"Are you with the police?"

"In a manner of speaking," he lied blithely. "I'm a psychiatrist in Illinois, at a facility called the Greater Chicago Forensic Institute. We work closely with the police."

Ms. Harvey became more respectful. "How long ago was the girl a camper here?"

"About three years ago."

"I wasn't here then. But Anita Pierce, that's the woman who used to run this place, lives near you. At least she did." Harvey named a small community about thirty miles northwest of downtown Chicago.

"Would you be good enough to give me her number?"

"Let's see, I should have it in the Rolodex. Here it is." She paused. "What's the name, if you don't mind my asking?"

"I beg your pardon?"

"The name of the girl who was victim of a violent crime."

"Shannon. Christina Shannon."

Gottlieb thought he heard her click her tongue against the roof of her mouth. "Figures. I figured it might be her."

"I, uhm, thought you said you weren't here when she was."

"I wasn't. But you could say she's become a kind of legend at this place."

He thanked her, hung up, and immediately dialed the number she had given him. A male voice had left a no-frills announcement on the answering machine. Gottlieb detected the rasp of a heavy smoker. "You've reached the Pierces. Leave a message at the beep." It was the weak, dry voice of an old man who hoped you *wouldn't* leave a message.

Unnerved, Gottlieb hung up. He took a moment to think about his opening gambit, wondering how much to tell her. The bare minimum, he decided. He dialed again. "My name is Dr. Harold Gottlieb. I'm trying to reach Anita Pierce. I wonder if you could call me tomorrow morning, anytime between eight forty-five and noon." He left the main number of GCFI and his extension there.

"If that's not convenient," he went on, "please leave me a voice mail message telling me when I might call you." He left a second number and thanked her in advance for her courtesy.

Three to one I never hear from her, he predicted to himself.

※

She didn't call the next morning, nor did she leave a message in his voice mail. He decided to try again on Thursday night. This time a man picked up. The same voice he'd heard on their answering machine, reminding Gottlieb of cinders being swept from a fireplace.

"Yeah?"

"Hello. I'm trying to get hold of Anita Pierce."

"Who are yah, mister?"

"My name is Harold Gottlieb. I'm a doctor—"

"Never heard of yah. Yah ain't *her* doctor." The smoker's rasp was much in evidence. Every few words he had to stop to catch his breath.

"No, but I need to talk to her about a patient. It's important."

A long pause followed. "Hold on, mister." Gottlieb heard the old man call out, "Anita, some fella—wants to talk—to yah. Says he's—some kinda doctor." Another pause, this one accompanied by wheezing.

"I'm Anita," a woman spoke finally. She sounded wary, tired.

"Hello, Ms. Pierce." He gave his name again. "I apologize for calling you at home, but it's the only number I have for you."

"What is it?" The voice of a woman who expected the worst from strangers, and possibly from friends as well.

"I understand you used to be a camp director. One of the girls who attended your camp has been the victim of a violent crime."

"Christina Shannon," she said without hesitation.

"That's correct. You may be aware of this already, but she was murdered a few weeks ago."

"Hard not to be. She's been in the news nonstop."

"I take it you remember her?"

"No one who knew her will ever forget her. *Ever.*" The statement came out as an absolute truth, as unarguable as the law of gravity.

"I, uhm, gather she made quite an impression on people." Pierce let this pass without comment.

"Why are you calling me?"

Gottlieb enjoined himself to keep it simple, keep it truthful. "I'm a psychiatrist who has gotten involved in the case. I've

been asked to evaluate and treat the man accused of killing her."
He chose his words carefully. "In the course of this evaluation,
we're trying to learn as much as we can about Christina herself.
We know she attended Green Lake Camp, and we know she left
under strange circumstances. We've no idea what happened
there, but we're wondering if it had some bearing on the case."

There were several seconds of dead silence, at the end of
which he heard her sigh. "I knew she'd come into my life again.
I hoped to God I'd never meet her, or hear about her, or have to
talk about her, but I knew I would. All right, mister . . . Doctor
. . . all right."

He pressed ahead before she had a chance to change her
mind. "When can I meet with you?"

"Tomorrow night's okay. You'll have to come here, though.
I don't leave the house too often. You'll understand."

They agreed upon a time, seven thirty and he jotted down
directions to her home. He was anxious to talk to her directly.
Perhaps, he hoped, some of the mystery about Christina
Shannon would finally clear up.

⸎

The latest heat wave was on the wane. A light breeze rustled
through the trees as Gottlieb made his way from the driveway
to Anita Pierce's modest wood-and-red-brick house. As soon as
he rang the bell, a tallish woman in her fifties came to the door.
Her salt-and-pepper hair framed a round plump face.

She nodded without smiling. "You must be Dr. Gottlieb.
Come on in."

When he did, he stopped in her narrow hallway. "Thanks for
agreeing to meet with me." He extended a hand to her, which
she ignored. While glancing in his general direction, she had a
way of looking past him.

It dawned on him that she was blind.

"We can talk in here." She indicated the living room with

the sweep of an arm. The room was filled with old-fashioned overstuffed chairs with frilly coverings on the arms and lace doilies on the backs of them. He tried to remember the name for the doilies. Antimacassars, that was it. He hadn't seen one in decades.

A pleasant room, notwithstanding the acrid aftermath of tens of thousands of cigarettes smoked there. Very little decoration, chiefly a scattering of family photos on the walls and tabletops. The wallpaper featured vertical rows of rosebuds against an off-white background. The hum of a window air conditioner filled the room. From another room came the sound of a baseball game on TV.

Gottlieb shied away from an immediate discussion of Christina. "So, Ms. Pierce, how long were you involved in the camping business?"

"Most of my life, on and off. I always loved Wisconsin. I was a camper there myself for three or four summers. In my teens I became a junior counselor. Counselors-in-training, or C.I.T.s, they called us. When I went to college, I became a full-fledged counselor. The money wasn't much, but I didn't care. I got to spend the summers in my favorite place, doing what I loved. I taught swimming and canoeing."

"And you kept coming back?"

She nodded. "Summer after summer. I became a teacher, third and fourth grades, which meant I had the summers off. I never married, so I wasn't tied down with a husband and children. In time I became the head counselor, and then the assistant director. I got more involved with the business end, hiring and purchasing and whatnot. Then I began to do more in the off-season, mainly talking to prospective campers and their families. Marketing. People don't realize how much goes into running a summer camp. It's a complicated business."

"I can imagine."

"Well," she went on, "it turned out I had kind of a knack for it. I don't know why. I don't have a background in business, but

I loved the work. And then the original owners wanted to retire. That would have been fifteen years ago, give or take. The camp was doing well. I had the opportunity to buy it for a pretty good price, so I took a chance on it. Quite a gamble for me. Took just about every penny I could scrounge up or borrow."

Gottlieb crossed his legs in one of the overstuffed armchairs and folded his hands on his lap. "So you finally had your own camp."

"Uh-huh. They were happy, those first years of running Green Lake. The happiest years of my life. I put together a good crew. We expanded our activities, made changes in the way we marketed. And I liked working with the campers. Nice girls, most of them. You'd be surprised how many of them still send a Christmas card, or a wedding or birth announcement."

Gottlieb felt she might be ready to talk about the murdered girl. "Perhaps you could tell me about Christina Shannon."

Anita's expression changed when he mentioned Christina's name. Her facial muscles contracted, she chewed briefly on her lower lip, her sightless eyes narrowed. She took a few moments before responding. "I remember my first reaction, which is probably the reaction most people had towards her. *What a pretty child!* I'm sure you've heard all that before, about her blonde curls and her blue eyes and so on. Suffice it to say, she was one of the most beautiful children I've ever seen. Those kids you see on TV, those child actresses, they haven't got a thing on her. The way she looked, it took you by surprise. It caught you off guard. It left you unprepared for the way she really was."

Gottlieb recalled that James Shannon himself had written similar things about Christina in his journal. "And how was that?"

"*Detached.* Above all else, detached, from everything and everyone. Impossible to engage, unreachable. And something else, amoral. It's funny, but I never knew exactly what that meant until I met her."

She went on, slowly and deliberately. "From the day Christina started camp, things started happening. Small things, odd things."

"For instance?"

"We noticed a lot of petty theft. You didn't see too much of that at a place like ours. For one thing, there isn't much to steal. No valuables, and the clothing's strictly sportswear, and there's no cash in the cabins. Campers' money is kept in the girls' accounts. But now, all of a sudden, there was theft. And this was striking, too, the things stolen made no sense. Photos, letters, and cards from home, books. Things of no value except to the owners. One girl lost her rosary beads."

The room was warm and close despite the air conditioner. Gottlieb loosened his tie and rolled up his sleeves. "Were most of the thefts in Christina's cabin?"

"Well, that's an interesting question. They occurred in all the cabins, but a disproportionate number occurred in hers. I should explain, the campers were housed in one of seven different cabins according to their ages. Each cabin had a counselor and a C.I.T. in residence. But we didn't keep the cabins locked, so campers came in and out as they pleased. The counselors and C.I.Ts were gone for much of the time, supervising the activities and so forth."

The quiet conversation was shattered by an old man's coughing in the next room. Anita turned her head towards it and cocked her ear. "You all right, Dad?" No answer. When it subsided, she resumed. "Throughout this time, by the way, Christina kept completely to herself. Her only activities were solitary ones. Swimming, canoeing, arts and crafts. The arts and crafts, that's another story I'll get to later. She refused to have anything to do with team sports. If you said hello to her, sometimes she'd say hello back, and sometimes she'd barely nod. If you asked a question, she'd give you a flat-out yes or no. She'd never elaborate, and she'd never ask a question in return. But . . . I know this sounds contradictory, but it's not like she was rude. If anything, she was exceptionally well-mannered. In some respects, a model camper."

Gottlieb remembered Malcolm Kenyon's words. *In some respects, she was a model child.* "A model camper? How so?"

"She was neat and clean. She never got into fights or squabbles. She didn't tease the other girls, didn't pick on them in any way. And she never complained. You're a psychiatrist, so you must know how young girls love to gripe about things. The others did, but not Christina."

Gottlieb waited for another fit of the old man's coughing to subside. "How did she get along with the counselors?"

"She did what she was told, and that was that. None of them engaged her, any more than the campers did. The counselor in her cabin, Kate Axelrod, had no idea what to do with her. I should tell you, Kate was one of the best-liked women on our staff, someone who had a wonderful way with children. At the time she was a premed at Marquette. She's in medical school now, and she plans to become a pediatrician."

"Did Christina show signs of being homesick?"

Anita scoffed. "If she was, she sure did hide it well. No one remembered her saying anything, ever, about her home or her parents or the rest of her family. She might have come from outer space for all we knew."

Plucking a handkerchief from a pocket of her house dress, Anita dabbed her forehead with it. "So, here was the situation. Items were missing. Senseless petty thefts were occurring, a disproportionate number in the cabin of this strange, reclusive girl who talked to no one. And then things began to die."

Gottlieb felt the hairs on the back of his neck stand up. "Excuse me?"

"Things began to die," she repeated. "Each of the cabins had what we called a nature plot. A kind of small garden where we kept different plants and wildflowers, and the girls in the cabin took care of them. The girls loved them. In fact, they've been one of our most popular attractions through the years. You see, we had a lot of city girls from Chicago and Milwaukee, and this was their first exposure to the real outdoors, to lakes and forests, no TVs or malls. Their first real taste of nature, their first chance to see things grow and bloom."

Gottlieb worked to keep an even tone. "And all of a sudden the plants and flowers were dying."

Anita nodded. "They'd been healthy and properly tended, and now they were literally shriveling up. Bear in mind that we're not talking about hothouse orchids. These plants were hearty. They'd grown in the wild, untended. So one day, while the girls were having their afternoon swim, Kate and I took a close look at the plots, trying to figure out what was happening to them. At one point Kate took a pinch of soil and tasted it. I'll never forget the look on her face. She said, 'Why, this has been salted!' I took a pinch of it myself. Sure enough, it was the saltiest thing I ever tasted. Someone had really done a job on it. And then Kate turned to me. 'Why would she want to do this?' She didn't ask *who'd* do this. We already knew the answer."

"Did you question Christina?"

She nodded again. "That same afternoon. We brought her to my office, and Kate asked her if she'd done anything to the nature plots. She stared at us with those big blue eyes of hers, as if we were both completely crazy, and she denied it flatly, over and over. We asked her if she knew of anyone else who might be trying to destroy them, and of course she denied that too. In all, we must have talked to her for ten minutes, closer to twenty. She didn't budge, didn't flinch."

"What happened next?"

"Next was the business with Critters Corner, our petting zoo. It was in a small enclosure near the dining hall. We had about what you'd expect there. Rabbits, guinea pigs, a chicken, a rooster, a couple of ducks. Our star attraction was a skunk named Petunia. The girls were crazy about her. Deodorized skunks make great pets, by the way. Then, this would have been in mid-July now, the animals started dying too. A guinea pig first, and then one of the rabbits."

"What did you do?"

She shifted in the armchair. "First, we called in a vet. He wasn't much help. Thing is, he mainly treated large animals, farm animals. And dogs and cats, of course. You knew he wasn't about to lose sleep over a dead guinea pig or rabbit, and no way was he about to do an autopsy on one. Only thing he suggested was to send the animals to Madison, to the vet school there."

"Did you?"

She shook her head. "We checked with the lab. Their fees were sky high. Besides, some of the tests took so long that camp would have been over by the time we got back the results. Instead, we decided to keep a closer eye on the animals."

"I assume you asked Christina about it?"

"Of course. And she did exactly what she did when we asked her about the nature plots. She stared at us as though we'd gone crazy, denying everything."

Gottlieb stroked his chin. "You kept a closer eye on the animals. Did you keep a closer eye on Christina herself?"

"Yes, as much as possible, but that was easier said than done. Summer camps don't have a lot of extra staff. It's a competitive business, and we all have to struggle to keep down costs. Besides, the extra staff attention usually goes to the younger children. They're the ones who need it most."

"Why do you think she wanted to kill those plants and animals?"

"You're the doctor, you tell *me*," Anita answered, snappish. She resumed a moment later, less combatively, "The only answer I can give you is that *she liked it when things died.* I know that sounds far-fetched, but it's the only one I can think of."

They fell silent. Despite the hum of the air conditioning, and the nearby clamor of the televised baseball game, Gottlieb made out the sounds of the summer night—crickets and cicadas, breezes wafting through the trees and bushes, an occasional dog barking in the distance. He found the sounds restorative, an antidote to mounting fatigue. Apart from his usual long day, the discussion of Christina drained him.

"You were going to tell me about the arts and crafts," he finally said.

Anita took her time before replying. "I guess she had some talent as an artist. She spent a great deal of her time drawing and sketching. Off by herself, of course. She didn't care what others did, or what they thought about her own work. To the contrary, she tended to be very secretive about it. She'd spend hours on a drawing, but then she'd rip it up and throw it out before anyone else saw it. Well, one night I was up late in the camp office finishing some paperwork when the arts and crafts counselor, Sherri Allard, rushed in to see me. Now, Sherri was usually very calm, a placid farm-girl type, but she was really in a state that night. She came over to my desk, holding several sheets of papers, so upset her hands were shaking. At first she couldn't even talk. Then she said, 'I think you ought to see these.' They were drawings she'd found in the trash bin. They'd been torn up, but it had been easy to tape them back together."

"What were they like?"

Anita squeezed her sightless eyes shut tightly, as if steeling herself to talk about them. "There were three of them. The first was a drawing of a guinea pig. A good, realistic likeness. Hooks, like fishhooks, had been driven through each paw, and each hook pulled in an opposite direction. The guinea pig was stretched across some torture device, like a rack. The whole drawing was bad enough, but the most awful thing about it was his eyes. You know how the eyes of an animal widen when it's terrified? Well, that's what this poor creature's eyes were like. Whoever drew it had captured them perfectly."

Gottlieb took a deep breath. "And the others?"

"The next one she showed me . . . it's still hard for me to talk about this. . . the next one was of a big angry dog. Again, a fairly realistic drawing, except for his exaggerated teeth, like fangs, and his eyes, as red as fire. In front of the dog, hunched over, was a woman. And this dog . . . this dog was having sex with her."

Anita blushed, and she took a moment to compose herself. "But the last one was the worst. She'd made a sketch of Jesus on the cross. His chest and trunk and limbs were done realistically, in fact very carefully. But his face was done as a caricature, as if he were some kind of drooling idiot. Around his neck hung a placard, with two words. *Fucking asshole!*"

A heavy silence filled the room. "I didn't sleep at all that night," she said eventually. As a rule, I sleep like a log, even when I've had an awful day, but not that night. All I could think of, over and over, was *I've never known a child like her.* By that time, I was already in my late forties. I'd spent the whole of my adult life dealing with children in one capacity or another. Most of them I liked very much. Some of them were difficult, of course. Spoiled, ill-tempered, rude, you name it. But Christina! I never knew one who'd been remotely like her. Still haven't, thank the Good Lord."

"Was that when you decided to send her home?"

Anita nodded. "The next morning I called a meeting. Carol Boyer, my assistant director at the time, and Kate Axelrod, and me. They agreed, she had to go. First time we'd ever done it. Oh, we'd sent them home before, but there'd always been a reason. Poor health, or intractable homesickness, or a death in the family . . . something. The thing is, there really was no reason with Christina. She had stirred up all kinds of suspicions, and there was certainly a bad feeling about her, but no one had ever proven that she'd done anything. But we were all afraid of what she might do next. If she'd hurt a guinea pig or rabbit, who could say she wouldn't hurt a child?"

"What happened then?"

"The next morning I had Kate bring her to my office. A rainy morning, I remember how the rain beat down against the windows as the three of us sat around my desk. I showed Christina the drawings without saying a word. It would have been a waste of time to accuse her of having made them anyway. She would have looked at us, innocence personified, and she would have denied it, the same way she denied the other things. So, I showed her the pictures without a word. And then I said, 'I think it's time for you to go home, Christina. It doesn't look like the camp experience is turning out to be very good for you.'"

"How did she respond to that?"

"She didn't argue," replied Anita with a shrug. "She didn't get angry or defensive, and she certainly didn't seem the slightest bit upset. As I recall, she looked at us, kind of blankly, and asked when she'd be leaving."

Anita took out her handkerchief again and wiped her forehead. The room was still warm despite the air conditioning. "I'm afraid I'm not much of a hostess. Can I get you something cold to drink? There's lemonade and iced tea in the fridge."

"Lemonade would be fine."

She got up and slowly but steadily made her way to the kitchen, guiding herself along the wall. A few minutes later she returned with two brimming tumblers and handed Gottlieb one. They sipped their drinks in silence. Then Gottlieb asked, "So, that was it? That was the end of your dealings with her?"

"Don't I wish. Dear God, don't I wish." For the first time since his arrival, she looked about to cry.

"I've always been fairly healthy," she continued, "but I do have my share of allergies. Nothing serious, but the symptoms can be annoying. Runny nose and red itchy eyes and so forth. I treat myself with over-the-counter medications, mostly nasal spray and eyedrops. Well, a couple of days after Christina left, my allergies started acting up. So I used my eye-drops, as I always did. But someone had put something in them. Lye."

Gottlieb jerked in the chair, as if an electric current had

passed through him. "What!"

"Lye," she repeated. "That's what the lab came up with. It's easy enough to get hold of. Drano, Easy-Off, and so forth. Lots of common products use strong alkalis, including ones we had around the camp.

"I don't know how much you know about eye injuries, but lye has a different effect on the eye than acid," she went on. "For one thing, it doesn't hurt as much, at least not right away. For another, there isn't such a telltale smell. So, if you've put it in your eyes, it takes a while before you know what you've done. Not long, but long enough to do yourself some terrible damage."

"But how—I mean, how was she able to get—"

"To get to the drops?" She scratched her nose. "Would have been a cinch for her. I should tell you about the camp's layout. There were four main structures apart from the cabins and activities buildings. The dining hall, the infirmary, and two that housed camp offices and living quarters for senior staff. All four are grouped around a central oval. We almost always kept them open. Up till then we'd had no cause to lock them. But even if we had, someone could still get into them easily. They're all one-story buildings, they all have ground-level windows. It's not exactly like Fort Knox up there."

"But even though you didn't feel the effects of it immediately, wouldn't you feel them a few seconds later? Wouldn't there be enough time so you'd avoid putting drops in both eyes?"

"Ordinarily, yes. But Christina thought of that, you see. She was a smart one, Christina. I'm sure you've heard that too. She put something else in my eyedrops. A topical anesthetic, Ophthaine. She probably snuck in and got it from the infirmary. Like I told you, we weren't Fort Knox. The Ophthaine killed the pain until it was too late. I'd already put drops in both eyes.

"What did you do then?" asked Gottlieb quietly.

"Well, the one good thing was, it happened in the bathroom.

As soon as I knew something was wrong, I stood at the sink, kept running water in my eyes. Then I called the infirmary. The camp doctor came right over. She took me to the nearest ER. From there they sent me to one of the University hospitals in Milwaukee. The doctor there was wonderful, a professor of ophthalmology at their medical school. By that time, he couldn't do much, though. I suppose I'm a little bit lucky. At least I can make out large shapes and light and shadow." She looked at him intensely. "I can see the outline of you, but I can't tell if you're a man or woman, or young or old, or black or white."

"Did you call the police?"

She shook her head. "You probably think I should have. Everyone else does. I'll admit, I was afraid of the terrible publicity. I told you, I'd sunk my life savings into the camp, and that kind of publicity could destroy it overnight. If I kept things quiet, at least I could unload it while it was still a thriving business."

She sipped lemonade. "Besides, I knew the police would come up empty. What did they have to go on? Just the eye-drops, nothing else. How could they prove she'd done it? Simple thing, to wipe a bottle clean of fingerprints. And even if they somehow tied her into it, what then? Remember, Christina was still a minor. She'd go to a juvenile facility somewhere, and then they'd let her out when she turned eighteen. Her records would be sealed. If you ask me, the law is way too lenient with juvenile offenders."

They fell silent as they finished their lemonades. Wild cheers exploded from the nearby TV, punctuated by the old man's coughing; the Cubs must have gone on a scoring spree. A few moments later Gottlieb continued. "So, you sold the camp?"

She nodded. "I sold it, and of course I quit teaching. Things were pretty rough back then. My mother had just died, and my father was having health problems of his own. For three or four months, I didn't do much of anything. I could barely force myself out of bed. Then I got tired of feeling sorry for myself. I learned Braille, got a part-time job with the local chapter of the National Federation for the Blind. Between that, and the disability checks and my father's pension, we get along. There's not much extra, but we manage. I still have times when I wonder if it's all worth the bother, but they pass."

She tapped the rim of the tumbler. "What do you think will happen to her father?"

"I don't know."

"No, of course you don't. And you probably wouldn't tell me if you did. But I'm guessing that they'll lock him up and throw away the key. That is, assuming they don't kill him. Too bad he can't afford a bunch of fancy lawyers. Do you want to know what I think? I think they should give him a medal for getting rid of her."

Gottlieb put down the empty tumbler on a coaster and prepared to leave. He looked forward to the long drive home, which would give him time to digest this wealth of new information. "I appreciate your meeting with me, Ms. Pierce. I can only imagine how hard it must be for you to talk about her. Before I go, is there anything else which might have a bearing on the case, anything I haven't asked you about?"

She shook her head no. "That's pretty much it."

He stood up and began to make his way to the door, then stopped and turned to her. "Just one last question. Have you ever had doubts, however fleeting, that she was the one who tampered with those eyedrops?"

"Never." She shook her head vigorously. "I should mention something else. You wouldn't believe how many times I've gone over it my head, gone over it until it's made me half-crazy. It was the day after we decided to send her home. We'd called her parents, made all the arrangements, and Kate and I were about to put her on the bus. And then, as she was walking to the bus, she stopped in her tracks and looked at me. She smiled at me. That alone was quite a shock, since I'd never seen her smile before. None of us had. She smiled at me, and here's exactly what she said— *'Well, I guess you won't be seeing me again.'"*

✦

Gottlieb had barely pulled out of the Pierces' driveway when his cell phone rang. He was startled. He rarely used the cell, and very few people had its number. Only his wife, and his answering service, and some people at GCFI.

He picked up the phone. It was Sharon. "Thank God I finally got hold of you, Hal! I've been so frightened!"

In the whole of their marriage, he could count on the fingers of one hand the times he'd known her to be truly frightened. Her fear spread to him, welled up in him like nausea. "What happened?"

"It's Peter. He's gone."

CHAPTER XVII

"GONE?" REPEATED GOTTLIEB, as if trying to process a word he'd never heard before.

"Gone." Her voice sounded close to breaking. "He went with Gordy to the mall this afternoon. Then he called from Gordy's house. He said they'd invited him to stay for dinner and he'd be home around eight."

"Sharon, let's not jump to terrible conclusions," he tried to soothe her, glancing at the clock on his dashboard. "It's only nine fifteen."

"I just called Ellen Wilder. *He didn't have dinner there tonight. He wasn't over there, period.*"

Gottlieb felt his throat tighten, and a pain in his stomach brought him close to doubling over. But he fought to keep his fear from her. *She doesn't need my own, on top of hers.* "Did they go to the mall at all?"

"Yes, but they split up at four thirty. Gordy went home. He hasn't heard from him since."

"Did you talk to Gordy?"

"I tried to. Jesus, what an inarticulate lump! He said that Peter was in some kind of mood and went off by himself. Peter wouldn't tell him where. And that was it, the last that anyone has heard from Peter. Five hours ago . . ."

The tightness in Gottlieb's throat increased. He was almost afraid to ask her, "Did you check his room?"

"Of course. The usual vile mess, no more, no less. He didn't leave a note, if that's what you mean. And his toothbrush was still there. All his clothes too, as best I could tell. But I did find something, a single sheet of paper crumpled up beneath his bed."

"What did it say?"

"Nothing. He hadn't written any words, but he'd filled the whole sheet with question marks."

Gottlieb fell silent, trying to collect his thoughts. "Hal? Are you still there?"

"Yes."

"Well, *say something*, Goddammit!"

He summoned as deliberate a tone as he could muster, hoping that it might assuage her fears, knowing that it wouldn't. "Listen to me, Sharon. He's probably off by himself somewhere, brooding, playing the tragic adolescent to the hilt. The odds are overwhelming that nothing bad has happened to him. My hunch is, he'll be calling momentarily. Let's try to stay calm. I'll be home in half an hour. I figure it's fifty-fifty he'll be there by then."

"Yeah, right. Fat fucking chance." She hung up the phone.

Fifteen minutes later his cell phone rang again. The edge-of-panic tone had given way to an icy rage. "He's back," she announced.

"Is he all right?"

"Yes. At least he looks no worse than usual."

"Where was he? What happened?"

"I haven't asked him yet. I'm waiting until you're here. We can ask him together."

⁜

The three of them sat at the kitchen table in high-backed chairs, Peter flanked by a parent on either side. He wore a dog-food-colored T-shirt, khaki cutoffs, and battered sneakers without socks. The kitchen light switch had a dimmer, and Sharon had turned it down. The room was almost as dark as the moonlit night outside.

"I just want to say one thing before we start," Sharon opened. She turned to her son. "This stunt you pulled tonight is unacceptable, Peter. It's the most thoughtless, shittiest thing you've ever done. To be gone for five hours, lying about your whereabouts, not bothering to call, and then to waltz in, without even bothering to apologize!"

"I guess I forgot to grovel," Peter mumbled.

"No one's asking you to grovel, you miserable creature, but when you've made the people who love you worry frantically, when you've deigned to come home with five hours unaccounted for, *it would be nice if you had the basic decency to say you're sorry!*"

Gottlieb assumed a calmer, more conciliatory tone as they fell into the good cop/bad cop roles, almost automatically. "Peter, this isn't a trial."

"Sure feels like one," he mumbled again.

"Well, it isn't. If you're in some kind of trouble, we'll do what we can to help you. We'll be there for you, as long as we live. But we need to know what happened." His tone was unthreatening but unyielding. "We want to know, we need to know, we have a right to know."

Peter, his eyes downcast, scrutinized the floor as though it held some hidden meaning. He hunched slightly forward, his arms folded in front of his chest as if to ward off blows. "The whole thing's so stupid. It's almost too stupid to talk about."

"Tell us," his father insisted.

"Okay. We went to the mall. We wandered around, the way we always do. That new book store, a couple of clothing stores. Nothing special."

"All, right, you're wandering . . ."

"We're wandering around, and then we got thirsty. We went to the food court to get something to drink. That was where we met them."

"Met who?" broke in Sharon.

"Rhoda Kramer and Deirdre Burke. Two girls we know from school."

"What happened then?" his father asked.

"We got Cokes and sat around talking. The three of them, that is. They talked while I just sat there, like a lump. Everything I thought about saying seemed boring and pointless. Or else it was too late."

"Too late?"

"They'd be talking about something, and I'd finally think of something to say, but by then it would be too late. They'd be talking about something else by then. The more they talked, the more I felt out of it. Feeling out of it . . . God, I hate that!" For the first time Peter's voice rose. "I hate that more than anything. And it's the way I *always* feel!"

"Peter, there's no one who hasn't felt that way," Gottlieb tried to comfort him.

"So what? It's still the worst feeling in the world."

"What were they talking about?" asked his mother.

He shrugged. "Ordinary stuff. Who's going out with who. Music, CDs, movies, clothes."

Gottlieb had a sudden flashback, as clear and realistic as a nightmare, to his own youth. He knew exactly what his son was talking about. He knew the racking silence that came with life on the social periphery, his customary station until he went to college. He knew the feeling that there was nothing he could say to his peers, whom he deemed vastly wittier, more sophisticated, and more socially adept than he could ever hope to be. He knew what it was like to write himself off as a bore, a clod, and a misfit. He wanted to hold his son in his arms, to hug and let him know how well his father knew the territory. *I understand, I was there.*

Sharon broke in, less angry now. "Did they say hurtful things to you? Were they mean?"

Peter shook his head. "As a matter of fact they were kind of nice. Every ten minutes or so, they'd notice me, pretend to, and try to include me in the conversation. Then they'd give up and go back to talking among themselves. Can't say I blame them."

The three of them fell silent. An awkward quiet engulfed the kitchen, damply oppressive, like a blanket left out in the rain.

"All right," resumed Gottlieb, "what happened next?"

"The girls left. Then it was time for Gordy's mother to pick us up. I told him I wanted to stay longer, that I needed to be alone. He asked me how I'd get home. I told him not to worry, I'd manage. We said good-bye and that was that. I walked around the mall some more, and then I walked home."

Gottlieb raised his eyebrows. "Peter, that's a six-mile walk! Maybe more!"

"Yeah, well, you're both saying how I never get enough exercise." He looked at his flabby midriff with self-loathing.

"This wasn't what we had in mind," said Sharon.

"I'm sorry, Peter," said Sharon, the icy rage completely gone now. "I'm sorry you felt so out of it."

"Not felt, *feel*. My natural state."

"It will pass. I'm sure you don't believe that, but it's true. Your father's right. There's no one in the world who hasn't felt that way. To go back to this afternoon—I'm sorry the whole thing happened. But it doesn't give you the right to do what you did to us. You don't know what that's like, Peter. To have no idea where your child is, or to fear he's in some kind of awful trouble. You don't know, and I hope to God you never do."

Peter looked about to say something but decided to hold his tongue. His father moved towards him and rested a hand on his shoulder. "I want you to think about something, Peter. Don't say yes, don't say no, just think about it. Maybe you need to see someone."

"A shrink, you mean."

"It doesn't have to be a psychiatrist. It could just as well be a psychologist or social worker. The main thing is finding someone you could talk to. No one cares about the degrees he has."

"*I'm not crazy!*"

"No," agreed his father, "but you certainly aren't very happy."

"Look, so I had a bad day. So what? Most of the time I do okay. My grades are okay. I stay out of trouble. I don't drink, I don't do drugs."

"But you're miserable," Sharon countered. "Your moods change at the drop of a hat. You have no friends except for Gordy. There's nothing you seem to give a damn about. I can hardly remember the last time I heard you laugh."

"So, I see a shrink and it would fix everything, right? I'd laugh all the time, like a friggin' hyena. Turn into the life of the party."

"No," his father acknowledged, "but at least you'd have a sounding board. Someone to help you find your own answers, even to help you formulate the questions." He thought of the sheet his wife had found, the crumpled paper filled with question marks.

Peter sprang off the chair and started to bolt from the kitchen. He stopped in the doorway and turned to them, his face flushed with rage. "I don't want to see some friggin' shrink! I don't want one, don't need one. I know you think it's the answer to everything but it isn't. I just want to be left alone. Is that asking for the world? Is that such a sin? *I JUST WANT TO BE LEFT ALONE!*"

⸙

Sharon went to the fridge and took out a can of beer. "Want one?" she asked listlessly.

Gottlieb shook his head no.

She took the beer to the patio outside their kitchen. He followed, two or three steps behind her. After taking a few swigs straight from the can, she stared up into the summer night. "All those stars," she mused quietly. "They must have planets, some of them. And some of the planets must have higher life forms. Maybe families, even. I wonder if there's a family just like ours on one of them. Parents fretting about some adolescent who stormed off in a huff, staring back at us across the void."

"Anything's possible."

She paced back and forth slowly while he stood immobile, leaning against the wall of the house. "I hate him sometimes."

"No, you don't."

"Goddammit, Hal," Sharon barked. "Don't tell me what I do and don't feel."

"Let me take an educated guess. You feel pretty much as I do. Angry, frightened, frustrated. Wanting desperately to see him happier but not knowing how to make that happen."

She spoke less heatedly. "If we have to go through this again with Sarah, I won't survive. I don't *want* to survive."

"He's right, you know."

"About *what?*"

"About his grades. About staying out of trouble."

"Forgive me if that doesn't make me jump for joy," she shot back. "He's a desperately unhappy recluse, with a room that looks like a toxic waste dump, and he's just come back from a five-hour fugue. But his grades are all right, and he doesn't have tracks or a rap sheet yet. Well, *whoopee doo!*"

"I didn't mean that he's in great shape now, and you know it. I merely pointed out that he was right. He *is* still capable of being right, believe it or not!"

"I suppose." She finished off the can of beer. When she spoke again, she sounded flat and defeated. "I'm going to bed. I want to put some closure to this day."

"I'll be up soon. Good night."

"'Night, Hal." She turned and went inside, walking very slowly, bent over like an arthritic crone, this woman who usually maintained the posture of a dancer or gymnast, who looked five or ten years younger than she was. Her eyes, as a rule bright and lively, looked dull and glazed; her shoulders slumped.

⸙

On the patio alone, he looked up at the uncountable stars,

each fixed in its place in the firmament. Or so it seemed. In fact, they were rushing away from each other, like points on the skin of an expanding balloon, as the universe encroached ever farther on the void. Nothing was as it seemed.

Gottlieb found himself thinking of a man named Warren Pasternak. He hadn't seen him for twenty years, and he might not think of him for six or nine months at a time. Even so, he'd been one of the half dozen most influential people in Gottlieb's life.

Dr. Pasternak, a professor of psychiatry at Gottlieb's medical school, had also been his therapist. He led him through a belated mourning process after the death of his much-loved father. He listened to Gottlieb's fears and self-doubts, hitherto shared with no one. He listened to an airing of his fondest dreams and most disturbing nightmares. He provided him the time and space to make sense of his life.

When a skeptical, reluctant Gottlieb began therapy with Warren Pasternak, he held psychiatry in low regard. With a condescension often seen in medical students as well as full-fledged doctors, he wrote it off as the dominion of the feckless, the timid, and the indecisive—for those who shunned the nitty-gritty work of medicine. If you lacked the manual dexterity to become a surgeon or the diagnostic acumen to become an internist, if you lacked the will or stamina for the ER or general practice, no matter. You could always make it as a shrink.

But, by the time he'd finished a course of therapy with Dr. Pasternak, he'd come to see psychiatry differently, as nothing less than medicine's most humanistic specialty. As something that was usually life-enhancing, and not uncommonly life-saving. As something that slaked his gut-deep need to alleviate pain, but also stirred his intellectual curiosity. He decided to become a psychiatrist himself, to his own astonishment.

Through the years, Gottlieb had sometimes yearned to resume seeing his old therapist. When a patient hurled trumped-up charges of sexual inappropriateness against him and sued him for malpractice, when his marriage foundered, when he and Sharon reconciled. Now, once more, he yearned again to see him, not so much as a therapist but as a wise and patient senior colleague. As a listener he couldn't shock, as a dispassionate but caring friend. As someone with whom he could share the paradox that nothing was as it seemed.

Nothing was as it seemed. The Gottliebs were an upper-middle-class suburban family, more fortunate than most, but otherwise unremarkable. Unremarkable, except that Peter grew more depressed and estranged each passing day. Unremarkable, except that Peter's parents found themselves pulling away from each other at a point when they needed each other more than usual, and his father inched towards his first affair after eighteen years of fidelity.

Nothing was as it seemed. A man dispatched his daughter in a heinous crime devoid of obvious motive, but the more Gottlieb delved into the case, the more the girl herself became suspect. Meanwhile the stars shone down, appearing fixed in their heavenly places, even as they rushed away from one another as they hurled themselves toward the void.

CHAPTER XVIII

GOTTLIEB SLEPT FITFULLY THAT NIGHT, tossing and turning like a great beached whale. Between his ragtag bits of sleep, a volley of disjointed thoughts and images jolted him. Images of Anita sitting in her genteel-shabby living room, her sightless eyes fixed on him; of Cassandra standing next to him in the cool dark corridors of the Shedd; of Peter, wretched and defensive in their kitchen. Images of Peter were the most vivid, the most distressing.

When he did doze off, he woke up a short time later with a start. Sometimes he found it hard to catch his breath. The pattern continued throughout the night. In all, he slept no more than three hours.

The next morning, he showered, dressed, and ate breakfast distractedly, saying little to Sharon as he drank coffee and munched on a croissant. Preoccupied, out of sorts, he made his way to GCFI in crawling traffic. The day had an unpleasant feel about it. The sort of day when you have a fender-bender, or trip and sprain an ankle, or receive an ominous piece of mail from the IRS. Nothing good would come from such a day, a conclusion he knew would likely turn into a self-fulfilling prophecy.

The day did not improve when he met with James Shannon. Gottlieb had come to look forward to their meetings. Shannon, so walled off at first, was open with him now (to a point); he also seemed to take more interest in their discussions. This morning, though, he looked uncharacteristically churlish from the moment he set foot in Gottlieb's office.

"You don't look very pleased about seeing me today," Gottlieb noted.

"I just woke up. I went back to sleep after breakfast. They put someone new in the cell next to me, and he screamed like a banshee all night long." Shannon said this in a vaguely accusing manner, as if the whole thing had been Gottlieb's fault.

"So they woke you up to bring you here. Well, I can see how you wouldn't care for that."

"There are times when I don't care about anything or anyone. Least of all, about what happens to me. There are times when I wish they'd give me a lethal injection and be done with it."

Gottlieb raised his eyebrows. "I thought you were opposed to the death penalty."

"I am, for other people. It's barbaric. But in my case it would be"—he chose his words carefully—"a way out."

"In other words, a state-assisted suicide."

Shannon scrutinized the floor. "I suppose that you could call it that. You could call it other things too."

"Such as?"

"Such as, an escape from an intolerable situation and intolerable memories. Such as, taking steps towards a reunion. A reunion with Margaret. I don't know any more about the afterlife than anyone else, but that's my fondest hope."

Gottlieb said nothing for a few seconds. "There's medicine for depression, Mr. Shannon," he resumed. "I know you haven't been interested in it up till now."

"I'm still not," he said, his tone close to belligerent.

"Why are you so opposed to it?"

"I just am. Do I have to give a reason?" He crossed his arms defiantly before his chest, in the manner of a pouting child. Gottlieb hadn't seen this side of him before.

"Listen to me," said Gottlieb, calling on his last reserves of patience. "You're facing the most serious charge there is. You're at the very center of a notorious case. Your life is completely different from what it was a few months ago. *It's understandable that you'd become depressed.*"

Crossing his legs and shifting in his chair, the psychiatrist continued. "I won't insult your intelligence by suggesting that medication is some kind of magic wand that's going to make everything all right. All it can do is to help you deal with what you have to deal with, nothing more. But that's still a lot."

Shannon broke the ensuing silence. "I'd like to go back to my room, if you don't mind. Nothing personal, I just don't feel like talking much today."

Gottlieb nodded. Ordinarily he might have tried to persuade him to stay longer.

After Shannon left, it occurred to Gottlieb that he hadn't mentioned the visit with Ms. Pierce. *Next time.*

⚜

Gottlieb saw three more patients at GCFI, including James Shannon's new neighbor, a teenage screamer who'd taken half a dozen hits of LSD and couldn't stop seeing worms oozing from his skin. He answered eight or ten phone calls, including a particularly tedious one from Shannon's lawyer, Brendan O'Connell. He shuffled through papers and dictated notes, as he plodded his way through the tedious morning. At one point, as he paused to sip tepid coffee, Norma Caldwell knocked on his door. "Got a minute?"

"Sure, come on in."

"Nothing important, I just wanted to—" She broke off as she studied him closely. "Are you all right, Hal?"

He nodded. "Why do you ask?"

"You look kind of gray. And your eyes are red. If I didn't know you so well, I'd wonder if you'd been on a bender."

"Nothing that interesting. I didn't get much sleep last night, and I'm having a lousy day. That's all."

"Anything on your mind?" She took a few steps towards his desk.

"Peter. Wondering if he's *trying* to drive us crazy, or if he's just innately good at it."

She laid a maternal hand across his shoulder and sighed sympathetically. "It's innate. All adolescents know how to push us to the edge. It's in their hard drive."

"You had three of them at the same time, didn't you?"

She nodded. "When Ray and I were married, we wanted children right away. We were twenty-two and twenty-one, and what the hell did *we* know? So, we had three children in five years. Which meant we had three teenagers all at once."

"How did you survive?"

"Golf!" Her eyes lit up. "It's totally absorbing, and you're outside where no one can reach you, and you get to hit that little white bastard as hard as you can. Great outlet. Of course, the Prozac helped too."

His lips squeezed into a poor semblance of a smile. "Maybe I should take it. Better yet, maybe Peter should."

※

He went through the rest of the morning and early afternoon in a thick dull haze. After a meeting with Dwight and Norma, he listened with scant interest as they argued about the merit of Spike Lee's movies. Norma considered him too strident. Dwight accused her of missing the point—if anything, he wasn't strident enough. Stanley Celinsky joined them in the lunchroom, his fine tremor apparent as he took spoonfuls of yogurt. Gottlieb himself had little appetite. He barely finished half a tuna sandwich and a few dollops of macaroni salad.

Leaving GCFI shortly after lunch, he put Ellington's "Mood Indigo" on the Saab's CD player. Even this, his favorite composition, failed to cheer him. Arriving at his office, he used about a hundredth of his brain as he checked messages, answered calls, and opened mail. When the parade of his afternoon patients began, he had to tap his feet and bite the lining of his mouth to stay awake. He envisioned each part of the day as another stretch along a dreary highway. He looked forward to going to bed that night with near-erotic anticipation.

At six thirty, when his last patient left, he picked up the phone and dialed Cassandra's number. He hadn't planned to call her, at least not that he knew of.

"Hi, Hal. What's the matter? You don't sound so great."

"I didn't sleep well, and it's been a long day." He launched into another telling of Peter's misadventures. As he did so, he suddenly found himself tired and sick to death of the Peter conundrum. Tired of his helplessness in the face of his son's depression, and tired of his son's indifference to his own plight, and tired of the pall he cast over the whole household. Tired, especially, of anticipating months or years of a situation more likely to get worse before it got better.

"I'd give anything to be with you awhile tomorrow," he said impulsively. He didn't realize how much he wanted to see her until the words flew out.

"I've got to do some things, but they don't have to be done at any special times. Come over when you want."

"You don't know how much I wish I could." He was feeling mildly sorry for himself. A rare occurrence, which he loathed.

"Full day?"

"Packed. Morning at GCFI, private patients in my office until almost seven thirty."

"Come over anyway. Come in the morning. Let the criminally insane fend for themselves for a few hours."

He pondered this. "Hmm. No real reason why I couldn't. I could call in sick. Something I've never done before."

"Never?"

"Never."

⁂

Gottlieb left the house at 7:30 a.m. the next morning, his customary time. At 7:33 a.m. he called Dwight Sanderson on the cell phone. The nurse's manner was friendly and breezy.

"Yo, Doc, what's happenin'?'"

"Hello, Dwight. I just wanted to tell you that I'm not feeling very well today, and I won't be coming in." This had an element of truth to it. Gottlieb did not lie easily or often. To do so now was giving him an upset stomach and a low-grade headache.

"Hey, 'bout time you did this," Dwight replied approvingly. "Took yourself a mental health day like the rest of us."

"Dwight, I really feel like shit," he said, awash in guilt.

"Yeah, whatever. Listen, Doc, if you're really sick I hope you feel better. And if you're not . . . what the hell, I ain't your momma, it don't matter none to me. See you Monday, okay?"

"Okay." He hung up the phone, mystified that so many people seemed to deal with guilt so effortlessly.

⁑

Cassandra came to the door wearing a lightweight blue cotton bathrobe, her hair wrapped in a towel. She reached up to kiss him. "Sorry I'm so slow this morning. I just got out of the shower. Make yourself comfortable. Freitag will keep you company while I throw on some clothes."

You don't have to get dressed on my account, he almost said, instantly discarding it as cheesy and adolescent. Instead, he sauntered to the sofa. In front of it sat a coffee table on which were strewn recent issues of *Atlantic Monthly*, the *Smithsonian*, and the *New York Times Review of Books*. There was also a massive tome on Bauhaus architecture and an oversized paperback on films of the 1950s.

While Freitag purred beside him, presenting an ear for stroking, Gottlieb picked up the book on films with his free hand. He opened it at random, found himself looking at a piece on *The Seven Year Itch*, and wondered if this was some kind of omen. The piece included a black and white photograph of an irresistible Marilyn Monroe smiling enticingly at a hopelessly smitten Tom Ewell.

The book contained concise descriptions and photos from some of the much-enjoyed, half-remembered movies of his youth. *The Crimson Pirate, The Incredible Shrinking Man,* and his all-time favorite: *Davy Crockett, King of the Wild Frontier.* His mother still had a picture of him in one of her albums, a little boy in a flannel shirt who wore the mandatory coonskin hat.

Utterly engrossed, he didn't hear her coming. He was startled when she came behind him and put a cool hand against his cheek. She wore white Bermudas and the same peach and plum blouse she'd had on at the Shedd.

"A bit jumpy, are we?"

It would have been silly to refute her, so he responded with a shrug. For want of something better to do with his hands, he picked up the book again. "I didn't know you were a film buff."

"I've loved the movies from as far back as I can remember. The perfect escape. Sometimes, when I was in graduate school, I'd go on a binge and see three or four in a week."

"What were you escaping from?"

"Everything. All the day-to-day aggravations. When I was young, the cold war between my parents, and my brother's benign neglect. That, and a sense that I was always different."

He closed the book and went back to petting the impatient cat. "What made you so different?"

"For starters, I was a first-generation American whose parents still spoke with an accent, and who came from a country we'd just been at war with. My father's patients may have worshipped him, but that doesn't mean they accepted him as a social equal. Another thing, I was pretty smart. Too smart to fit in and go along with things, but not smart enough to figure out how to make myself happy."

"It's not an epiphany . . . it evolves."

"Maybe so, but you don't know that when you're twelve or thirteen."

He turned his attention back to the book. "Most of these

films were made before you were born."

"I've seen a lot of them, though. I've rented them, or I've caught them at revivals. I like the fifties films. There's an innocence about them. No bad language and God forbid, no nudity or sex, but there's often more depth to them than meets the eye. They hold up well, the best of them. A couple of months ago I rented *Twelve Angry Men*. Ever see it?"

"Yes, but I don't remember it too well. About jurors, isn't it?"

She nodded. "Very simple format. The whole thing takes place in a jury room. No high tech glitz, and certainly no romance, but it's the best thing I've ever seen about a jury deliberating. A hundred times better than *A Time to Kill*."

She joined him on the couch, a noisily purring Freitag wedged between them. They glanced through the book together, sharing comments and reminiscences about the movies mentioned. Gottlieb found himself distracted by the freshly showered smell of her. She'd used a shampoo that reminded him of the ocean. Salt air, with a hint of citrus.

"Did you have breakfast?" she asked him a few minutes later.

"Toast and coffee."

"I don't have too much in now. I planned to shop later. But there's fruit salad and bagels and whatnot. Or I could fix us some eggs or pancakes."

"Fruit salad and a bagel would be fine."

He followed her into the kitchen and sat down while she brought out a dish of fruit salad from the fridge, put bagels in the toaster oven, and made a fresh pot of coffee.

"Anything I can do?" He wasn't used to sitting idly while others waited on him.

"Relax, Hal. You don't always have to be *doing*." She put cream cheese and orange marmalade on the counter, touching his shoulder as she passed by him.

After they ate—unhurriedly, as the knot in Gottlieb's stomach slowly disappeared, as they sat at the counter finishing their coffee — he loosened his tie, pushed back the chair, and crossed his legs. "It still feels strange to be here. Less so, though."

She regarded him with a quizzical half-smile. "I don't know. You look pretty comfortable to me."

He stared at the nearly empty coffee cup with more intensity than it merited. "Last night, when I couldn't sleep, my mind was spinning like a pinwheel. I was thinking about. . . oh, God, about all kinds of thing. About you, and us, and the two of us at the aquarium."

Gottlieb looked at her, hoping that she'd pick up the thread of the conversation. She held her silence, though, refusing to take him off the hook. He continued, "It was the first time I've kissed another woman in more than twenty years."

"What was it like for you?" she asked, in what he'd come to think of as her clinical mode. *She would have made a hell of a therapist,* he thought, not for the first time.

He searched for the proper simile. "It was like jumping out of an airplane," he replied finally, "or my guess of what it must be like. Jumping out, and that interval before the parachute opens."

She threw back her head and tossed off a brief laugh. "Come, now!"

"I mean it." He tried not to sound hurt.

"Well, it's actually quite flattering. I've never heard a kiss described that way before."

Exposed and vulnerable, he wanted to throw the focus back to her. "What was it like for *you*?"

"Overdue."

With that, she moved towards him, framed his face with her hands and kissed him. Her lips parted, and her tongue flicked and darted as it sought out hidden places in his mouth. His hands came to life, at first unsteadily, moving down her cheeks to her neck and shoulders, coming to rest on the breasts that swelled beneath the plum-and-peach blouse. He felt her nipples rise and stiffen. They kissed again, and then for a third time, and a fourth.

So it went for a few minutes, or maybe five or ten, until she pulled away from him. Without speaking, she led him to the bedroom. For once passive and docile, he felt relief that she was willing to take charge. His sense of time and distance had gone awry. The bedroom seemed a block away, and it took them forever to get to it.

Once there, they stood by the side of her unmade bed while she shed her clothes with fluid ease, and then she turned her attention back to him, kissing and stroking him while she unbuttoned his shirt and unbuckled his belt. His eyes feasted on the firm smooth contours of her body, while his hand made its way (slowly, slowly) from her face to her nipples to her belly to her crotch. In spite of himself, he took note of how her body differed from his wife's. Her firmer breasts, and the slightly more lateral pitch of them, the better definition of the muscles of her trunk and thighs, the lack of stretch marks. The curlier, more abundant thicket of blonde hair that marked the cleft between her legs.

He was too absorbed with her to give mind to his own nakedness, for once. Intensely self-conscious about his bodily failings—his weight, his lack of muscle tone, his too-hairy arms and legs—he still felt ill at ease, *still,* when his wife saw him nude. Whenever possible, he dressed and undressed while she was out of the room.

Holding his hand, she splayed herself on top of the crumpled sheets of the unmade bed and pulled him towards her. As they lay side by side, he returned her kisses more avidly, while his free hand explored the warm blonde thicket. She answered by stroking the most robust erection he'd had in years. That was when the walls began to close in on him, and the room began to spin and jolt. He was seized by the notion that centrifugal force would lift him from the bed and flatten him against a contracting wall. The absurdity of this notion did nothing to dispel it. The walls themselves came in out of focus. They oscillated, their surface marred by eruptions of spark-like incandescent dots.

No matter how forcefully he inhaled, he felt on the verge of suffocation. He felt as though a great weight lay across him, precisely where his neck met his chest. Within the next few minutes he would die. He was sure of it, without a shred of doubt. He would die, and they would find his hairy, fat, buck-naked body in her bed. His heart raced, his hands shook, his palms turned clammy. And, the coup de grâce, his erection vanished in the twinkling of an eye.

And even as these thoughts and sensations assaulted him, a more analytical corner of his mind took them in dispassionately. *For years my patients have told me about their panic attacks. So, this is what they're like.*

He turned on his back, put a hand over his eyes, and groaned. She shot up in the bed and leaned over him. "Hal! What's the matter?"

"Room spinning . . . can't catch my breath . . ." He groaned again. It was an act of will for him to talk, since every word took prodigious effort.

"I'll call 911." She reached for the bedside phone.

"No, don't. Not a heart attack."

"Are you sure?"

"I'm sure. Just give me a minute or two."

"Do you want a glass of water?"

He nodded. At least it would get her out of the room, if only for a moment. He found himself with a sudden desperate need to be alone. He wished he had a desert island to escape to.

She bolted from the bedroom, returning with a glass of water and dampened washcloth. As he drank, she placed the washcloth across his forehead. The room was becoming stationary again; the walls no longer oscillated. When he finished drinking, she sat next to him on the bed, as his breathing returned to normal and his pulse slowed. The dread passed, leaving in its wake a leaden awkwardness and embarrassment.

He forced himself to turn towards her, to look her in the eye. "I'm sorry."

"Makes two of us."

"Nothing like this has ever happened to me. It's the worst feeling imaginable."

Her tongue made a clucking sound against the roof of her mouth. "Well, it's a first for me too. At times I've had a strange effect on men, but I've never caused anything like *that* before."

"You didn't cause it. The truth is, it had nothing to do with you."

Her eyes bore into him, her pupils narrowed. "That's funny, I thought it might have, since it happened in my bed, right before we were about to make love for the first time."

"That's not what I meant," he said helplessly.

"What *did* you mean? No, wait, I don't think I want to know the answer." She turned away from him and looked dispassionately out the window. "I think you should get dressed now. Go home—go home to your wife. Hmm. I wonder if anything like this happened to her, when she was having *her* affair."

He sat up in bed sharply and put a hand to his face as though she'd punched him. "That was cruel."

"I guess it was." Her tone conveyed no trace of an apology.

⸎

Gottlieb dressed quickly, as they maintained a total silence. He couldn't wait to be outside, to feel the late summer breeze against his cheek, to flee the confines of this apartment, to flee the presence of this woman. At the same time, it occurred to him that once he did leave, he might not see her again. An intolerable thought.

Finally, he was ready to make his exit. He glanced at his

watch. It was not quite ten o'clock. He'd been there for less than ninety minutes. It felt like half an eternity.

His hand on the door, he turned back towards her, as she stood in the middle of the living room, her arms akimbo. "May I call you?" he asked, as tentatively as he'd ever asked anyone for anything.

She maintained a stony silence before answering. "I suppose," she said at last. "But let's give it a while, okay?"

CHAPTER XIX

RARELY DID GOTTLIEB HAVE SIGNIFICANT BLOCKS of free time during the day. He was therefore at loose ends when he left Cassandra's apartment, lacking goal or purpose, still smarting from humiliation and failure.

To the extent that he felt like doing anything, he felt like driving. Almost automatically he headed for Lake Shore Drive. He couldn't estimate how often he'd traversed it through the years. Five hundred times? A thousand? It didn't matter; he never tired of the sleek soaring architecture on one side, the blue-green glory of Lake Michigan on the other.

But even Lake Shore Drive gave no solace. Once on it, he found himself indifferent to it. For all he cared, it might have been the ugliest stretch of highway in the world, a collection of low-life bars and cheap motels and pawn shops.

Demoralized and distracted, he considered his options. He could always go to GCFI. Tell them he'd made a miraculous recovery, and he'd decided to come in after all. Too late for that, though. GCFI was far away—by the time he arrived, it would almost be time to leave again. Besides, and more to the point, he didn't want to go there. GCFI was, in fact, the last place he wanted to be just now, with the exception of Cassandra's apartment.

Half tapping, half pounding the steering wheel, Gottlieb weighed his other options. He could do what she said: go home to his wife. Except that Sharon wouldn't be at home. She'd be at work. Sarah would be at day care. Only Peter would be there, probably just emerging from his den. Miserable, profoundly shaken, Gottlieb realized that he simply lacked the heart to see his son just then.

He could go to a restaurant, get something to eat. Not a bad idea, except that he wasn't hungry. He could kill an hour or two in one of the nearby museums, the Field Museum or the Museum of Science and Industry. Another reasonable option, but he had no interest in them. Or he could go early to his office, rearrange the piles of papers on his desk, and pretend to read some journals. If all else failed, he could play solitaire on his computer.

Beset by colossal indifference, he pulled off Lake Shore Drive and headed to his office. He couldn't recall a time when the day passed so slowly, so oppressively. The thought came to him, as undeniable as it was unwelcome—*I need help. I need to talk to someone.* The realization made him blush and clench his teeth. Gottlieb had grown used to a caretaking role. He was the strong one, the one whom others turned to. He hated few things as much as admitting that he needed help himself. The illogic of this made it no easier to stomach. He sought help only when he had no choice.

As soon as he got to his office, Gottlieb took the *Yellow Pages* from a drawer. With a sigh he turned to the listings for physicians, searching for Warren Pasternak, the psychiatrist he'd seen a quarter of a century ago.

There was no such listing, as he'd expected. The man had almost certainly retired, off to Florida or California. Or else he'd died. He'd been in his midfifties when Gottlieb had consulted him. That would make him close to eighty now.

On a hunch, Gottlieb picked up another phone book, the *White Pages*. Pasternak would likely have had an unlisted home number while he still practiced. Once retired, though, he wouldn't need one. A long shot, but Gottlieb was desperate enough to try anything. He turned to the *P*'s. Pace . . . Paget . . . Parker . . . *Pasternak, Dr. Warren V.* The listing gave a Sheridan Road address.

He dialed the number right away, lest he give himself an opportunity to back down. The phone rang half a dozen times before a man answered—*Hello?* The voice was clearly Warren Pasternak's: older now, but with the same tone, mildly questioning. The same cadence; the same hint of a subtle, not displeasing accent. Gottlieb recalled that he'd immigrated to America as boy, arriving here with no English. His parents, Austrian Jews, had seen the writing on the wall. Like Cassandra's parents.

It occurred to Gottlieb that he didn't know what he'd say. He hadn't thought it through that far. "Dr. Pasternak?"

"Speaking."

"Dr. Pasternak, I don't know if you remember me. My name is Harold Gottlieb. I was your patient many years ago."

"Gottlieb. Harold Gottlieb . . ." The old man pondered this awhile. "Why, yes, I do remember you. I saw you when I did some work for Student Health Services. You were in medical school, yes?"

"That's right. I saw you for—oh, four or five months, I think it was. You helped me very much."

"Well, this is always nice to hear." He sounded pleased. "We don't get those quick dramatic outcomes, like the surgeons."

"So I've noticed. I became a psychiatrist myself."

"Really! Where do you work?"

"Here, in Chicago." Gottlieb was starting to feel less tentative, less needy. "I do a fair bit of forensic psychiatry. I'm on the staff of the Greater Chicago Forensic Institute. I also do some teaching, and I have a small private practice."

"I hear from everyone how hard it is these days to practice," he said. "Myself, I was very fortunate. I quit ten years ago, before this foolishness with managed care became too bad. Before the bean counters and failed nurses began to watch over us like birds of prey."

"Have you retired completely?"

"Just about. I do a little work for Jewish Family Services, six hours a week tops." He paused. "So, Dr. Gottlieb—"

"Hal. Please call me Hal."

"So, Hal, what leads you to call me after all these years?"

A truthful answer might have gone along these lines: *Because I have a case I don't know how to deal with, a life-or-death case which is taking me into dark uncharted waters. Because I need to talk about my son, my one-time greatest joy in life, who throws me completely for a loop right now. Whenever I come home, I half expect to find that he hanged himself. Because I had my very first panic attack this morning, in the bed of a woman not my wife. Because my life no longer makes much sense to me. There hasn't been a great disaster, at least not yet, and God knows it could be infinitely worse, but it simply doesn't make much sense to me at all.*

What he said instead was this: "I'm dealing with a very unusual case right now, a criminal case, and I'd appreciate your input. I'm also dealing with some, uhm, difficult personal issues. Talking with you has helped me clarify things before, and I thought it might again."

Pasternak seemed to deliberate before replying. "Well, Dr. Gottlieb—Hal—as I told you, I closed my office long ago. But I'd be happy to meet with you here, in my home. Informally."

Gottlieb felt a tidal wave of gratitude pass though him. "I can't tell you how much I'd appreciate that."

"When would you like to come?"

"As soon as possible, whenever it's convenient."

"Come tomorrow morning if you'd like. Ten thirty?"

"Perfect."

Gottlieb thanked him again, said good-bye and heaved a huge sigh of relief. For the first time in weeks he felt something akin to calmness.

⁂

Warren Pasternak lived on the eleventh floor of a high-rise at the southern end of Sheridan Road, a short distance past the terminus of Lake Shore Drive. His apartment included a small patio off the living room, facing the lake. He and Gottlieb sat there, on opposite sides of a serving table that held their glasses of iced coffee and a plate of macaroons. It also held Pasternak's smoking accouterments. A pouch of tobacco, a pipe tool, and a lighter. He smoked an elaborately carved meerschaum. A light breeze from the lake failed to dissipate an aromatic haze that lingered above the patio.

"This is my favorite place on earth," began Pasternak, after an exchange of pleasantries. "I sit here by the hour. I read, I watch the colors of the lake change, I observe its moods. I watch the boats and planes." He pointed towards the sky. "This is one of the approaches to O'Hare."

"It's very pleasant."

"I think we moved here because of the patio. I wasn't much older than you are now. Our children were grown, and we wanted someplace smaller than the house we had in Evanston. We looked at different condos, but none of them had a view like this one."

He still wore a wedding band, Gottlieb noticed, but the condo showed no sign of a woman's presence. "Is your wife living?"

"Barely. She's in a nursing home. Advanced Alzheimer's. Once in a while she knows who I am, but not usually. She spends the day wandering up and down the corridors. You know how Alzheimer's patients tend to pace. Sometimes she'll watch a video of tropical fish swimming in a tank. No plot, no dialogue, just the fish. It was made for cats. Now this was a lawyer, someone who graduated from the University of Chicago cum laude. They made her an editor of the *Law Review*."

"I'm sorry. It must have been awful for you."

He acknowledged the condolence with a nod. "The first stage was the worst. She was still intact enough to know what was happening. She'd cry for hours, sometimes for days. None of the antidepressants made a whit of difference. All they did was give her side effects. Blurred vision, lightheadedness, upset stomach, dry mouth. You name them, she had them."

He drew on the pipe. "Well, Hal, it's what that woman said—Hannah Greene, her name was? No one promises us a rose garden."

They fell silent as a trio of sailboats swept across the horizon, their sails gleaming in the bright sunlight. Pasternak put down the pipe and tapped the edge of it against the ashtray. "Tell me about this case you're so concerned with."

"Have you followed the Christina Shannon murder?"

"Not closely. When you reach my age, you grow tired of the atrocity of the moment."

Gottlieb paused to organize his thoughts. "I told you, I do a lot of forensic work. James Shannon, her father, is our patient." He gave a quick review of the key facts of the case, including results of the workup to date. "It's a matter of life or death, literally," he concluded. "Our evaluation may play a role in whether or not he's executed."

"I see. And you say you've found no evidence of a major psychiatric illness?"

"None. That isn't just my own opinion. Everyone at GCFI who spends time with him feels that way. It's also been corroborated by friends and family members."

"Hmm. Very interesting." Pasternak refilled his pipe and lit it, expelling a spiral swirl of smoke. He asked many of the questions which Gottlieb had asked himself. Did Shannon have an undiagnosed physical problem? Did he have a rare reaction to some prescription medication? Did losing his wife set in motion a psychotic depression? Was Gottlieb convinced he didn't drink to excess or use drugs?

Gottlieb answered the questions as he sipped iced coffee. "Shannon once described himself as the most ordinary man in the world," he remarked. "And he is, except for having killed his daughter in cold blood, for no apparent reason."

"Tell me what you know about the girl."

"She was neat and clean, polite and obedient, and no one

liked her. It goes beyond dislike. She was universally despised by just about everyone who knew her. Hated, even." He summarized the meetings with Malcolm Kenyon and Anita Pierce, ending with an account of Anita's blindness.

The story prompted Pasternak to inhale sharply. "You're suggesting that she blinded this woman—*blinded* her!—because they asked her to leave the camp?"

"I know, it sounds preposterous. But the more I hear about her, the less preposterous it sounds. One thing's certain. *Someone* put something in those eyedrops, and there weren't any other candidates."

Gottlieb finished the iced coffee, then resumed. "From early childhood she seems to have enjoyed inflicting pain on others."

"Well, there are sociopathic children, no doubt about it." The old man stroked his chin. "Did you ever read *The Mask of Sanity*? That book must be fifty years old now, but it's still the best account of antisocial types I've come across."

"But she wasn't a classic sociopath. For one thing, she was never impulsive. She thought things through, she'd bide her time, she'd plan. She didn't smoke or drink or use drugs. She didn't act out sexually, at least not that we know of. I never saw her report cards, but I'd be surprised if there was any mention of poor conduct." He set down the empty glass. "She was also more sadistic than most of the sociopaths I've known." He recounted the story of the goldfish, and her reaction to her mother's burns from the spilled coffee, and the drawings they'd found at Green Lake Camp.

They fell silent while a 747 flew directly overhead, effectively drowning out all conversation. "The more I learn about her," resumed Gottlieb, "the more it sounds as if she might have been a genuinely evil person. Whatever *that* means."

"Are you sure she hadn't been abused?"

"I'm not very sure about anything these days, but her father is the least likely candidate for child abuse I've ever known."

"What about abuse from others? A grandfather or an uncle? A cousin, a neighbor? Or a priest?"

Gottlieb shook his head. "I can only say that I don't think so. Neither did Dr. Kenyon."

"Hmm." Another swirl of pipe smoke rose above them. "Interesting, what you said about evil people, *whatever that means.* There was a time when I was preoccupied with understanding evil. Obsessed with it. I'd just started medical school. It was towards the end of World War II, following the liberation of the death camps. We were just learning the full extent of the Nazi horrors. To put it simply, I couldn't fathom how such things were possible. So I read . . . I read everything I could get my hands on. Books on psychology, philosophy, religion. I read about evil until it made me slightly crazy, but the more I read, the more it bewildered me. As they'd say today, I couldn't get a handle on it. Now this is strictly my own opinion, Hal, but I think there's something about the nature of evil which always eludes us, no matter how hard we try to understand it. Perhaps it always will."

"Do you believe there's some ultimate source of evil? Some embodiment of it?"

He set the meerschaum in the ashtray carefully. "I don't believe, I don't disbelieve. Such a belief makes no sense to me, of course. Devils with pitchforks are for children on Halloween. But through the years, I've heard things that are hard to understand in rational terms."

"Such as?"

Pasternak folded his hands placidly on his lap. "Let me tell you about a patient I used to have. We'll call him John. An ordinary fellow, probably much like your James Shannon. Middle-aged, a strong Catholic background. A tool-and-dye maker who worked for the same company for twenty years. John's wife left him for another man, and I was treating him for depression. One day we were talking about his family of origin. He had two sisters and a brother. I asked him why he never talked about his brother. John said he hoped he'd never see him again, that he considered him a lost cause. And these were his exact words—*I did everything I could for him. I even went to the exorcism.*"

"I beg your pardon?"

"You heard me. *Exorcism.*"

Gottlieb sat listening, enthralled. "Go on."

"Needless to say, that gained my attention. And then John told me the whole story. He described his brother speaking in a language he'd never heard before, in voices he'd never heard before. He described the most terrible, vilest smells imaginable, different from anything he'd ever known. He described him as having the strength of a bull, how it took four big men to hold him down. By the way, his brother was only five foot seven, about 150 pounds and slightly built. And then he told me about the levitation—"

"What!"

"Levitation," Pasternak repeated. "His brother's body lifted off the floor. More than once, in fact. It stayed in the air for five or ten seconds at a time."

"That's impossible."

"It would seem so," replied Pasternak, unruffled. He picked up the pipe but didn't light it. "I asked John the obvious questions. Had he been drinking? Using drugs? Could someone else have drugged him? Could his brother have learned a foreign language without his knowledge? Could he have soiled himself and become incontinent, could *that* have caused the smell? Could there have been some kind of hidden supports, like wires from the ceiling? Was he too far away to see what was really happening? And the answer was always no."

Pasternak paused briefly. "I should tell you something else about John. He wasn't an imaginative fellow. He had no flair for melodrama. Phlegmatic, a little on the dull side. I don't think he *could* have made this up, even if he'd wanted to."

"Had he told anyone else about it?"

"No. And I don't think he would have told me, if I hadn't stumbled into it, and if I hadn't pressed him."

Pasternak broke off when a helicopter flew noisily over the beach front. "I don't know what really happened that day with John's brother, any more than you really know what the Shannon girl was all about. I'll only say that things happen that can't be addressed by our ordinary logic. Things that go beyond our ordinary realm of experience. How did Shakespeare put it in *Hamlet*? When Hamlet tells Horatio that there are more things in heaven and Earth than are dreamt of in your philosophy. I forget the exact words."

They fell silent. Gottlieb studied the lake, darker now, a deeper green than it had been before. He remembered what Pasternak had said about the lake's different moods and colors. The lake's mood had changed, subtly but unmistakably. More restless now, on the verge of angry.

"I'm afraid I haven't been much help to you," the old man commented.

"Yes, you have. It helps just to bounce this off someone else."

The old man turned towards him. "When you called," he prodded gently, "you said there were some other issues. Personal ones."

"I'm terribly concerned about my son," said Gottlieb. "He's fifteen now, with all the signs and symptoms of a serious depression. Each day he pulls farther away from the rest of us." Gottlieb gave a rapid account of Peter's metamorphosis from the happy little boy with dark cherubic curls to the silent, sullen lump who sat alone in his hovel of a room.

"I see him headed for terrible trouble," concluded Gottlieb, "and I don't know how to stop it. He's dead set against any kind of therapy. He won't tell us what he wants or needs. Perhaps he can't because he doesn't know himself."

"What did you want when you were his age?"

Gottlieb shut his eyes as he tried to conjure up the past.

"God, it was so long ago, I can barely remember back that far. What did I want? Well, the main thing I wanted was for my father to get well." By the time Hal reached his teens, his father had already become incapacitated by the multiple sclerosis that ultimately took his life.

"Yes, but what did you want for yourself?"

"Above all else, I wanted to feel I wasn't so terribly *different.*" He recalled, in passing, that Cassandra had told him much the same. "That I wasn't the only one who was too fat, with acne, who masturbated all the time. Who was sure no woman would ever look twice at him. I wanted not to feel everyone in the world was better than me. Better looking, more confident, more socially adept. I felt condemned to be the outsider, not just then, but forever."

Gottlieb's eyes welled up. "I don't think about those things too often. I forget how painful they once were."

"If you consider what you were like at that age yourself, and what you needed then," reflected Pasternak, "that alone will help you to help your son."

Gottlieb took a macaroon, not because he was hungry, but because it gave him something to do, to focus on. Something to keep him from crying.

"There's another thing," he resumed after a lengthy silence. "Yesterday morning, a few hours before I called you, I had a full-blown panic attack. The first one I've ever had." Too embarrassed to look at Pasternak directly, he scrutinized the lake as he haltingly delved into the circumstances.

"Who is she, this other woman? What is she to you?"

"Her name is Cassandra. She's a historian, in her late thirties. Nice looking, very smart. As is my wife, I should add, on both counts. What is she to me? The first word that comes to mind is *friend.* Although I'm not sure friendship is an option now . . . not after *that.* I've told her things about myself that I haven't told anyone else, and vice versa. I don't know if we've known each other long enough to develop what constitutes a true friendship. It hasn't even been two months, but she has gotten to be terribly important to me."

The old man pressed his fingertips together. "You know one of things that has always struck me about psychiatry, Hal? It's this paradox: we study the brain in all its infinite complexity, and we put together these great theories of personality and behavior, but much of it comes down to little more than common sense. For example, let's consider what happened to you yesterday. We could talk about it fancifully. Midlife issues. Doubts about your own attractiveness to women, stemming from your own adolescence and rekindled by what's happening to your son now, and so on. We could talk about it in these terms, but do we need to? The gist of it seems pretty clear, I think. *Infidelity makes you terribly uncomfortable.* You may be drawn to the fantasy of it, like most of us, but you shy away from the reality of it."

He uncrossed his leg on the hassock before him and went on. "Now I know there are people who carry it off with relative ease, or at least who appear to. They indulge themselves. They hop from bed to bed without a second thought. Maybe they're lucky, and maybe not. I must say, I haven't known too many of them who struck me as terribly happy. But it's irrelevant, since you don't happen to be one of them."

"I suppose," said Gottlieb quietly, "that I knew that all along."

"Listen, Hal, since you're not my patient any longer, not officially, I have the luxury of giving you direct advice. Be this woman's friend, and let her be a friend to you. Assuming that the friendship will survive, and my hunch is that it will. But let it go at that. Stay faithful to your wife. There are worse things than staying faithful to a woman you still love. That is, if you still do, of course."

"I do. I always have, almost from the day I met her. I always will, incurably."

Pasternak gave his knee a small fraternal pat.

Their conversation shifted to a lighter vein. The weather, local politics, Gottlieb's plans to attend a seminar in forensic psychiatry, Pasternak's plans to spend Labor Day weekend with a daughter in Maryland.

Gottlieb checked his watch. It was a few minutes after noon. "I really didn't know it was so late," he said apologetically. "I hope I haven't imposed too much."

Pasternak cut him off with a wave of the hand. "Not at all, not at all. It was very nice to have you here. I hope you'll keep in touch and not wait for twenty-five more years to pass. God forbid that I should be around then."

"I won't. And thank you."

"You're welcome."

Pasternak began to walk him to the door but stopped abruptly. "Something just occurred to me about that case, the Shannon case. Why did he kill her when he did? Why not three months earlier or six months later?"

"I don't know. Whenever we've talked about it, I've mainly been concerned with motive."

"Never underestimate the importance of timing, Hal. Things happen for a reason, but they also happen *when* they happen for a reason. I know, it's a basic point, but it's easy to overlook."

Gottlieb raised his eyebrows. "I'll ask him about it. I'll ask him the next time I see him, on Monday morning."

They shook hands by the door. Standing, Warren Pasternak looked older than he had on the patio, stooped and wizened. But his gaze remained clear, his handshake firm. "Keep in touch," he repeated.

"I will," Gottlieb vowed again.

He found himself wondering what the old man's life was like—living alone, his children living with their families far away. Watching the lake, smoking his pipe, reading. Living alone while the wife he clearly loved spent her final days in a nursing home, pacing the halls and watching a videotape of tropical fish, a video made for cats.

CHAPTER XX

THE NEXT SUNDAY, THREE DAYS AFTER his meeting with Warren Pasternak, Gottlieb found himself with a surfeit of nervous energy. While not lazy—he had more than a touch of the workaholic in his nature—he usually avoided household chores. A Jewish medical princeling, his wife called him, a man who believed beds made themselves and clothes laundered themselves. But this Sunday he lunged into a series of mundane tasks with near-zeal. Washing and waxing the Saab (Sharon's Acura too, for good measure), cleaning the garage, and weeding the margins of the driveway.

Sarah helped him, in a manner of speaking. She scrubbed the Saab as far as her short arms could reach, stuffing debris into heavy-duty trash bags while singing fragments of songs from *The Lion King*. Every so often, as her father hosed down the car, he'd turn the water on her, to her great enjoyment.

Watching her pretend to run away from him, as seemingly happy as a child can be, Gottlieb had a fleeting memory of Peter at that age. He'd been just as happy as his sister, just as carefree. Comparing them forced Gottlieb to contemplate Sarah's adolescence. It was still a long way off, but not long enough to suit him, not nearly long enough. *Maybe it won't be as bad as his*, Gottlieb allowed himself to hope. *If it is, I could join the French Foreign Legion.*

Peter himself was spending the day with Gordy Wilder, with whom he was on good terms again, more or less.

Gottlieb and his daughter worked steadily, from right after an early lunch until close to three. It was cooler than usual for this time of year but still muggy, and it grew muggier as the day went on. "Daddy, it's too hot to work like this," complained

Sarah.

"I know, sweetheart, but we're almost finished." They had just filled their third large plastic bag with the last of the debris from the garage.

"Could we go to a movie?"

He pretended to ponder this at length. "Well, I don't see why not," he answered finally. "Let me finish up the odds and ends in here and then we'll check the paper."

Inside the house, they skimmed the entertainment section. The cinematic fare consisted mainly of action sequels. *Speed II, Jurassic Park II,* the latest *Batman.* There were also several comedies of the *Porky's* genre. Then he noticed that *101 Dalmatians* had been brought back by one of the smaller nearby theaters. The next showing was at three fifty. Sarah had seen it on TV a year ago, and enough time had passed for a second viewing.

He asked Sharon to join them but she declined, as he knew she would. Sharon's Sunday afternoon routine bordered on the sacrosanct. She sorted through papers and paid bills while listening to *Car Talk,* taking a walk if the weather permitted, taking a nap. Despite little interest in automotive matters, she listened to *Car Talk* faithfully, mainly because of an infatuation with Tom and Ray. She told Hal that she intended to run away with one of them if anything happened to their marriage. Either one; it didn't matter.

They set off in the Saab, sparkling clean now, as they headed for the theater. Gottlieb, contented for a change, was unburdened by the pinwheel of dark tangential thoughts that had lately become the bane of his existence. He took a deep if simple comfort in listening to his daughter prattle about going back to school . . . about Disney World, and couldn't they *PLEEZE* go there . . . about her friends and her dolls and her stuffed animals.

He enjoyed the movie more than he expected to. As much as the movie itself, he enjoyed his daughter's reactions to it. He turned in the darkened theater to steal glances at her face, which registered concern when the Dalmatians were in danger, severe disapproval of Cruella De Vil, and joy and relief when the pups prevailed.

On the way home they stopped to have dinner at a nearby deli. She sat across from him in a booth, munching on a grilled cheese sandwich and sipping a glass of chocolate milk.

"Daddy, I think we should get a dog," she said gravely.

"You do, do you?"

"Uh-huh. A puppy."

"You weren't thinking about a Dalmatian puppy by any chance, were you?"

"How did you know?"

"Just a hunch."

She broke into a huge smile. "Those dogs in the movie were *soooo* cute!"

"I know, honey, but a movie's different from real life. Having a pet means lots of work and responsibility. You'd need to give it food and water, and clean up after it, and train it. You'd have to take it out for a walk, even when you didn't feel like it, even if it's raining or snowing. There's more to having a pet than just playing with it."

"*I'd* take care of it. I'd feed it every morning, and give it water before I went to school. Peter could help me."

Gottlieb took a forkful of herring salad. "But after a while, the novelty would wear off."

"What's novelty mean?"

"It's when something's new and exciting. Trouble is, it doesn't last. What used to be novelty becomes familiar, and then it's not a novelty anymore. It's not so exciting." *Like a marriage, for instance.*

She considered. "But something that's familiar can still be fun, can't it?"

"Well, yes, of course it can."

"If we had a puppy he'd become, you know, like part of the

family," she countered. "We'd love him, so it wouldn't matter if he was a novelly or not."

"Novelty," he corrected her.

She batted her eyes at him. *"You know what I mean."* He did, indeed.

"It would be a wonderful birthday present," she pressed on. The following December she'd turn six.

"Honey, we'll have to think about this very carefully. It's a big decision. Dogs live a long time. Some of them live almost twenty years."

"I *hope* so. It would be awful to have a dog that died."

He sighed. "I'll talk to Mommy about it. But no promises, okay?"

"Okay." She nibbled at the sandwich before she played her final card. "It would make me the happiest girl in the world!"

"I thought you were already."

She weighed this carefully. "Well, *almost.*"

The conversation moved on to other things, like was it better to have a dog or cat, and why couldn't you have one of each, and did he have a dog when he was growing up, and what about Mommy, and there was a friend of hers, Betsy Powers, who had a dog and a cat *and a pony*. And Gottlieb knew that sooner or later a Dalmatian pup would very likely take up residence with them. It didn't matter that Dalmatians had a reputation for being temperamental and high-strung. Nor did it matter that the complications of the Gottliebs' lives, already considerable, would burgeon. There'd be trips to the vet and dog obedience school, and they'd have to make boarding arrangements when they went away, quite apart from the day-to-day care of an untrained puppy. Expensive too, when you added up the dog food and vet bills, and maybe electric fencing.

Nor did it matter that Sharon would most likely shit a brick when he brought it up. Sharon waged a constant battle to simplify their lives. But if Sarah really wanted something, he would try to find a way to make it happen. He could no more resist her than he could resist the allure of a warm sunny day in the dead of winter.

＝

Just as they got home, Sharon was leaving, her car keys clutched in a tight fist, her face as livid as Gottlieb had ever seen it. She accosted her husband without looking at him. "I have to get away from him. He's in his room. *You* deal with him!"

He flew out of the car and ran after her. "Sharon, wait! What happened?"

"Ask him. Listen, Hal, *I really have to leave.*"

"Where are you going?"

"I have no idea." She got into her Acura, slammed the door, started the car, and shot out the driveway like a rocket.

They went to the house, Gottlieb holding Sarah's hand, squeezing it to the edge of discomfort. She looked at him, bewildered. "Daddy, what's the matter?"

"I don't know yet, honey. Listen, why don't you watch TV for a bit while I talk to your brother?"

"Okay." She trudged off to the family room as he took a deep breath and steeled himself for his son.

Gottlieb went upstairs and tapped at Peter's door. No answer. He knocked again, more forcefully. "It's me."

"Go away!"

The sound of his voice, however angry or despairing, brought Gottlieb an iota of relief. *At least he hasn't hanged himself in there.*

"Peter, I just got home. I have no idea what happened here today. Suppose you tell me."

"Suppose you go away and *LEAVE ME THE FUCK ALONE!*"

Gottlieb's cheeks reddened. "Damn it, Peter, I wasn't even here this afternoon! Why are you mad at me?"

"Can't you please just go away?" This time Peter's tone

expressed less rage; it was more imploring. He sounded close to tears.

"No, Peter, I can't. I need to know what happened here today. I need to see you face to face. I need to reassure myself that you're okay."

Gottlieb tried the doorknob but the door barely budged. He didn't understand—the bedrooms had no locks. Then he realized that his son had barricaded himself.

"What did you put against the door?"

"A chair. My desk."

"Peter, why are you doing this?" he asked, very quietly. His son made no reply.

After a lengthy silence, Gottlieb sat on the floor, resting his large frame against the wall adjacent to the door. "Listen to me, Peter. I'm still here, and I'll be staying here. I'll be staying here all day. All night, if need be. I'm staying here until you let me in."

Again, no answer.

"What time did you get home from Gordy's? Things were okay before you left, at least they seemed to be. Did something happen there?"

Still no answer, but Gottlieb thought he heard a muted sob, barely more than a whimper. "Whatever happened there this afternoon, whatever happened here, let's talk about it like two reasonable human beings," he went on. "Let's talk about it, without a door between us."

His son maintained the same unyielding silence.

Gottlieb fought against the swells of frustration that rose within him. He fought against the brief but powerful desire to break the door down, as in a TV cop show, which he could have done easily. Instead, he began to talk, to ramble.

"All right, Peter. If you won't talk to me, I'll talk to you. You don't have to answer, you don't even have to listen, but I'll keep on talking anyway. What to talk about, though? Let's see . . . how about parenthood? Why not? As good a topic as any.

All right, then, parenthood it is. What it's like, what it's meant to me. Let me try to sum it up for you, okay? I've had good and bad days in life, like everyone. A lot more good than bad ones, I've been luckier than most, but the two best days were the days that you and your sister were born. Nothing else compares with them. Not the day I graduated from medical school, not even the day I married your mother. Nothing else compares with them, and nothing ever will. You don't know what that's like, you *can't* know, until you're a parent yourself. All of a sudden there's this astonishing new creature in your life, beautiful and innocent, and full of all the potential in the world. When you were born I felt *fulfilled*, in a way I'd never felt before. If I'd died on the spot, I would have considered my life a complete success. Your mother feels the same. We've talked about it."

He broke off as he heard the sounds of furniture being dragged across the floor. Peter opened the door slowly. His father, unprepared for what he saw, tried not to gasp. Peter's eyes were red, and the sallow skin below them was swollen as if he'd been pummeled. His curly black hair was matted. Both forearms showed deep scratches, long parallel lines, which he'd made with his dirty fingernails. His only clothing: baggy, unkempt boxer shorts. It looked as though he'd worn them two or three days running.

But Peter himself was in splendid shape compared to his room. Dirty clothes lay all over the floor, on top of the unmade bed and on top of the bookcase. The bookcase itself was now devoid of books. Peter had hurled them in all directions. The debris was punctuated by empty yogurt cartons, empty bags of potato chips, the core of an apple, the rind of an orange. The room had an indefinably rank smell to it. The smell of sweat and semen, of dirty clothes and rotting food, and, incongruously, the antiseptic aroma of a disinfectant spray.

Gottlieb moved gingerly towards his son, but the boy retreated, waving him off with a brusque nod. He changed course, cleared a pile of underwear and pajama bottoms from the desk chair, and sat down. Peter, meanwhile, sat on the bed, his arms wrapped around his knees.

"I'm glad you let me in."

Peter said nothing, but he uttered a small low grunt.

"Feel like talking about what happened today?"

Peter shook his head no, his eyes fixed to the floor.

"Just tell me this. Did something happen at Gordy's?"

He didn't answer, didn't even shake his head this time, but his eyes welled up.

Gottlieb tried to convey a casualness he didn't feel at all. "Well, maybe you'll feel like talking about it later." He shut his eyes, trying to think clearly and dispassionately, trying to rid his mind of the room's bad aura. Trying to find a way to break through the wall his son had built around himself. Then he recalled his conversation with Dr. Pasternak.

"Yesterday I saw an old friend, a man I haven't seen for many years. We talked about . . . oh, about a number of things. One of the things we talked about was you. I told him how much I was worried about you. Not only worried but stymied. I told him I had no idea how to reach you now, and no idea of what you wanted. My friend asked an interesting question. He asked me what I wanted when *I* had been your age."

Peter's eyes rose from the floor. For the first time, he looked at his father directly. "What did you tell him?"

"Above all else, I wanted not to feel so different." He recounted as much of the conversation as he could.

Peter listened closely, once in a while leaning slightly towards him. "You felt that way too?"

"Absolutely."

"But at least you knew what you wanted to do. I remember, you told me once that you wanted to be a doctor from almost as far back as you could remember."

"Yes, I did, but so what?" He crossed his legs as he sat in the narrow desk chair. "You can know what you want to do but still feel as though you don't fit in. Worse than that, you can feel you never will."

Out of nowhere: "*I hate him! God, I hate his goddamn guts! I wish he'd get hit by a car or get brain cancer!*"

"Gordy?"

Peter nodded.

Gottlieb drew in his breath. "Tell me about what happened."

Peter squeezed his eyes shut tight, as if the faintest ray of light would make it impossible for him to tell the story. He looked as though he had to steel himself before launching into it, as though it took his every bit of will. "His parents went out," he began slowly. "They went to see his grandparents. His sister was out too. So we had the house to ourselves. At first it was okay. We listened to some new CDs he got, we sat around talking. And then . . . do you remember what I told you about the mall last week? Remember what I told you about those girls?"

"Yes. Go on."

"He called one of them. Deirdre. Asked her to come over. She's older than we are. She got her license this summer. She's got a car, so she can come and go as she pleases. So, good old Deirdre came over. The three of us talked. It was obvious they didn't care about me, like at the mall, but they tried to be polite. For a while, at least. And then—" Peter buried his face in his hands, his voice so muffled that his father could barely understand him. "I don't wanna talk about this anymore."

Gottlieb pushed ahead, with quiet relentlessness. "They tried to be polite," he recounted. "And then?"

Peter shut his eyes again. "And then they started to fool around. They were on the sofa in the family room, wrapped around each other. They were kissing, and then he began to feel her up, and then she had her hand inside his pants. *They didn't care that I was there.* I didn't want to watch, but I couldn't help it. Maybe they liked my watching, in fact I think they did. It was like they were putting on a show. So finally . . . so finally Gordy said they'll be gone for a while, they were going to the bedroom.

They both had these big shit-eating grins on their faces. Gordy's bedroom is right next to the family room. I heard the whole thing, heard her giggle, heard them groan and moan, heard the bed shake and the springs creak. Once she said, 'Shh, Peter's right outside.' He said, 'That's okay, he'll enjoy it, he'll get his rocks off.' And that's what I did, that's exactly what I did. I got my rocks off, standing outside the bedroom door with my dick in my hand. Hating them, but hating myself even more, feeling like this fat ugly fly on the wall, getting my rocks off while they fucked. Oh, God, Dad—"

He began to cry, to sob. Gottlieb went over to him, and this time Peter didn't pull away. He buried his head against his father's shoulder. Gottlieb said nothing, did nothing, except for patting the back of Peter's neck with his large hands as his son's tears soaked his shirt and undershirt. The torrent of tears gave way to a torrent of words.

"I'm fat and ugly, I'm such a goddamn geek . . . no woman's ever gonna look twice at me, I'll still be jerking off when I'm forty. I'll never get a girl like Deirdre with her blonde curls and freckles and her perfect tits, and I wouldn't know what to do with her anyway, I'd just fuck it up, the way I fuck up everything. I am the biggest waste of time who ever lived . . . so they finished, FINALLY, and they came back out to the family room, and the three of us went on talking, like nothing happened, except every so often they'd smile at each other, pat each other's leg and things like that. GOD, I hate them, I don't know which of them I hate more . . . I didn't know it was possible to hate someone so much! If I had a gun, I really think I might have shot them . . . and then Deirdre gave me a ride home, and the whole time she had this smug little smile across her face, and she'd hum to herself, but of course she didn't talk to me because she thinks I'm not worth talking to, which is probably the case . . . and then Mom said something totally innocent, like did I have a good time there. That did it . . . I went off on her, I ran up to my room, and I wouldn't let her come in, and I wouldn't come out, and I wouldn't tell her why, because I couldn't. It wasn't her fault, I knew that. I'm not completely stupid, but it didn't matter. She was the only one I could take it out on. Wrecking the room made me feel better, I don't know why . . . it just did, and I felt better when I scratched myself. It hurt, and the pain took my mind off the other thing . . ."

When he finished, he pulled himself away from his father's embrace. With a dull thud, he set himself down in the middle of the floor, clearing a spot for himself with a wave of his hand, amidst the books and dank clothes and remains of food. He sat with his hands around his knees, staring blankly straight ahead.

"This has been the most awful, most miserable day of my life," he brought the story to a close. "I wish I could crawl into a hole and die."

Gottlieb sat on a corner of the bed, on top of a heap of crumpled sheets and blankets. "I have only three things to tell you, Peter. First, I think I understand how bad you feel now, more than you imagine. There were points when I felt as terrible as you do now. I didn't think I'd survive them. I didn't *care* if I survived them. In fact I didn't want to, but I did. Second, in time what happened today will become a very dim and distant memory. It will become no more painful or important than a bad dream you once had, or a toothache you vaguely remember. I know you don't believe me, but it's true. Third, I still love you very much. So does your mother."

"She hates me!" broke in Peter. "I don't blame her. I said some pretty awful things to her."

"She's smart enough to know you didn't mean them." Gottlieb said this with more conviction than he felt.

"Where is she?"

"I don't know," he answered noncommittally. "She was driving off just as Sarah and I were coming home."

"Listen, Dad, I know it's a lot to ask of you, but could you please not tell her about Gordy and Deirdre and me? About what happened there?"

His father considered. "All right. I guess she doesn't have to know everything we talk about, any more than I have to know everything that you and *she* talk about."

Peter didn't say *thanks* out loud, but his lips formed the word, unmistakably.

"I have a proposal for you," Gottlieb said. "I'll help you clean up here if you'll let me."

"It's not your mess. Why should you?"

"Because no one should have to live this way. Because it's a two-man job."

Peter glanced around the room. "It's so bad, I don't know where to start."

"We'll start by getting laundry baskets from the basement and some trash bags from the kitchen. I'll do that while you bring up the vacuum cleaner. It was in the downstairs hall closet the last time I saw it."

They spent the next two hours putting books back on shelves, filling plastic trash bags, vacuuming, and doing laundry; they even used furniture polish on the desk and bureau and cleaned the windows. Gottlieb went down to check on Sarah once. She'd fallen asleep in front of the television. Later, he and Peter ate leftover pizza. Those were their only interruptions. By the time Sharon came home, they were nearly finished.

She stood in the doorway. Her jaw dropped when she beheld the clean neat room with its freshly made bed, its books back on the shelves, its spotless floor visible for the first time in months. Her jaw dropped further when Peter came over to her and kissed her on the cheek.

"I'm sorry, Mom. I didn't mean those things I said."

CHAPTER XXI.

A T NINE FIFTEEN ON MONDAY MORNING, as James Shannon sat opposite him, Gottlieb was struck by how much his patient had aged since he'd come to GCFI. His hair was grayer; the lines etched around his eyes had deepened. His mustache, trim and shiny when they'd met, appeared unkempt and dull. He'd lost weight, especially in the face, and his depleted jowls gave him a hangdog look. *You'd think that he'd been here for years instead of months*, thought Gottlieb. *By Christmas he'll look like an old man.*

"The last time we met, I was short with you," Shannon opened. "Our parents tried to drum it into us that there was never cause for rudeness," he went on. "Especially our mother. She was close to eighty when she died and I don't recall her being rude to anyone, not once."

"Confinement doesn't help our manners."

"I suppose not." He paused distractedly. "We did our best to teach Christina manners. Our one success with her. Unfailingly polite she was, I'll give her that."

Gottlieb sought to keep the focus on her. "Your one success with her. There weren't others?"

"None." Shannon spoke with the certainty of an Old Testament prophet.

"I wonder if other people would agree with that. People who knew her, who knew the family."

Shannon shrugged. "That's not important, is it? Even if she fooled the entire world with her model child act, so what?"

"How *do* you think others regarded her?"

He rubbed his temples, as if trying to recall the very distant past. "I suppose they were impressed with her. At least at first.

Understandably—she was smart enough, and pretty and polite. Who wouldn't be impressed by that? The good impression never lasted, though." He broke off the narrative, as if he were too exhausted to continue.

"Go on."

"Of course people never told us they disliked her, not directly. We *were* her parents after all, so they pulled their punches. But they managed to get the point across. When we went to her school for parent-teacher conferences, the teachers always had those fake stiff smiles. Awkward, kind of pained. You could tell they'd rather not be talking to us."

"What kinds of things did they say about her?"

Shannon put his hands together in his customary prayerful fashion. "They said she was a diligent worker, they agreed on that, but they all said she needed to work on her social skills. A nice way of telling us that she didn't get along with other children. It's interesting. She didn't *not* get along with them. It's not that she got into fights and such. It's more that she was unmindful of them. One teacher used just those words. *Unmindful of them.*"

He went on to give a more detailed account of how she did in school. Of teachers who praised her clear, precise handwriting, and her invariably neat homework, invariably turned in on time (she'd never asked for an extension). Of her methodical if superficial book reports. Of her quiet demeanor in the classroom and her perfect attendance. The faint praise was offset by comments about her aloof nature, her coldness, her intolerance of criticism. And every teacher brought up her dislike and indifference towards any group activity or effort. *She's just not a team player*, one of them had summed it up. "The biggest understatement I ever heard," said her father in a rare display of hyperbole.

"By the way," said Gottlieb casually as he could, "since we're talking about how others reacted to her, I should tell you that I had a conversation with one of the women who knew her at Green Lake Camp." Shannon said nothing but he arched his eyebrows, almost imperceptibly. "A woman named Anita Pierce," Gottlieb went on. "The camp director. You never met her, but I believe you spoke with her on the phone."

Shannon looked annoyed. "Now why did you have to go bothering *her?*"

"Because I needed to learn more about your daughter, in order to learn more about you."

The annoyance passed. "Well, I hope you had better luck than we did. When Margaret and I spoke with them, right after they decided to send her home, they weren't one bit helpful."

"What did they tell you?"

Shannon sighed. "I thought we went through all this before. They said she couldn't adjust to life at camp, but they were vague on the particulars. That she kept herself apart from other girls. That she was homesick. I might have told that already, I can't remember. In any case, we knew that was a load of hogwash. Not the homesick type, Christina."

"There *was* more to it than what they told you."

"Like what?" Shannon's tone remained the same, but Gottlieb sensed that he was listening raptly.

"They suspected Christina's involvement in a number of strange occurrences. Instances of petty theft. Doing damage to a garden plot, hurting animals in a petting zoo." He gave a summary of what he'd learned from the former camp director.

"I should add that this is all conjecture," concluded Gottlieb. "No one ever proved she did those things."

"Of course not. Christina would have been too clever to get caught. Too clever and too careful."

"You don't doubt these allegations?"

"Not for a minute."

The psychiatrist hesitated before continuing. "There was another incident. It happened after she went home, but they thought she might have done it anyway. They thought she put something in Ms. Pierce's eyedrops. Something that caused a permanent injury."

Shannon wasn't given to emotional displays, but he did sit up with a jolt and inhaled sharply. His sallow complexion became a shade paler. "Oh, God. I should have known. I should have tried to do something! Oh, God!"

"Why should you have known?"

"Because of what she said when she came back, as I was driving her home from the bus station. She was sitting on the front seat next to me, very quiet as usual. Wouldn't say much more than yes or no when I asked about what happened there. And then, all of a sudden, she broke into a smile. Not a very happy smile; if anything, it was kind of vicious. And all she said was, '*She'll be sorry.*'"

Oblivious to Gottlieb, he seemed to be talking to himself. "I should have known Christina was up to something, I should have tried to warn that woman. But what could I have said? Christina would never have told me what she'd done, not in a million years. But I should have tried to warn her anyway. At least I should have told her to be careful. I should have *tried.*"

Gottlieb picked up a rubber band from his desk, twisting and stretching it. "I want to make sure I'm understanding you correctly, Mr. Shannon. When I told you about the petting zoo, you weren't surprised at all. You believed she was quite capable of hurting animals for no reason. And now you're not surprised to hear she might have caused a serious permanent injury to Ms. Pierce."

He nodded. "If you'd asked me what she was capable of, I could have told you long ago. I could have saved you the trouble of playing detective."

Gottlieb let a few moments pass as he continued to play with the rubber band. "So, she was capable of hurting people, perhaps of hurting them very badly. Does this have anything to do with why you killed her?"

Shannon looked away from him and stared out the window, stared out at the GCFI parking lot and a stretch of the expressway.

Gottlieb pushed on, harking back to his conversation with Warren Pasternak. "When we do things is as important as why we do them. More so, sometimes. Take you and Christina, for example. There's the question of why you did it, but there's also the question of why you did it *then*. She was pretty much the same, I gather, for quite a while before she died. For practically her whole life, in fact. But one June night, one ordinary night, you killed her. Why then? Why not a month later or two months earlier? Why not last year, or next year?"

Shannon said nothing as he continued to stare out at the parking lot and Expressway.

"There's a great deal I still don't know about you," the psychiatrist went on, "but I think I know you well enough to say that wouldn't have done it without extraordinary provocation."

Shannon kept his silence, but he began to chew on his lower lip. He also moved his head from side to side, almost indiscernibly.

"Why are you still protecting her? Does she really merit your protection? *Why?*"

Still no answer, but the chewing on his lower lip became more violent, and the side-to-side movements of his head began to quicken.

Gottlieb's professional sense of timing, honed by his decades of experience, told him to push ahead, to offer his patient no avenue of retreat. "That night in June . . . what pushed you to the edge?"

Until now, Shannon had always stayed put in his visits to Gottlieb's office. He'd parked himself in one of the chairs beside the desk like a docile schoolboy. Rarely did he even fidget. Gottlieb was therefore caught off guard when he stood up now and began to pace, his head bowed, his eyes downcast. From time to time he dug his heels into Gottlieb's carpeting.

He wants to tell me, Gottlieb thought. *He's almost ready. One more push.* "Why then?"

Shannon stopped pacing. He brought his gaze up from the floor and looked at Gottlieb directly, his eyes glazed. "It has to do with Margaret," he answered. "I just found out she killed her."

CHAPTER XXII

THROUGH THE YEARS, GOTTLIEB HAD TRAINED himself to keep from showing much emotion, no matter what his patients threw at him. A man once told him how he broke his grandmother's fingers, smashing them with a brick during a bad LSD trip. A tormented adolescent put her brother's pet gerbils in a blender and turned it on, full blast. A woman told him how she caught her husband, a software wizard who made ten million dollars before he'd turned thirty, having sex with the family's German shepherd bitch. In all these instances, and others like them, Gottlieb maintained his professional persona. He might nod; he might give a tacit invitation to continue; he might say nothing. If he felt astonishment or disgust, if he felt on the verge of tears or laughter, he kept it to himself. He didn't blush or scowl. He might wince (rarely), but otherwise his face remained a mask. His self-concealment would have done credit to a professional actor.

Even so, in the wake of Shannon's revelation he had to take a moment to compose himself. "Tell me about it," he said finally.

His patient sat down. Assuming his docile schoolboy manner, he spoke in his customary way, quiet and deliberate, hands folded on his lap. "It was the first week of June, right after the school year ended. A Saturday afternoon. Christina had gone out. She went on her bike to a 7-Eleven that's a mile or so from us. I was doing a bit of work around the house, and I'd just taken out a load of laundry. We used to take turns doing it. That week it happened to be my turn. Sometimes I wonder what might have happened if it had been *her* turn. Maybe I wouldn't be here now. But it doesn't help to dwell on what might have happened, does it?" He seemed to expect no answer.

Beads of sweat began to line his forehead. He wiped them off with the sleeve of his gray sweatshirt. "Ordinarily I'd leave the laundry basket in her room and let her put the clothes away herself," he resumed. "But I was at loose ends that afternoon. Restless. So, mainly for lack of something else to do, I decided to put the things away for her. It's strange, as I look back on it. I'd never been in her bureau drawers before. I had no cause to be. It's not that I was looking for alcohol or drugs, or anything in particular."

He looked at Gottlieb directly. "I don't know what prompted me to go into that particular drawer, on that particular day. But it's beside the point. I did."

Falling silent, he covered his eyes with his hands. Gottlieb prodded him to keep going. "So. You were putting away the laundry."

"I found a notebook. An ordinary spiral notebook." He seemed embarrassed. "I make a point of respecting the privacy of others. But I'll admit, as soon as I saw it, I was terribly curious. Christina had always been such a mystery to me, to both of us. I thought the journal, or whatever it was, might shed some light on her. So I sat down on her bed and read it."

He stood abruptly and headed back towards the window. "I'll put this as simply as I can. Reading it was the worst thing that ever happened to me. It was even worse than when Margaret died."

"What was in it?"

"Among other things, an account of how she killed her mother."

Shannon's eyes welled up, but he didn't cry. "Do you remember my telling you about Margaret's diabetes?" Gottlieb nodded.

"They diagnosed her when she was a child. They put her on insulin right away. I didn't know her then, but apparently she did all right with it. Always the responsible patient, even when she still in grade school. She gave herself injections regularly, and she followed the diet strictly. She also had an excellent doctor, a pediatrician who specialized in juvenile diabetes. Once in a while she'd overdo it, she'd exercise too much and her blood sugar would drop too low. But she'd drink juice or eat candy, and everything would be all right. By the time I met her, her condition was as stable as anyone could hope for. She knew a good deal about the illness . . . she knew the risk of blindness and kidney failure and the rest of it, and she wanted to stay healthy. I should mention that Margaret was optimistic, much more than I am. She refused to dwell on the bad things that might happen. She believed that if she took good care of herself, ate properly, and paid attention to the doctor, she'd stay healthy. She also was a woman of great faith, a woman who believed that God would always be there for her—that He would help her deal with anything that came along."

Shannon moved away from the window, sat down again, and continued. "For the last six months or so before she died, Margaret began to have much more trouble with the diabetes than she'd ever had before, even during her pregnancy. No matter how strictly she kept to the diet, no matter how closely she monitored herself, she couldn't seem to get it stabilized. Her doctor didn't understand it either. What none of us knew, of course, was that Christina had been playing with her insulin. Emptying part of the vials, filling them up with water. But sometimes, just to keep all of us off base, she left them alone. That way, when Margaret increased her dosage, she would get more than she needed. Her sugar would swing the other way, and she'd become hypoglycemic."

He paused, as if to summon the wherewithal to go on. "This must sound far-fetched to you, or even ridiculous. Well, maybe not so ridiculous after what that camp director told you. It's simply not that hard to tamper with someone's medicine. Besides, Christina was very smart. I'm sure you've gathered that by now. And she knew a lot about her mother's illness.

She'd been exposed to it all her life."

He paused again. "So that's how it went, for weeks, for months. Margaret's sugar would shoot up, and then it would be okay, and then it would drop down, and then it would be okay again. She began to have symptoms she'd never had before. Numbness in her hands and feet—neuropathy, you call it? Ulcers on her heels. She was always tired, no matter how much she slept, and she never slept well. Her vision started to deteriorate. At times she'd get confused. She couldn't concentrate on things. You're a doctor, you know about diabetes, you know how devastating it can be."

Gottlieb nodded but said nothing. He didn't want to break the flow.

"I started making calls to 911. I started bringing her to the ER. I took her to other specialists. An eye doctor, a skin doctor, a neurologist. They did their best, and I'm sure they all were competent, but how much could they really do?" His eyes welled up again.

"And then?"

"And then Christina called me at work one afternoon, which she almost never did. She was still at home, on Christmas break. December 29. She said she'd just called 911. Margaret had gone into a coma. By the time they brought her to the hospital it was too late. The ER doctor pronounced her DOA."

For the first time since Gottlieb had met him, Shannon began to cry—quietly (except for a few choked sobs, he made no sound at all) and with obvious embarrassment. Gottlieb handed him a Kleenex from a box on his desk, which his patient accepted without looking at him.

"And all that was in the spiral notebook?" Gottlieb asked finally.

"All that and more."

"What exactly did she write?"

"I'd tell you, but you'd think I was making it up. You should read it for yourself."

"Where's the notebook now?"

"At the house. There's a small space behind the fuse box in the basement, just to the right of the washer and dryer. I put it there."

He suddenly sounded tired. More than tired; he sounded as exhausted as anyone that Gottlieb had ever talked to. Like a man who could sleep around the clock for days on end. "My sister has a key to the house. Ask her for it," he gave instructions in a hollow tone. "Tell her I want her to meet you there and let you in." His voice had trailed off into a whisper.

"I don't want to talk anymore," he concluded. "I feel talked out."

Gottlieb nodded. He stood up, walked over to him, and put a hand on his shoulder. "I'll walk you back to your room." As soon as he got back to his own office, he called Rita.

⚜

Gottlieb had a light afternoon, by his standards. He finished in his office at a quarter after five. As soon as the last patient left, he headed off to seek Christina's notebook. Slightly more than half an hour later, he pulled up to the small beige-shingled ranch where the Shannons had lived, the house where both Margaret and Christina died.

Rita Tierney was waiting for him, leaning against her car. She shook hands with him in a dutiful manner, and they walked to the front door. "I don't understand what this is all about," she protested.

"Your brother mentioned something he found by accident, something Christina wrote. It might have a bearing on what happened. It might also be important when he gets to court."

"Do you think it could help him?"

"Possibly."

"All right," she sighed. She reached into her purse, pulled out a key, and let him in. "I'll wait outside for you." She regarded the house with unconcealed loathing.

He was surprised to find the Shannons' living room rather cheerful. Orange and lemon slip covers on the chairs and sofa, yellow-and-white-striped wallpaper. A few watercolors of floral arrangements, mainly roses and daisies. A small bookcase containing a Bible, a dictionary and several volumes about Ireland. It also held an illustrated book on San Francisco. Gottlieb recalled his patient's account of their honeymoon.

There were knickknacks. Vases and dishes, a pewter dog and cat, a hurricane lamp, a music box. Family photos. Among these was a small color photo of Christina, in a gold frame, next to a Waterford candy dish. The photo captured a girl of eight or nine, quite beautiful but serious and distant, a child ill at ease in the camera's eye.

The house already had the smell that comes with prolonged vacancy, a smell of dust, stale air and mold in a place where no doors or windows had been opened. A smell intensified by the hot, humid summer.

Gottlieb went quickly through the rooms, looking for the door to the basement stairs. He found it in the kitchen next to the fridge. The steps creaked as he descended. At the base of the stairs, he felt along the wall in near-complete darkness, trying to locate a light switch. When he found it, a sixty-watt bulb lit his way to the washer and dryer. Just above it was the fuse box. A small gap existed between the fuse box and the wall, just large enough for a six-by-nine-inch notebook.

He pulled out the book and went upstairs. A few moments later, he rejoined Rita in the small front yard. He patted the notebook. "I found it."

"Anything else you need, I'd appreciate it if you took it now," she bit the words off. "I'd just as soon not come back here. Suppose we'll have to, though, if things don't go well for Jimmy. We'll have to get it ready to put on the market."

"No, I don't need anything else just now."

"Let's go, then."

"All right."

They walked together to their cars. As she was about to get in, she turned to him. "I didn't mean to be abrupt. It's not you, it's the house. I hate that house, I hate what happened there. I wish it would burn down."

"I can see where you would."

"Well, then." She shook hands with him, a bit less coolly than when he'd arrived. Then she pointed to the notebook. "I hope it's useful. In any case, thanks for trying to help him."

She got into the car and drove off without looking back.

⁑

Gottlieb sat in his own car, the notebook in his hand, barely able to contain his curiosity. In half an hour he could read it at home, in the comfort of his living room, but he didn't want to wait that long. The summer twilight still made it bright enough for him to read it in the car. He took off his sports coat, folded it on the seat next to him, and opened the notebook.

Things to do Saturday
*   change sheets make bed   clean bathroom sink*
*   empty wastebaskets   take back library books*
*   start history project . . .*

Notes for history report on Pres. Andrew Johnson
*   born in Raleigh No. Carolina 1808*
*   humble beginnings, didn't go to school at all*
*   worked as tailor's apprentice*
*   married a school teacher who taught him how to read & write*
*   started political career in Tennessee-House of Representatives*
*   a Southerner who opposed slavery & favored Union . . .*

It's so nice to sleep late on Sun. & lie in bed while they go to Mass. Why do they do it, why do they bother?? What do they get out of praying to that man, & do they really believe he's the son of god? Can they really be that stupid?? She's more stupid than he is, even. Jesus this & Jesus that. It's enough to make you want to throw up!!

> *Wed. night, good program on cable about Fr. Revolution. Would like to have been there watching when they sent 1000s of people to the guillotine. Must remember to look up more about guillotine in school library, but they probably won't have too much on it, too gory for children. What did it feel like to let go of blade & watch it come down? What was it like to lie there & wait for the blade & actually hear it coming?*

On the bottom of the page, in careful detail, she'd sketched a guillotine.

Mommy had another episode last night. Rapid breathing, & it was hard for her to catch her breath. She was sweating like a pig even tho it was pretty cold, in the 50s. She's not walking too well either, needs a cane now. She tried to explain it. Neuropithy, she called it. The nerves in her feet aren't right because of the diabetes. It's really neat to see how taking away just a bit of insulin has such a big effect . . .

Things to do on Saturday
change sheets make bed   do laundry put away clothes
make brownies (yummy!)   vacuum dust room neaten up
buy birthday card for Aunt Rita

Under the notation about Rita's birthday card was a drawing of her, a recognizable caricature. Christina had exaggerated her features. Her small eyes were rendered as barely visible dots, her thin lips as mere lines, and the small hump of her nose had been blown up way out of proportion. Rita was naked from the waist up. She tried to cover her drooping breasts with wrinkled, old woman's hands.

Why are people so afraid of dying? If they believed god was really so great & good like they're supposed to, you'd think it wouldn't bother them too much. I think they're afraid because they <u>know</u> he's not all-powerful. Maybe they don't want to but they do anyway. I challenge god, if he's so powerful, let him strike me dead right now. I DARE HIM!!

Here she'd drawn a hand, quite realistically, with the middle finger extended towards the sky.

Recipe for dark chocolate fudge from paper (looks easy)
1½ cups semisweet choc. chips
½ can sweetened condensed milk
½ cup chopped nuts
¾ tsp. vanilla extract
dash of salt

Melt chips in saucepan with condensed milk & salt over low heat . . .

Tues., more fun & games with Mommy's insulin. After I'd been diluting it she took more of it than usual, much more than she needed. So she got a real big dose, & <u>WOW</u>! She started staggering around like she'd drunk too much, & she was babbling like an idiot! & then Daddy tried to give her orange juice but she couldn't keep it down. So he had to call 911. Usually he stays calm but he was really scared for once. I had to keep from laughing when one of the ambulance guys put his arm around me & gave me all this soothing crap 'cause he thought I'd be bent out of shape. If he only knew!! Wonder how it would feel to screw up her insulin so much it would kill her.

3 weeks 'til Xmas. Have to buy presents & put on same old show. Ideas for gifts
  Mommy—scarf
  Daddy—new gloves
  Grandma Lucy—calendar with pictures of cats
  Uncle Tim & Uncle Vince—CDs
  Aunt Rita—religious book

Things I'd really like to give them
  Mommy—big box of chocolates, do a number on her diabetes
  Daddy—bunch of dirty magazines with lots of pictures
Xmas has to be the biggest joke there is!

Here she'd drawn a picture of Santa Clause with a little girl, naked, kneeling in front of him. Both figures were done realistically. Santa sports a huge erection. The girl is reaching out to it.

Project for French class due March 1. Pick a city in France, not Paris, & do report on it. Write to municipal offices, students & school libraries there, get info. Ms. Levesque will help us do this. All letters to be written in French. List of cities to consider:

Besancon	*Nancy*
Carcassonne	*Nimes*
Cherbourg	*Rennes*
Limoges	*Strasbourg . . .*

Aunt Rita came by last night with Mary and Danny and The Brat, to drop off Xmas presents. They are all such idiots, especially Mary and Danny. As we sat around drinking tea and eating fruitcake, I wondered if they ever suspected that I had something to do with the fire. Probably not in a million years.

It's so easy to burn a house down. A candle, a few strips of paper soaked with lighter fluid, and you're in business. Too bad none of them were killed, tho. Maybe next time.

Gottlieb remembered Rita's story of the fire, and how Margaret had done everything she could to help the family.

I'll bet it wouldn't be all that hard to start a fire in the basement of a small hospital. You couldn't do it in a big one like Cook County because there'd be too much security. But a smaller one, that might be easy. Better yet, a nursing home!! Think of them trying to bring out all those sick old people . . .

Things to do
  change sheets   make bed
  clean sink   scrub bathtub
  write thank you notes for Xmas presents . . .

YES!! SUCCESS!! I replaced almost 2/3 of her insulin with tap water. WOW!! Around 9, an hour or so after she gave herself the regular AM injection, she began to have stomachache & feel queasy. 30 min. later, she's very weak, throwing up now, beginning to have heavy breathing. Gave herself another injection, but she only got about 1/3 of what she thought she was getting. By 10 or 10:30 she's really *sick & Daddy's at work, not here to help her. At 11, just before she goes into coma, she asks me to call 911. Which I do, at noon, after making myself a tuna salad sandwich & taking walk. By 1:30 or 2 it's all over. I put on a sad face . . .*

Recipe for peanut butter & jelly bars
  1½ cups flour   ¾ cup grape jelly
  ½ cup sugar   Reese's peanut butter chips, 10 oz.
  ¾ tsp. bak powder   1 egg, beaten . . .

CHAPTER XXIII

EARLY THE NEXT MORNING, AS GOTTLIEB SAT by himself in the GCFI canteen, Norma Caldwell came over to his table. "Mind if I join you?" He signaled for her to sit across from him.

She studied him carefully. "I must say, Hal, you're terribly subdued today. Off in your own world somewhere."

He glanced at her, preoccupied. "I had an unnerving experience last night."

"Don't tell me, let me guess. Peter did something to make you crazy again." She clucked sympathetically.

"No, he's been fine for a couple of days, knock on wood. A paragon of adolescent virtue. No, this has to do with Shannon."

"I've never seen a case take hold of you like this before."

"I've never had a case like this before." He tapped a staccato beat across the tabletop. Can you come into my office? I want to show you something."

"Sure." They picked up their cups of coffee and sauntered down the corridor. "So, Hal, what's all the mystery about?" she asked after settling into the chair beside his desk.

"Last night I read Christina Shannon's notebook. It clarifies a few points, including why her father would want to kill her."

"Are you serious?"

He nodded. "Take a look." He slid the spiral notebook across the desk to her.

She skimmed the first few pages quickly. "A list of chores? Notes for a paper on President Andrew Johnson?"

"Keep going."

He sat back in the desk chair as she read, watching her interest deepen, the pupils of her eyes widen. Every so often, she jerked her head back sharply. When she finished, her hand trembled as she set the notebook back down on his desk. "Jesus Christ." She seemed eager to get rid of it, as if it were a snake or rat.

She glanced at the notebook and shuddered. "Jesus Christ," she repeated. "I don't recall the last time I felt this way at nine in the morning, but I could really use a drink. *Why*—?"

"Now there's the real mystery, isn't it? Her mother was very good to her, by all accounts. She loved her, unlovable as she might have been. She doted on her. They both did. If there was the smallest provocation, we don't know about it."

"It almost sounds as if she did it on a whim. Or else out of boredom or curiosity, as a kind of experiment."

Gottlieb clasped his hands behind his neck, threw back his head back and scrutinized the ceiling. "As far as I'm concerned, the most eerie thing about it is the lack of anger. Christina doesn't *hate* her mother, doesn't even seem to dislike her. She just doesn't care about her, period. If her mother had gone on living, I don't think it would have bothered her too much."

"Why would she leave it there, in a place where he could find it so easily?" Norma shook her head in disbelief. "It's common knowledge that parents go through their children's drawers. Say what you will about Christina, she wasn't stupid, but it was an amazingly stupid thing for her to do. Especially considering the contents."

"I don't know. Don't forget, Christina knew the kind of man her father was. She would have known he had a great respect for privacy. He'd never gone through her things before. Why would she think he'd start then, all of a sudden?"

Norma hesitated. "Could she. . . I know, this is crazy . . . could she have *wanted* him to find it? We know how errant children have a genius for getting caught."

"Anything's possible, but I doubt it. She knew how her parents felt about each other. She would have known that even her father had his limits. Besides, no one ever caught Christina doing anything. At the camp, it was a matter of strictly circumstantial evidence. If they hadn't found those drawings, she might have finished out the summer there."

Norma shuddered again. "Speaking of drawings. It takes a lot to shock me, Hal, but she managed it."

"Those sketches . . . it's interesting, she obviously had some talent. But her drawings are more than merely dark. There's a deadness about them. Have you ever seen pictures of Hitler's drawings?" She shook her head. "He did them in Vienna, before World War I. He was living in poverty there, trying to earn some money making sketches and postcards. His drawings were finely detailed, and they showed a certain talent too, but they had that same kind of darkness. Deadness."

They fell silent. "So now we know why he did it," she said finally. "Could make a big difference in how his case plays out. Maybe they'll give him a gold medal for getting rid of her."

"Funny you should say that. Kenyon said the same thing, more or less."

"Who?"

"Malcolm Kenyon. A child psychologist who tried to treat Christina once. I met with him, oh, four or five weeks ago."

"Not a fan of hers, I gather."

"I've yet to find anyone who was." He tipped his chair back and rested his feet against the edge of the desk. "About the notebook. Of course it *could* help him, but that's not a certainty. It's so outrageous that a jury might not buy it. Besides, a jury might not take it well if the defense tried to turn the case around and put a murdered girl on trial."

"So he's in the same bind. A sane defendant in a capital case, guilty of what looks like a terrible crime."

"Yes, but I have an idea that could help him. A long shot, but it might be worth a try. That is, if his lawyer buys it."

"Oh?"

"He's sane. We all know that. But there's a big distinction legally between his sanity and his competence. "

"You're telling me you suddenly doubt his competence?" She sounded skeptical.

"No, as a matter of fact I don't. But I think the issue might reasonably be raised. And I'm willing to do as much, if it will help him."

Her skepticism deepened. "Even if it means you'd be taking a few liberties with the truth?"

"Not so much taking liberties with it as shading it. Using some chiaroscuro here and there."

"Chiaroscuro? What the hell is *that?*"

"It's an art term. Means the use of light and shadow in an impressionistic way, not altogether accurately, to create a dramatic effect. Something like that."

⸙

By Wednesday noon, Gottlieb had finished a seven-page report on James Patrick Shannon, patient number S09921 at the Greater Chicago Forensic Institute. It gave a detailed account of his alleged offense and his behavior at the time of his arrest, as well as his subsequent behavior in the police station, jail, and hospital. It gave a history as reported by the patient himself, supplemented by collateral information from his brother and sister.

The report included these segments:

Ever since his admission to the Greater Chicago Forensic Institute, Mr. Shannon has shown signs and symptoms compatible with a severe depressive disorder. These include pervasive sadness, a sense of helplessness and hopelessness, a loss of the ability to experience, recall or anticipate pleasure (anhedonia), an altered sleep pattern, indifference to his fate and passive death wishes if not frank suicidal ideation. While his depression has no doubt been exacerbated by the real and undeniable difficulties of his present situation, there is reason to believe that it began well before his present incarceration, and before the commission of the crime of which he stands accused. Most likely, it was precipitated by the death of his wife . . .

It should be noted, moreover, that Mr. Shannon has a fixed belief that the alleged victim, his daughter Christina, was responsible for the death of his late wife, an insulin-dependent diabetic. He believes that Christina knowingly and willfully altered Mrs. Shannon's insulin, thus causing her to go into the irreversible diabetic coma to which she ultimately succumbed. He maintains this belief even though he can give no motive for his daughter's action, and even though he knows such an action would be virtually unprecedented for a girl of Christina's age. Such a conviction qualifies as a delusion, defined (according to a standard psychiatric reference work) as "a false belief not shared by others, that is firmly maintained, even though contradicted by social reality." Another source [The Oxford Companion to the Mind] elaborates further: "Unlike normal beliefs, which are subject to amendment or correction, a delusion is held to despite evidence or arguments brought against it. *Delusions are usually taken to indicate serious mental illness.*" [emphasis mine] . . .

Delusional thinking may often emerge in the course of severe depression, as one of many signs and symptoms of a full-blown psychotic process. It follows that a delusion such as Mr. Shannon's would provide ample motivation for commission of a violent crime against an agent he believed responsible for the death of a loved one. This motivation would be strengthened by the concomitant belief that the same agent was capable of committing further heinous acts against others, which appears to be another key part of his delusional system . . .

In conclusion, the undersigned believes that the severity and chronicity of Mr. Shannon's depression, and its likely, virtually certain, delusional component, render him presently incompetent to stand trial. While competence is based on several determinants, such as an awareness of the charges one faces, and a basic knowledge of the legal system, the most important determinant is the ability of the accused to defend himself in a court of law in a meaningful fashion and to work constructively with counsel. A man who is depressed to the point where he has become completely indifferent to his fate, whose thinking remains delusional, and who often wishes that the State, in fact, would kill him, can scarcely be considered competent . . .

Respectfully submitted,
Harold E. Gottlieb, MD
Senior Consulting Psychiatrist,
Greater Chicago Forensic Institute

＊

Later that afternoon Gottlieb phoned Brendan O'Connell. "I thought you'd like to know that I've finished the competency evaluation of your client," he began. "Of course it has to go through channels."

"Of course."

"It goes first to my immediate superior, Dr. Stanley Celinsky," went on Gottlieb. "He, in turn, will pass it along to the DA's office. The mayor's office wants a copy too, I understand. I'm sure that none of them will like it, but I intend to submit it anyway. In any case, I thought you might be interested in taking a look at it beforehand."

"Well, uhm, why, yes. I'd appreciate that very much." The offer seemed to nonplus him.

"I'll fax it to you this afternoon. Then, when you've had a chance to look it over, perhaps we could get together and talk about it."

"Whenever you want," he said eagerly. "I assume you want me to come to the Institute?"

"No, as a matter of fact, I'd prefer that we meet in my private office. Friday afternoon would be good. Two thirty, say?"

"I'll be there. O'Connell gave Gottlieb his fax number, and Gottlieb gave O'Connell his address.

"One more thing," Gottlieb added. "I want to send you some other documents which have a bearing on the case."

"Sure, fine. Out of curiosity, what are they?"

"Excerpts from Christina Shannon's notebook."

$$\doteqdot$$

They sat together in Gottlieb's office, oblivious to the pleasant day outside. It was cool and sunny, with a foreshadowing of autumn in the air. O'Connell, hard-pressed as usual to sit still, tapped a foot vigorously against the floor.

"It's a good report," he volunteered. "Very thorough, very clear. I like the way you stay away from jargon." Gottlieb acknowledged the compliment with a nod.

"It's a good report," the lawyer repeated, "but five to one the court won't buy it."

"Why not?"

"For one thing, the DA's office will have a fit. They'll say it would set a terrible precedent in that it would allow anyone accused of a major crime to raise an issue of incompetence because he's depressed. They'll say anyone who faces a severe punishment has a *right* to be depressed, that depression is an appropriate response to what he's facing. Moreover, most of them would maintain the view that the perpetrator of a heinous crime *deserves* to be depressed."

"You might think that anyone accused of a major crime would almost certainly become depressed. Surprisingly, that's not the case, though," Gottlieb countered. "Most defendants are angry and frightened when they're looking at felony charges, but relatively few of them go into a full-fledged depression."

"Besides," O'Connell talked through him, "Christina's murder is a hot potato. I'm sure you can appreciate that. Lots of emotion and publicity. There'll be tremendous political pressure to bring him to trial. Robin Aveiro, the DA assigned to the case, won't give an inch. They wouldn't *let* her give an inch, even if she wanted to, which she doesn't. Have you met her?"

Gottlieb shook his head.

"She's young, thirty-one or thirty. Ambitious and pretty smart. She'll want to prove she's got the balls to send a man to Death Row."

"On the other hand," Gottlieb noted, "she won't want those revelations about Christina to come to light."

O'Connell scowled. "Christ, what a hateful little shit! Do you believe what's in that notebook?"

"Well, let's talk about the notebook. How would you like to be Ms. Aveiro if its contents became public knowledge?"

"I wouldn't. Truth is, Doc, I'd rather not be on either side of this one. I want it over and done with. I love Jimmy Shannon, but I wish to God he'd taken my advice and let me get another lawyer for him. All I want right now is to go back to wills and closings, with a few drunk drivers for a change of pace."

The lawyer said this quietly and slowly, in a voice that had none of his customary feistiness. The voice of a dispirited man, someone who'd seen too much of the worst of human nature and needed a long respite from it, but who had none in the offing. Gottlieb knew that he was fifty-five, James Shannon's age, but he looked older now, like a man of sixty-two or sixty-three. In fact, he looked a good deal older than when he had when they'd met for the first time, less than two months ago.

This case is taking its toll on all of us.

O'Connell resumed the nervous tapping of a foot. "Why are you doing this?" he asked.

"Doing what?"

"You know. Going out on a limb for him like this. Talking to me ex parte. Giving me tips, so to speak, on how to defend him. Writing that report, which just might get you fired."

"I don't think it will. I've been around awhile now, and I have a pretty solid reputation. They're not about to fire me because of a single report they don't care for. It wouldn't be that easy for them to fire me anyway. I put in enough hours at GCFI to make me civil service."

"I hope you're right," O'Connell muttered. "Myself, I tend to be a cynic . . . suppose it's an occupational hazard. While I don't have much direct experience with the local politicians, they have a reputation for getting what they want. If they really want to get rid of someone, they'll find a way."

"If they do, they do. I've been through worse."

His foot still tapping, O'Connell went ahead with his cross-examination. "You still haven't answered me, haven't told me why you're going to bat for him like this."

"Because I like him. Because I see him as an inherently decent man who has been through an agonizing time. Because he doesn't pose a threat to anyone now, and there'd be no purpose served by a long prison term. Or, worse, by his execution."

He picked up an eraser from his desk, played idly with it and continued. "And because of something else. It goes back to the first thing he told me, right after they transferred him to us, when he finally began to talk again. I asked him why he did it, and this is what he told me: *to save the world from her*. Well—I can't believe I'm saying this, but I'm starting to see his point."

O'Connell nodded, his face a picture of distaste. "If she could do that to her mother, God only knows what she could have done to the rest of us."

"Plenty. Let me tell you more about Christina." Gottlieb gave him a summary of her time at camp, of Anita Pierce's revelations.

When he finished, the lawyer looked more shaken than at any time since Gottlieb had met him. "She was what, twelve or thirteen when she did that? What the hell would she have done later?"

"Her father's point, exactly. Staggers the imagination, doesn't it?"

He stroked his chin thoughtfully. "I think I'll arrange to meet privately with Ms. Aveiro. It might make her a trifle more receptive to your report if I show her the pertinent parts of Christina's notebook. I'd rather not put the girl on trial, but it's possible that I'll have no choice."

"Perhaps not."

"If Aveiro still balks," he went on, "I could mention the story you told me about Ms. Pierce. Tell her we plan to have her testify. A woman who'd been blinded would have a powerful effect upon a jury."

"But no one ever proved Christina did it."

"True, but Aveiro doesn't have to know that now." He continued to play with the scenario. "The case comes to trial. Pierce takes the stand and talks about the eyedrops. Aveiro objects on grounds of conjecture and the judge upholds her objection, but the words can't be negated. They've already made their impact."

Gottlieb considered. *Maybe he's a better lawyer than I thought he was.*

O'Connell continued to think aloud. "But let's assume, for the sake of discussion, that they do find him incompetent. So, they'll send him to a funny farm somewhere. They'll force him to take medication, put him in a locked ward with a bunch of raving lunatics. Restrict his moves, refuse to give him passes, and refuse to give him any rights at all." A somber expression crossed his face. "It could turn out to be a de facto life sentence anyway, the way it was with Hinckley when he shot Reagan."

Gottlieb shook his head. "I doubt that. The fact is, he's not Hinckley; he didn't try to kill a head of state. Yes, they would send him to a hospital, but they'd also have to reevaluate his mental state from time to time. Sooner or later someone would have the courage to say that he was fit to go."

"I don't know. People fall through the cracks."

"That would depend on you, in part, or on his subsequent attorney. Besides, his brothers and sister have a little money and at least a degree of sophistication. I don't see them allowing that to happen."

"What *do* you see happening?"

"I've been wrong too many times to make predictions where the courts are concerned, but my best guess is that they'll hospitalize him for a couple of years. Then, like it or not, they'll have to release him."

O'Connell looked at him in a way that was close to imploring. "So you think there's a reasonable chance he might be free someday?"

"In a manner of speaking."

"What do you mean?"

Gottlieb folded his hands on his lap. "Well, I wonder how free you can ever be when you've killed the daughter who killed your wife. When the media has turned your case into a circus, a feeding frenzy. When just about everyone in Chicago—for that matter, the whole state, and much of the rest of the country— knows who you are and what you did. When your life has been shaken to the core, stripped of everything familiar, and you've been locked up for years."

✦

The Gottliebs were spending the Labor Day weekend at the Wisconsin retreat of one of Hal's brothers and his family. Adam Gottlieb owned a home on Lake Geneva, a simple but spacious white raised ranch. Adam, a financial planner, and his wife, Lois, a self-employed caterer, had done it up in shades of light orange, browns, and greens. They'd tried to create a woodsy ambiance, in keeping with the Wisconsin forests that surrounded them.

Their two older daughters had already left for their respective colleges. Only the youngest, Emily, still in high school, would be there with them. A serious, heavyset girl with thick glasses and a kind, round face, she had always taken a warm sisterly interest in her slightly younger cousin Peter. Like her parents, she fussed shamelessly over Sarah.

They swam and water-skied behind Adam's runabout, Hal showing grace and skill on skis despite his girth and customary awkwardness. Hal and Sharon doused themselves with OFF! and took walks along the lakefront, the mossy paths as soft as carpeting beneath their feet. When they weren't hiking, swimming, or in the boat, they sat talking on the screened-in patio, replenishing themselves with Lois's gazpacho and lobster pasta salad, washed down with Adam's sangria.

Peter and Emily split off by themselves. From the patio, Hal and Sharon could see them talking earnestly on the pier, their feet dangling in the cool, clear water. Peter, for once, didn't seem self-conscious about his body. From time to time, he and Emily laughed together. Gottlieb realized how starved he'd become for the sound of his son's laughter.

On Sunday night, following another day of swimming, boating, and hiking, Adam broiled steaks on the outdoor grill. After dinner, they adjourned to the living room, chatting while Brubeck and Ellington CDs played in the background. Adam shared his brother's taste for the legendary jazz figures.

Sarah, happy but worn out, fell asleep right after dinner. Peter and Emily headed for the pier again. It was still early, not much past nine thirty, when Hal and Sharon went to bed themselves.

The house sat perched on a knoll. From the guest room window, they could see moonlight play against the lake. A breeze rustled through an abundance of birch and spruce. Sharon nestled against his chest and gave a contented sigh. "This is the most relaxed I've felt in months. It's so peaceful here! I know we're just an hour or so from home, but it feels like we're a million miles from everything and everyone."

He ran a finger through her short blonde hair. "We need a vacation, not just a long weekend. Hard to remember when the last one was. Toronto . . . that was it, Toronto. It was nice enough, that trip, but I'd hardly call it restful."

"A classic understatement!" In May, they'd driven to a psychiatric convention there. Along the way, they'd stopped to visit friends outside Detroit. They'd also made a side trip to Niagara Falls.

"Face it," she went on, "it was your typical Hal Gottlieb marathon. Nonstop activity, with that famous disapproving look of yours if I slept late or, God forbid, did nothing for two hours."

"I thought you liked that trip." He sounded disappointed.

"I did, of course I did. Toronto's a wonderful city, what's not to like? But the concept of relaxation still gives you a lot of trouble, especially when you travel. And I wish you wouldn't make me feel like the ultimate spoiled JAP if I dared to order room service. Just once before I die, I'd like to have breakfast in bed when we go away."

"When we go to Bermuda next spring, we'll have breakfast in bed every day if you want it. And there'll be no meetings, no seminars, no force-fed culture."

"Promise?"

He reached over and kissed her. "I promise."

"Be still, my heart."

They fell silent, listening to wind rustling through the trees and the occasional distant rumble of a motorboat. At one point, they heard laughter from the pier. "Peter does appear to be enjoying himself," he commented. "I'm glad Emily's here. They've always liked each other."

"I have to say, he's been much better lately. Ever since that awful day I ran away from home."

"Hmm, so it seems."

"Well, I'm quite impressed." Her fingers stroked his chest. "What *did* you say to him that day?"

"Nothing miraculous. Mainly I just listened to him."

"Sometimes your patience awes me, Hal. I wish I had a fraction of it."

"Well, this summer has been an eye-opener. One thing I'll say for Christina Shannon, she made me realize how much worse things could be with him."

Her body tightened. "I hoped against hope that we might get through the weekend without mention of the wretched Shannons."

"Do I really talk about the case that much?"

"Are you kidding? You mention it almost every day. You're *obsessed!* You don't even have to say a thing. I can tell when you're thinking about it. There's a certain look you have. Vaguely worried, distant. *The Shannon look*, that's how I think of it."

"I didn't know it was so obvious." He shifted in the bed. "The thing about it that takes hold of me is this — it hits on one of the three or four most basic questions of them all. Whether or not there are inherently evil people. Doesn't that seize your interest too?"

"Not particularly."

His voice rose slightly as he tossed the words back at her. *"Not particularly?* How is that possible?"

"Because I have a less speculative mind than you do. Not as good, I suppose, but often better grounded in reality. I don't much care about the Big Bang, or quarks and black holes, or the ultimate nature of good and evil, or those other things you like to brood about. I don't believe we're meant to understand those things, and they don't have a great bearing on my life in the first place. I guess I just don't speculate a lot. Oh, I'd like to know more about the assassination of JFK, who *really* was behind the assassination and stuff like that, but I never felt a need to look for all the answers. If that makes me a dolt, so be it."

"You're the least doltish woman I've ever known."

"Gosh, I bet you say that to all the girls. You're such a masher!" She giggled, something she did every year or two.

"Many things I've been called, but not that," he said, bemused.

She yawned. "It's getting hard to stay awake."

"Go to sleep, then." He kissed her goodnight, and she curled herself against him, her face on his chest while he wrapped one of his arms around her midriff. Not yet quite ready for sleep, he listened to the familiar murmur of her breathing, soft against the counterpoint of the breeze and the waves splashing against the shore while he watched the play of moonlight on the lake.

☨

The rest of his life—James Shannon and the other tortured souls at GCFI, his private patients, his quasi-affair with Cassandra—dwindled into insignificance. What mattered was Sharon, the wife who slept next to him, the partner in their bloodied but durable marriage. What mattered was Peter, happier now, at least for a week or for a day. Peter, who might finally be emerging from his adolescent angst and torpor. Peter, the same age as the late Christina Shannon, a mere four months older. What mattered was Sarah, the light of his life, a phrase he'd deemed trite and hyperbolic until she came along.

Sharon had the right idea, most likely. Put aside the huge unanswerable questions, stay grounded in reality, stay grounded in the here and now. Par for the course: Sharon usually had the right idea.

CHAPTER XXIV

JAMES SHANNON SAT IN GOTTLIEB'S OFFICE, his fingertips touched lightly together in his typical prayerful fashion. He'd continued to lose weight: he looked diminutive and almost elfin in his bulky regulation sweatshirt. It was the Tuesday after Labor Day. Discussion focused on Christina's notebook.

"How did you feel when you read it?" Gottlieb asked.

"How do you think I felt?" shot back Shannon. "How would *you* have felt?" He paused. "I told you. It was the worst experience imaginable.

"I think I went into a kind of shock," he went on, less brusquely. "For hours, maybe even days. I kept trying to find a way to make some sense of it. Telling myself *I'm imagining this,* even though I knew I wasn't."

"What did you do?"

He rubbed his fingertips against his temples and shut his eyes, as if trying to recall events of twenty years ago. "I don't know, I'm not really sure. Everything seemed unreal to me. I think I went into my bedroom. Of course I didn't sleep, that was out of the question. I just lay there on the bed. A couple of times I threw up. Every so often, I went back to the notebook. I reread bits and pieces of it, a few pages at a time. Some of it . . . you must have noticed this yourself . . . some of it seemed so *innocent.* Lists of chores and recipes and so forth. So innocent and ordinary. But then there were those other things, and those drawings . . ."

"Did you confront her?"

"Not right away. I couldn't." Shannon crossed his arms in front of his chest. "Maybe it was cowardly, but I'll admit I lacked the stomach for it. I didn't say a thing to her for the rest of the afternoon. When she came back from her bike ride, I avoided her. Later, five or six, it must have been, I told her I wasn't feeling well and didn't want to eat. I told her to fix herself some dinner. After she ate, she went off to watch *Jeopardy* the way she usually did. She liked to play along with the contestants. Then, when the program was over, I finally confronted her."

"How did she react?"

Shannon's tone remained the same, but his body language changed. He sat rigidly but defensively, as if expecting to ward off blows, and his right hand became a hard tight ball. "You won't believe this—well, maybe now you will—but *she* was angry! More than angry, furious. The angriest I've ever seen her. I should tell you, Christina didn't show anger the way most people do. She didn't yell or scream. If anything, she spoke in a softer, more deliberate way than usual. She didn't make threatening movements with her hands or get red in the face. Except for those hate-filled eyes of hers, and a certain way she had of squeezing her lips together, she didn't even change expressions. I'll remember what she said if I live to be a hundred. '*Daddy, didn't they teach you not to snoop?*'"

"What happened then?"

He shut his eyes again. "I don't recall too much of what she said, aside from *you don't understand*. She said that several times. She was right, of course. I didn't understand. Could anyone? I asked her, over and over, how could she do it. *Do what?* she'd ask, bold as brass. At one point, she even told me she'd been jotting down notes for a writing project. A story about a girl who killed her mother, a mystery story. For a split second I almost believed her. I *wanted* to believe her. I wanted to believe anything except the truth."

"Did she ever admit to having caused her mother's death?"

"Not directly, but she came close to it. She said no one would believe a girl like her would do a thing like that. I suppose she was right. Who'd believe something so far-fetched? She said she'd stick to her guns, no matter what. She'd been jotting down notes for a mystery story, and that was all there was to it."

Shannon stood up and walked over to the window, glancing outside, his eyes slightly glazed. "I remember something else she said, the most extraordinary thing of all. She looked at me directly, stared at me, with her hands on her hips. 'Look at it this way, Daddy, she just would have gotten sicker and sicker. Losing her toes, maybe even her whole foot. Going blind, or maybe going on that kidney machine. She's better off dead. Besides, you won't have to spend the next ten years or so taking care of her now.' I lost my temper then. 'How dare you!' I yelled at her. Then I slapped her, hard, across the face. The only time I ever hit her."

"What did she do then?"

"Nothing. She didn't blink an eye, didn't move a muscle. When she spoke, her voice was so low and quiet I could barely hear her. *'You'll regret that,'* she told me. I'm sure I would have. Christina had no interest in forgiveness."

Gottlieb strove to keep an even tone. "Was that when you began to think of killing her?"

"I don't recall exactly. If not then, the next day, or the day after that. I think it came to me gradually. It wasn't some bright idea"—he snapped his fingers—"that came to me in a flash."

Shannon looked out the window and took a few deep breaths, as if to settle himself. "It's important that you understand this, Dr. Gottlieb," he said when he resumed. "I didn't kill her for revenge. I've never been a vengeful person. I never will be. In fact, it's hard for me to tell you why I did it . . . it's hard to find the words. I think I did it out of something like a sense of duty. What I told you that day I began to talk again, to save the world from her. I didn't understand her, didn't have a clue about her, but it no longer mattered. What mattered was, I knew her capabilities. She would hurt people, kill them, as the result of the smallest passing fancy. Without a qualm, without regret. There was something wrong with her, something that went to the very center of her. There always had been, but I couldn't deny it any longer. Her malice had no limits, and I saw no chance she'd change. Her intelligence made it all the worse; it would have made her all the more dangerous."

He sat again. "If someone didn't stop her, she'd spend the rest of her life striking out at others as she pleased. I had to be the one to stop her. No one else could. Besides"—he blinked back tears—"there was something else. I'm ashamed to admit it, but it's true. I was afraid of her. I was afraid of my own daughter. For two reasons. First, I knew she killed her mother, and now she knew I knew. I had the notebook. My having it posed a threat to her, however slight. To kill me would eliminate that threat."

"And the second reason?"

"I'd dared to cross her. I'd even dared to slap her. Christina never would have let that pass. She would have retaliated tenfold, a hundred fold. I didn't know what she'd done to Anita Pierce, not then, but I knew she'd do something similar to me. Something terrible, when I least expected it."

They fell into a protracted silence as Gottlieb sipped tepid coffee from a nearly empty cup. This had been the most, by far, that Shannon had ever said about his daughter. *Let him go on*, Gottlieb told himself. *Let him say as much about her as he needs to.*

But Shannon showed no inclination to talk about her further. Instead, he brought up the competency report. "Brendan told me what you wrote," he said. "He told me not to get my hopes up, but he said there is a chance I'd go to a hospital instead of a prison. Even a chance I'd get out someday."

"It's possible."

He unclasped his hands and idly tapped the arm of the chair with his right hand. "I assumed I'd spend the rest of my life locked up. I assumed that from the start. I didn't want to tantalize myself with foolish hopes." He went on, pensively.

"The idea that I might get out someday takes some getting used to."

"Suppose you did. What do you think it would be like for you?"

"Very strange, I imagine. Especially strange to have some choice again. To be able to go here or there, or do this or that. To take a walk when I pleased, or a shower. To choose the food I ate, to go out for pizza or Kentucky Fried Chicken. Interesting, how quickly a person becomes . . . what's that word, institutionalized?"

"I think I'd leave Chicago," he went on. "Go downstate to one of the smaller cities. Springfield or Decatur or Carbondale, some place like that. Some place where Christina's murder hadn't been on the top of the news for weeks on end. Where it would be remotely possible that not everyone had heard about me."

"What would you do?"

"What I did before, if I could. Work in the office supply field, put in my years before retirement. Keep to myself and mind my own business. It wouldn't be a real exciting life. I don't want that kind of life. I never did."

Shannon grew more animated; his speech became almost pressured. "Of course I'd stay active in the church. Become a deacon if they'd let me. I also might do some things I never got around to. Learn about gardening, start a garden of my own. That would be very nice, I think. Putting on old clothes and getting down on my hands and knees and getting my hands dirty. To watch the flowers bloom, maybe grow my own vegetables. And something else, I'd like to go back to school someday. Take a course or two at a community college, just because the subjects caught my interest. I'd like to take a course on different religions. I know about my own but scarcely anything about the others."

It was the first time Gottlieb had ever heard him talk about the future with any interest, much less enthusiasm. Gottlieb was pleased, but he also felt a certain apprehension. They might refuse to accept his report. The prosecutor might decide to fight it all the way, notwithstanding Christina's notebook, and the judge might agree with her. If that happened, his patient could become as despairing as before. More so, because he'd dared to begin to hope again, only to have his hopes come crashing down around him.

"There's a fine line," said Gottlieb carefully, "between maintaining one's hopes and counting on them. What I wrote may help you, but that's not a given. The process will be long and complicated, and none of us can predict the outcome now."

Shannon looked at him with a hint of a rueful smile. "Have you had many Irish patients, Dr. Gottlieb?"

The question surprised him. "Well, yes, quite a few through the years."

"Then you've probably learned this about us. We tend not to get extravagant about our hopes."

They moved on to less weighty matters. Shannon asked him if he'd enjoyed the Labor Day weekend, and Gottlieb asked him about his brother's visit. His sister's migraine headaches were acting up, so she couldn't come. He asked Gottlieb to order a laxative for him. Gottlieb went through his standard questions. How was his appetite? His sleep? His concentration and attention? His energy? And then Gottlieb checked his watch. The signal that their time was drawing to a close.

Shannon stood up, said good-bye, and moved slowly towards the corridor. When he got to the door, however, he turned around. "Thank you. Not just for the report, but for everything. You've gone to a lot of trouble on my behalf. More than anyone else, except for my family and Brendan."

Gottlieb stood up and strode over to him. "You're welcome. I hope things work out all right for you. My hunch is that they will, eventually." In fact, he felt by no means convinced of this, but he said it anyway.

He laid a hand on Shannon's shoulder very lightly, very

quickly. Even through the sweatshirt, he could feel the shoulder tighten. *Not a man who is used to touch*, he thought. But the tightness passed, almost immediately, and Shannon gave what might have been an appreciative nod.

Gottlieb stood in the doorway and watched as Shannon headed down the corridor, walking slowly, at times nearly shuffling, his head bent. His hands were loosely joined behind his back, as if held in place by invisible cuffs.

CHAPTER XXV

GOTTLIEB, LIKE A NUMBER OF PSYCHIATRISTS, had mixed feelings about the Twelve-Step programs. On the one hand, he often sent patients to AA and the NA and the rest of them. Recovering alcoholics and drug addicts and compulsive gamblers, in his view, could provide enormous help to one another. They understood each other as no one else did. Those with years of sobriety or abstinence could demonstrate to newcomers that, yes, it's possible to break free from an addiction.

On the other hand, he recoiled against the stridor and rigidity of the groups' more dogmatic members, the AA and NA Nazis with their clichés and one-liners, their rejection of psychiatry in general, and psychiatric medication in particular. Gottlieb failed to see the rationale for withholding a mood stabilizer from a bipolar patient, or an antipsychotic from a schizophrenic, just because he happened to be a drunk.

But in the balance, he felt the groups did much more good than harm. He liked their simple truths, and the not-so-simple wisdom which lay beneath them. *One day at a time. Live and let live.* And his personal favorite: *This, too, shall pass.* More than a tidbit he passed on to his patients, it was an integral part of his personal credo, and it had helped him through the worst times of his life. However bad things seemed to be, they wouldn't last. Nothing did.

This, too, shall pass. His personal choice for the four most important words in the English language. These words became his mantra in the firestorm that followed the release of his report on James Shannon.

⊹

At GCFI, he, Norma Caldwell, and Dwight Sanderson often had a table to themselves in the canteen, since the rest of the staff tended to keep their distance from him. Some of them looked away from him, refusing to meet his gaze. Dwight tried to cheer him. "I wouldn't lose no sleep if I were you 'cause a bunch of spineless mo'-fo's are givin' you the cold shoulder, Doc."

Stanley Celinsky and Howard Pincus cajoled and badgered him to change his findings. Celinsky told him bluntly that he'd been duped. Shannon, in his view, had concocted a few delusions and exaggerated his depression in a shrewd attempt to save his life. Gottlieb politely asked him what he based this on, since he'd never interviewed the man himself. More than once, Pincus reminded him that the mayor's office still followed the case with interest, and alluded to the possibility of "serious ramifications" if Gottlieb stuck to his guns. Gottlieb asked if that was a threat. "I'll let you draw your own conclusions," Pincus answered darkly.

The Shannon case, relegated to the media back burner for a month or two, was thrust again into the forefront. SHRINK SAYS MURDERING FATHER SHOULD BE IN HOSPITAL, screeched a typical headline. James Shannon's face, flat and expressionless, reappeared in the local newscasts, as did Gottlieb's. One of the Chicago papers carried an editorial about the uses and abuses of psychiatric testimony. The editorialist fretted about the prospects of "our worst criminals avoiding punishment because of the chicanery of expert witnesses, a disturbing trend in high-profile cases."

The coverage fueled a small but steady stream of hate mail, always anonymous. *Gottlieb*, ran one letter, *you have to be stupidest fucker who ever lived. Or else your just another liberal pansy who thinks taxpayer $$ should be wasted on scum like Shannon who deserves to rot in hell. Either way your disgraceful!*

Most of the mail was in this vein, but not all of it. Some of it lauded him for standing up to the press and politicians, for refusing to join a lynch mob. Some of it—more than he would have expected—expressed sympathy for Shannon, clearly a sick man, since only a sick man could do what he'd done. A brief note arrived from Malcolm Kenyon, hand-written in a meticulous script. It praised Gottlieb's willingness to take an unpopular position and having shown the fortitude to stick with it. And there was this, a simple message on a postcard, dictated by Anita to her father: *My daughter says to say thank you,* the old man had written in a shaky scrawl. *Sincerely, Richard Pierce.*

Away from the sound and fury, Brendan O'Connell met with Robin Aveiro. At times they talked quietly; at times they bellowed at each other as they rehashed the case until they both were sick to death of it. They pored over Christina's notebook, page by page and line by line, and its contents soon became common knowledge throughout the district attorney's office.

Occasionally, she came close to expressing a measure of sympathy for her father. "All right, I'll grant you, Christina may have been the world's worst child," she admitted once. "That *still* gives him no right to bludgeon and strangle her."

O'Connell ignored her. "Too bad we can't prosecute the dead for murder, isn't it? By the way, what do you think of how she waited an hour or so before calling 911 the day her mother died? Cute kid, eh? And what about the way she contemplated setting a fire in a nursing home? I wonder how a jury would take to *that.*"

In the course of their third meeting, O'Connell told Aveiro about Christina's summer at Green Lake Camp, including an account of Anita Pierce's blinding, an ace up his sleeve that he'd been saving. "I don't want to drag this unfortunate woman into it," the lawyer concluded, "but I will if I have to."

"I need to think about this," Aveiro answered, "and to talk it over with the brass." Her dark eyes fixed on Christina's notebook as if it were a pile of maggots.

"You do that," agreed O'Connell amiably.

The next day she talked at length with her boss, and the day after that he talked with his boss. A few more days passed, and then Ms. Aveiro issued a terse statement to the press. While she herself continued to harbor serious doubts about Mr. Shannon's incompetence, she had studied his medical records thoroughly, conferred with her colleagues, and reluctantly decided not to contest Dr. Gottlieb's findings. Mr. Shannon would be remanded to a state hospital for further evaluation and treatment, and the matter of his competence would be reviewed at regular intervals. This did not mean, she emphasized, that the charges against him would be dropped. Nor did it mean that the district attorney's office would take a softer, more lenient approach towards the perpetrators of heinous crimes. It meant only that Mr. Shannon's charges would be held in abeyance until his psychiatric evaluation had been completed and his mental state had stabilized. In the brief Q-and-A that followed, she declined to speculate on how the DA's office might react to an insanity defense or an allegation of diminished capacity.

This, too, shall pass.

⸙

Slowly, week by week and day by day, Gottlieb's life returned to normal. He evaluated patients at GCFI and attended the usual round of meetings there. The shunning ebbed, and co-workers resumed talking to him. His private practice flourished, the bad press notwithstanding. He continued to teach medical students and residents at the university hospital where he made rounds. He also began to jot down notes for new articles.

In his spare time, he took walks with Sharon after dinner. It was a pleasant way of unwinding from the day, especially as the evenings grew crisper and cooler. He read bedtime stories to Sarah and continued to reach out to Peter. The boy responded to his overtures, at least most of the time. Peter and his cousin

Emily made frequent calls to each other, and his mood always brightened after them.

One night, as he and Sharon took their walk, she turned to him. "Peter asked me about inviting your brother and his family to come down and have Thanksgiving with us. I said fine, I didn't see why not. And then I teased him, I told him I thought he had a crush on Emily. And he *smiled*, Hal, he actually *smiled*! It's so wonderful to see him smile again. I was beginning to wonder if he still knew how . . . I was afraid those muscles might have atrophied."

"He'll be all right," proclaimed his father.

"I'm actually starting to believe that."

⋛

Gottlieb's work kept him busier than ever, and family and social life filled up the balance of the time, but often his mind still drifted to Cassandra. Small things might trigger thoughts of her—a reference to the Holocaust in a book or TV show, someone mentioning the Shedd Aquarium, a woman in a store or restaurant with a squarish face framed by shoulder-length blonde hair, or even just a woman of her height and build. But the thoughts might come to him without an obvious trigger, when he shaved or showered, or when he drove between his home and one of his offices. Or as he lay in bed next to Sharon trying to fall asleep, with mixed results.

Several times, he almost called her. Sometimes he dialed the first few digits of her number, but invariably he hung up before he dialed the rest of it. So many things he would have liked to talk about, to ask her. How was the biography of Goebbels coming along? What books had she read, what notable movies had she seen? How was Freitag? When did she plan to leave for Germany (if he'd ever known the exact date, he had repressed it), and could they maybe have a drink before she went, just a drink? Did she still brood about her Uncle Franz? Did she ever think about their visit to the Shedd? Did she miss him? (He knew he'd never ask her that. The sting would be too sharp if she said no).

What he wanted to ask her, above all else: had she forgiven him for the fiasco in her bedroom, for his flagrant display of ambivalence and guilt? Patients often told him how they'd give anything for Gottlieb to erase their most hateful memories, the way a surgeon might excise a cancer. He understood the futility of such a hope with new empathy.

In spite of himself, he still yearned for her. He could shut his eyes and summon up a vision of her lying naked next to him, before the walls of her bedroom closed in on him, and it made him close to giddy with desire. He followed up these visions by reminding himself of Warren Pasternak's verdict, too obvious to argue about. *Infidelity makes you terribly uncomfortable.* He also bore in mind his old therapist's dictum. *There are worse things than staying faithful to a woman you still love.*

Perhaps he'd steel himself—take a few deep breaths and maybe a Xanax, and then call her before she left. Assuming that she hadn't left already. Perhaps.

He thought of her, and he thought about his wife and children, about his private patients and his clientele at GCFI. His thoughts might take him anywhere and to anyone, but most frequently they took him to James Shannon. James Patrick Shannon, with his inherent decency, and his inability to deal with a daughter who altogether lacked it. The man who was reading the book of Job the morning of their first meeting. Surely he must have identified with Job. Shannon, like Job, had managed to hold on to his faith throughout his tribulations. Shortly after they first met, Gottlieb reread the book of Job himself. Among the passages that stayed with him: "*This would be my consolation; I would even exult in unrelenting pain; for I have not denied the words of the Holy One.*"

James Shannon, as ordinary a man as Gottlieb had ever known, a schoolboy whose idea of acting out was cutting classes to go to a Cubs game. A man of simple tastes and pleasures, who recalled with poignant gusto a lamb stew his dead wife had made decades ago. A man who dreamt his daughter would jump joyfully into his arms one day when he came home from work, a dream as unrealistic as finding a pot of gold on his doorstep. A man with as mundane and uneventful a life as anyone could imagine, except for fathering a monster and then killing her.

Gottlieb recalled with particular vividness the last time he saw Shannon, walking down a corridor, his hands behind him as if held in place by invisible cuffs. He wondered how the man would fare in a state hospital, a place where his story would be common knowledge before his arrival, where his caretakers, as well as his fellow patients, had likely formed the worst possible opinion of him. They might pump him full of meds that would turn his face into a flaccid puff, and make him walk like an octogenarian, and render him so tremulous that he could scarcely brush his teeth. Meds that might make his arms and legs writhe uncontrollably in his old age, assuming he would last that long. Meds he didn't need in the first place.

Gottlieb was pretty sure he wouldn't kill himself. The bedrock of his faith, if nothing else, would keep him from it, though others might do the job for him. The perpetrators of vile acts against children don't fare much better in state hospitals than prisons.

Still, Gottlieb thought Shannon might survive— might even get out eventually—might go ahead with his plan to move downstate and live in semi-anonymity. He'd never be happy (too much had already happened to him), but he might yet derive a measure of contentment from his life. He could take a walk in a park on a cool sunny day, he could spend Christmas or Thanksgiving with his family, he could go to a movie or eat in a restaurant, if he felt like it. He could go to a church of his choosing; he wouldn't have to take communion in a dank auditorium that doubled as a prison chapel. He could regain at least part of his former life.

Notwithstanding the horrendous stories his patients told him through the years, and notwithstanding his own experience with angst and trauma, Gottlieb had managed to on to a certain optimism. The horrendous stories were leavened by others that imparted great kindness and self-sacrifice, not to mention an extraordinary ability to survive. And James Shannon had good credentials as a survivor. He'd survived Christina, after all. No trivial feat, thought Gottlieb. There was a chance—a halfway decent chance, in the psychiatrist's opinion—that Shannon might emerge from the darkness of prison and an unneeded hospitalization, of being reviled and condemned by millions of people who never knew him, and survive to see once more the light of day.

ACKNOWLEDGMENTS

Writers who venture outside their fields of proficiency are courting disaster. In my case, I hope this risk has been lessened by the input and advice of experts. Three names in particular come to mind. Reverend Barry Cass tutored me on the theological underpinnings of the concept of evil, especially as it pertains to the New Testament. Dr. Joseph Segal provided me with valuable and pertinent information regarding eye injuries and their treatment. I should add that any errors should be attributed to me and not them.

The third name is a poignant one for me. Samuel Edgar Wilhite was my guide and teacher in matters of criminal law. Ed Wilhite and I met during Eisenhower's second term; we were college roommates; we remained companions and confidants for many years thereafter. Our friendship lasted until he died, much too young, in the first decade of the new millennium.

Three more notes of gratitude: to my friend and colleague, Dr. Sam Silverman, who read the entire manuscript of Model Child, and who suggested several big and small changes. The result, I believe, is a better and tighter book. I also would like to thank the people at SideStreet Press, Dennis Foley in particular, for their willingness to take a chance on an unknown novelist they'd never met and who lived close to a thousand miles away from them. I am greatly indebted to Cynde Acanto, for her invaluable encouragement and advice, especially regarding the book business, (still a terra incognita for me, for the most part).

The final note of gratitude goes to my wife, Judy Goodwin, who has been, in simplest terms, my most merciless critic and staunchest supporter through the years.

BOOKS BY SIDE STREET PRESS

The Drunkard's Son by Dennis Foley

Echoes from a Lost Mind by Carl Richards

We Speak Chicagoese—stories and poems by Chicago writers, Edited by Bill Donlon, et al

And These Are The Good Times by Patricia Ann McNair

Model Child by R.C. Goodwin

forthcoming

The Blue Circus by Dennis Foley